STABBED
IN THE
BAKLAVA

**The Kitchen Kebab Mystery Series
by Tina Kashian**

Hummus and Homicide

Stabbed in the Baklava

Published by Kensington Publishing Corporation

STABBED IN THE BAKLAVA

Tina Kashian

KENSINGTON BOOKS
KENSINGTON PUBLISHING CORP.
http://www.kensingtonbooks.com

KENSINGTON BOOKS are published by

Kensington Publishing Corp.
119 West 40th Street
New York, NY 10018

All Kensington titles, imprints, and distributed lines are available at special quantity discounts for bulk purchases for sales promotion, premiums, fund-raising, educational, or institutional use.

Special book excerpts or customized printings can also be created to fit specific needs. For details, write or phone the office of the Kensington Sales Manager: Attn.: Sales Department. Kensington Publishing Corp., 119 West 40th Street, New York, NY 10018. Phone: 1-800-221-2647.

Kensington and the K logo Reg. U.S. Pat. & TM Off.

First Printing: September 2018
ISBN-13: 978-1-4967-1349-0
ISBN-10: 1-4967-1349-4

eISBN-13: 978-1-4967-1350-6
eISBN-10: 1-4967-1350-8

10 9 8 7 6 5 4 3 2 1

Printed in the United States of America

For John,
for believing in me

CHAPTER 1

"Did you see who's at table three?"

Lucy Berberian set down a tray of wrapped silverware and looked where her sister, Emma, pointed from behind the waitress station.

"Isn't that Scarlet Westwood?" Lucy asked. The attractive blonde was a famous Philadelphia socialite and the daughter of a hotel mogul. Her picture was splashed across tabloids at the checkout counter of Holloway's, the sole grocery store in the small Jersey shore town.

"In the flesh!" Emma's voice rose an octave and she dropped the towel she'd been using to wipe down tables.

"Who's the older woman with her?" Lucy asked.

"Probably her personal assistant. Socialites don't go anywhere without them." Emma nudged Lucy. "They asked for you when they came in."

Lucy blinked. "Me?"

"That's right. They want to talk to the manager. That's you now, Sis."

Less than two months ago, Lucy had quit her position as an attorney at a large Philadelphia law firm, packed her bags, and returned to her small hometown of Ocean Crest, at the Jersey shore. She'd only planned for a temporary visit home until she could get back on her feet and find a new job, but she'd ended up staying and having a go at managing Kebab Kitchen, her family's Mediterranean restaurant. Her semiretired parents continued to work part-time, but Lucy was taking on a bigger role each day.

Lucy toyed with a cloth napkin on the tray. "Did they say what they wanted?"

Emma shook her head. "No. But don't keep Scarlet Westwood waiting. I don't think the celebrity types have a lot of patience."

Lucy snatched an order pad from the counter and headed for table number three, the best seat in the house, which overlooked the Atlantic Ocean and the Ocean Crest boardwalk. The table was also tucked away in a corner, semiprivate, and often requested by romantic couples. It was a hot and humid June afternoon, and sunlight shimmered on the ocean like shards of glass. Umbrellas and towels were scattered across the beach like a colorful quilt. Children frolicked in the surf and played in the sand while sunbathers reclined on beach chairs. In the distance, Lucy could see the amusement pier with its old-fashioned wooden roller coaster and Ferris wheel.

Lucy took a breath as she approached the table, wondering why they'd asked for her. Did wealthy socialites expect to be served by the manager and not the waitstaff?

"Good afternoon. My name is Lucy Berberian. How can I help you?"

Both women looked up. Scarlet Westwood removed her sunglasses and tucked them into a slick, black Chanel purse. She was stunning, just as she appeared in the celebrity photographs. She was in her late twenties with long, blond hair that brushed her shoulders and sky-blue eyes. Her makeup was expertly applied, and her trademark lips were big and glossy. Lucy had read that Scarlet liked her Botox, and her full lips were a result of a skilled doctor's injections.

"I was told you are the new manager here," the older woman said.

Lucy turned to the woman seated across from Scarlet and studied her for the first time. She appeared to be in her midfifties, old enough to be Scarlet's mother, with a brown bob and shrewd, dark eyes. Dressed in an elegant champagne-colored suit, she drummed long red fingernails on the pristine white tablecloth.

Lucy tucked the order pad back in her apron. "Yes, that's right."

The woman shot her a haughty look. "We're here on business and don't have much time today."

"Of course. Our kitchen is quick. Would you like to hear our lunch specials? Or if you prefer there's a hummus bar that offers a variety of hummus and vegetables for dipping. Pita bread is served warm from the kitchen and—"

"Not that type of business."

Then what? From what Lucy had read in the gossip rags, Scarlet liked to party and enjoyed expensive food, wine, and couture clothing. Kebab Kitchen was a pleasant family establishment, certainly nothing as trendy as the upscale establishments to which Scarlet was accustomed.

Scarlet flipped an errant blond curl across her

shoulder. "I'm getting married at Castle of the Sea in Ocean Crest. I want Kebab Kitchen to cater my reception. This is my wedding planner, Victoria Redding."

Lucy's insides froze for a heart-stopping moment. Her first thought was that it would be a once-in-a-lifetime opportunity to cater the socialite's wedding. Her second thought was how would she pull it off? She was still learning the business, and she'd recently hired her ex-boyfriend, Azad, as the new head chef to take her mother's place. Things were as sticky as baklava syrup between them and Lucy was taking it day by day.

Which led to a bigger question: why would someone of Scarlet Westwood's status want to have a small, family-owned Mediterranean restaurant cater her reception?

"I'm flattered that you chose us, but I have to ask—"

"Why?" Scarlet finished for her.

Lucy shrugged. "Well, yes."

"I've vacationed at the Jersey shore since I was a child, and I recently purchased a summer home in Ocean Crest."

"I see." But that still didn't explain it.

"I plan to film my first movie, and a scene will take place on the beach here. My fiancé is Bradford Papadopoulos, the show's director. Bradford has Mediterranean roots and he loves the cuisine. He also raved about the food when he last ate here."

That made more sense. Lucy remembered hearing about a possible movie being filmed on the beach from her best friend, Katie Watson, who worked at the Ocean Crest town hall. And if the groom preferred

Armenian, Greek, and Lebanese food, then Kebab Kitchen was the best in all of South Jersey.

Lucy cleared her throat. "Congratulations on your engagement, and I'm honored you want us to cater your wedding."

"We realize this is a big opportunity for you," Victoria said, her voice stern. "And we have certain conditions."

Lucy may have been taken aback at Victoria's caustic tone, but she schooled her expression. The business would be great for the restaurant's catering arm. She could put up with a bridezilla, or in this case, an aggressive wedding planner, if it meant helping the business and proving her worth to her family.

"First, we intend to have two hundred and fifty guests. Have you ever catered for that large a number?"

"Of course," Lucy lied as her pulse pounded like an overloaded food processor.

She'd never catered at all. Her mother had handled the catering end of the business, and as far as Lucy knew, the largest order she'd filled was for a hundred people. But Lucy was stubborn and determined. Azad was an experienced chef, and together with their line cook, Butch, and her parents' part-time help, she was confident they could handle two hundred and fifty guests.

"Second, the wedding will take place in two weeks."

Only two weeks to prepare? The pressure tightened in her chest, and her mind whirled with all the details that would be required. The labor would be a problem, but she'd come up with something. Katie was always willing to help out, and there were college kids looking for summer jobs.

"And most important, news of the wedding must be kept as secret as possible, understand?" Victoria said.

Now this posed a different type of challenge. Gossip in Ocean Crest traveled as fast as greased lightning. It didn't help that the *Town News* was run by Stan Slade, a former New York City reporter who was always hungry for a story. Lucy recalled how hard it had been to keep things under wraps two months ago when the town's new health inspector had been murdered. It had been pretourist season then and Ocean Crest had been quiet, but now that it was late June, the town swelled with tourists and it was impossible to find a vacant parking spot. Talk was sure to start if anyone spotted Scarlet on the street or the boardwalk.

"I'll do everything in my power to keep it quiet. Only my staff will know, and they can be trusted. But what if you're seen in town? Surely people will ask questions."

Victoria cleared her throat. "Yes, but like Ms. Westwood said, she now owns a shore home in town. People have no reason to suspect she's getting married."

Both women stood. Victoria handed Lucy a business card. "Here's my personal cell number. I'll be in touch to go over the menu for the cocktail hour and the reception. Some of the guests have dietary restrictions that must be accommodated."

"Of course," Lucy said.

Scarlet reached into her purse and slipped her sunglasses back on. Lucy thought the disguise did little to conceal her true appearance. "You must wonder why I would want my wedding kept a secret when I live in the limelight."

"No." *Yes.* Scarlet's escapades and lavish lifestyle were

blasted weekly in the tabloids and television celebrity shows. Bad publicity only served to add to her impressive number of young fans.

"A large part of my life is for public display," Scarlet said, "but my wedding is different. I want that one day for myself."

Good luck, Lucy almost slipped, then bit her lip. It would take a small army of personal bodyguards to keep a wedding of that size secret. Even the guests could leak details of the wedding to the press. Nothing was off limits when it came to Scarlet and publicity. Did she plan on blindfolding two hundred and fifty people and driving them in large buses to the wedding? On an off-season day, that felt like much of Ocean Crest's entire population.

As soon as the women left, Emma and Sally, a long-time waitress at the restaurant, rushed over. Both wore their uniforms—black slacks, button-down white shirts, and red aprons—and their faces were anxious with anticipation.

"Well? What did Scarlet Westwood want?" Emma asked.

"She wants Kebab Kitchen to cater her wedding." Lucy still couldn't believe it.

"That's fantastic!" Sally said.

"It's for two hundred and fifty guests. We only have two weeks to prepare." Lucy felt a bit light-headed.

"You're kidding?" Emma asked.

"Nope. That's what she said."

Emma pursed her lips. "Well then, you'd best talk to Azad."

Lucy's gut tightened at the mention of her ex. *Really, Lucy. He works for you now.* She had to keep things in perspective. It was just a wedding, and so far, she'd insisted on maintaining a professional working relationship with Azad, the restaurant's new head chef.

It wasn't as if *they* were getting married.

Her legal training would kick in to full gear. Lucy had always excelled at organization, and she just needed to come up with a battle plan for Azad, her parents, and the rest of the staff to efficiently tackle each task. She'd give Scarlet Westwood a perfect reception.

After all, with organization and hard work, what could go wrong?

"You're doing it wrong."

Lucy turned at the masculine voice to see Azad Zakarian looking over her shoulder. Tall, dark, and good-looking, the sight of her ex-boyfriend still made her heart pound a bit too fast.

She straightened her spine and wrinkled her nose. "How? There is no wrong way to chop garlic." Lucy knew the basis of Mediterranean cuisine was garlic, onions, and olive oil. It may give you killer breath, but it was one of the healthiest diets around.

Over the past two weeks, everyone at Kebab Kitchen had been working overtime to prepare for Scarlet Westwood's wedding. The kitchen had been a whirlwind of activity—the ovens heated the kitchen, the constant whirling of the industrial-sized mixer never seemed to end, and the delicious smells of freshly baked pastry and breads floated through the restaurant.

Lucy eyed the bowl of unpeeled garlic cloves

soaking in cold water on the kitchen worktable. The garlic was needed for several of the dishes that would be served at the wedding reception, and Lucy had thought to peel and chop the garlic to relieve Azad from the menial task. But from the tense look on Azad's face, it was clear he didn't want her assistance.

"Yes, there's a wrong way," he said. "You're going to slice off the tips of your fingers. That chef's knife is wicked sharp and dangerous in the hands of an amateur."

In the hands of an amateur.

How many times had she heard similar comments over the past weeks? Her mother, Azad, and even their line cook, Butch, all seemed to remind her of her culinary shortcomings on a daily basis. She knew she wasn't a chef. When she'd worked as a city lawyer the extent of her culinary talent was to memorize the take-out numbers of all the restaurants within a two-mile radius of the firm. But since returning to Ocean Crest and deciding to take a stab at running her family's restaurant, she'd been determined to learn how to prepare basic Mediterranean dishes.

Lucy frowned up at him and set the knife on the cutting board. "Fine. Show me, then."

Azad plucked a clove of garlic from the bowl, efficiently peeled the skin, and placed it on the cutting board. "First, keep the tip of the blade on the cutting board at all times, then press downward and use the full length of the blade to slice your food."

He took the knife and began deftly to mince the garlic. His knife worked at breathtaking speed, and Lucy could barely follow his movements. Her gaze moved to his muscled forearms and rose to his chest.

His broad shoulders strained against his shirt. She could see the day's growth of stubble on his chiseled cheeks and the sexy dimple in his chin. He wore his dark hair a bit long and it brushed his collar. Despite her determination to maintain a working relationship, she couldn't help but acknowledge that there was something irresistibly sexy about a competent male in the kitchen.

"There are five ways to mince garlic. Knife-minced, garlic-pressed, mortar and pestle, knife-pureed, and microplaned," he rattled off as he continued to work. "Each has different qualities and unique tastes for dishes."

"What about the jars you can purchase from Holloway's grocery store? The garlic comes perfectly minced."

Azad's knife halted in midchop and he gave her an incredulous sidelong glare. "You're kidding, right? Your mother would have a fit."

It was true. Everything was made from scratch at the restaurant. Her mother, who had been the head chef before Azad took over, even insisted on grinding her own meat for her dishes. *"It's never as fresh if you don't do it yourself. Fresh is everything,"* Angela Berberian had often said.

"I never said I was a chef. That's why I hired *you*, remember?" The words came out a bit harsher than Lucy wanted.

He flashed a grin, and the dimple in his cheek deepened. "Don't get all bent out of shape. I'm just showing you proper technique."

Lucy felt her face grow warm. They'd dated back in college, and when they'd graduated, their relationship turned serious. Or at least, *she'd* been serious.

Azad had broken her heart when he'd suddenly ended things and they'd gone their separate ways— Lucy to law school and Azad to culinary school. She was older, wiser, and now his boss. So why did she let him get under her skin? One charming grin and she felt like a hormonal teenager gazing longingly at the star quarterback at a high school football game.

Ugh. She'd have to try harder to hide her emotions.

Only a few months ago, Azad had wanted to buy Kebab Kitchen. But Lucy's "temporary" visit home, after quitting the firm, had turned into a permanent stay, and she'd come to realize how much she'd missed her family, her friends—and surprisingly— how important Kebab Kitchen was to her. So Lucy had stepped up. Her parents were more than happy to teach her the business as they worked part-time and eased into retirement.

At least it had seemed the perfect arrangement for her. Azad may not view it that way. He'd left his sous chef job at a fancy Atlantic City restaurant to become head chef of Kebab Kitchen. She knew he'd initially wanted to buy the place from her parents and make it his own, but he'd changed his mind after Lucy had stated her intentions to remain in town.

Azad set the knife aside and wiped his hands on a dish towel. "Now do you remember how to knife-puree it?"

"Sure. Start by crushing it with the back of the blade."

Determined to show him she could do something, Lucy picked up the knife, pressed the back of the blade flat on a clove, and slammed her fist down to squash the garlic on the cutting board. But instead of cooperating, the finicky garlic clove shot from the board and flew across the kitchen like a smelly projectile.

Oh, no. Her eyes widened in dismay. What the heck went wrong? He made it look so simple.

She was saved from another culinary lecture by the sound of footsteps on the kitchen's terra-cotta floor.

Her mother, Angela, appeared behind an industrial mixer almost as tall as her five-foot frame. Her signature beehive, which had gone out of style decades ago, added a few inches to her height. The gold cross necklace she never left the house without caught a ray of light from an overhead kitchen window.

Angela frowned as she bent down to pick up the wayward piece of garlic from the floor. "You're doing it wrong, Lucy."

"She forgot to add salt," Azad said.

Salt! That was it. Lucy resisted the urge to smack her forehead with her palm. Salt made it easier to crush the garlic.

Angela's face softened as she looked at Azad in approval. She tossed the clove in a trash can and approached to pat Azad on the arm. "Listen to Azad, Lucy. He knows how to cook."

Lucy fought the urge to roll her eyes. If her mother had her way, Lucy would be baking her own baklava to celebrate her nuptials with Azad. It was no secret Angela Berberian wanted more grandchildren. Lucy had turned thirty-two and Angela firmly believed that her daughter's biological clock was set to explode. It wasn't enough that Emma was married to Max, a real estate agent in Ocean Crest, and they had a ten-year-old daughter, Niari. Lucy's mother wanted more grandkids, and fast.

"Now, do you have everything planned for that woman's wedding?" Angela asked, her tone a bit chilly.

"Her name is Scarlet Westwood," Lucy pointed out.

Angela folded her arms across her chest and arched an unamused brow. "Hmph. I know her name. I don't have to like her. She's done nothing to earn her fame except to be born into a wealthy family."

Lucy set aside the knife. "I know, Mom, but think of it as great publicity for the restaurant."

"Bah! Kebab Kitchen has done just fine for thirty years. Plus, that woman is a home wrecker."

Her mother was referring to several of Scarlet's past relationships with engaged or married men. Almost all were older and wealthy. Lucy wondered how much of what was reported was true and how much was sensationalized. "Since when do you watch the celebrity news channels? I thought you only liked the cooking channel and that good-looking chef."

Angela looked affronted. "What's wrong with Cooking Kurt? At least he's honest and single."

Lucy couldn't help but smile. One of the things she'd discovered since returning home was that her mother liked watching cooking shows while she worked. But she wasn't as interested in the new recipes as she was in watching the hot, sexy star of one of the shows.

"What's this about Cooking Kurt?" her father's voice boomed.

Lucy and her mother turned. Raffi Berberian stood between the swinging doors leading into the kitchen. Arms crossed over his thick chest, her father was a large, heavyset man with a balding pate of curly black hair and a booming voice. He held a stack of papers.

Her mother waved her hand dismissively. "We've been over this. You won't take me to Cooking Kurt's book signing at Pages Bookstore," Angela said. "Now I have to ask Lucy to take me."

Raffi's brow furrowed. "The man is a fraud. I doubt he even wrote one recipe in that cookbook."

Her mother planted her hands on her hips. "Of course, he wrote it. Isn't that right, Lucy?"

All eyes turned to her, and Lucy squirmed beneath her parents' gazes. "I guess so, Mom. If he didn't, his name wouldn't be on the cover."

A glimmer of satisfaction lit her mother's face, and her gaze returned to her father. "See? Lucy would know."

"Harrumph," her father said, dismissing the subject in his own way.

Lucy coughed to hide a smile. Despite their bickering, she knew her parents loved each other.

Her father sifted through the papers in his hand. "I double-checked the remaining wedding invoices you prepared. Everything looks good." He'd been in charge of the finances and the day-to-day business aspects of running a restaurant. Her mother had been in charge of the cooking.

"Thanks for double-checking, Dad," Lucy said.

"Is everything ready to be loaded into the catering van?" her father asked.

Two tall, rolling, catering carts with Dutch doors stood ready in the corner. One was heated to keep prepared food warm, the other was refrigerated for the cold items. The meat kebabs and vegetables had been marinated and would be grilled at the reception.

"We're ready to go," Azad confirmed.

"Do not forget that everything has to be served minutes from the grill." Her mother's laser-like gaze landed on Lucy. "I don't know who the servers will be, so it's up to you, Lucy, to be sure the food arrives hot to every table. The reputation of Kebab Kitchen is on the line."

Lucy swallowed as her nervousness slipped back to grip her. Her mother, despite her five-foot frame, could be quite intimidating. The wedding was a test and she was determined to prove that she had what it took to be a successful restaurateur.

At Lucy's nod, her mother continued. "Good. I'll stay behind with your father, Emma, and Sally and run the dinner shift. You go with Azad in the van and take all the food. Butch will meet you there."

"Katie is helping." Her friend didn't normally work weekends and had agreed to help Lucy oversee the reception. They didn't need any more staff. Castle of the Sea had a full staff of servers, dishwashers, and bartenders. Kebab Kitchen was responsible for the *mezze*—or appetizers—for the cocktail hour, the main course, and baklava for dessert. The wedding cake was made by Cutie's Cupcakes bakery, and Lucy knew that anything Susan Cutie made would be a stunning and mouthwatering confection. The lemon meringue pie was Lucy's favorite.

Her mom shook a finger at her. "Remember what I told you. Don't interfere with Azad while he's cooking. I know how you two can be at times. You need to oversee the servers and make sure the dinner hour runs smoothly. Don't argue with him or get in his way."

"Why would I argue with him or—"

Angela clutched Lucy's chin and lowered her face to place a kiss on her forehead. "I'm proud of you, Lucy. Now go give that home wrecker a perfect wedding. If her marriage goes bad, it will be her fault, not ours."

CHAPTER 2

"It's stunning! No wonder they call it Castle of the Sea." Lucy's gaze was riveted on their destination as Azad drove them in the catering van up a long, winding drive. The sprawling mansion resembled a southern plantation with its white Corinthian columns, front portico, and wrought-iron balconies. But instead of an expansive front lawn, the mansion was located at the top of a hill overlooking the sparkling Atlantic Ocean. It was early afternoon, and the sun was a flaming ball in the sky. Gulls circled above, and a cool ocean breeze carried through the open window and brushed tendrils of wayward curls that had escaped Lucy's ponytail.

Azad wound around the building and turned up a hill to the service entrance. "Wait until you see the inside of this place."

"You've been here before?"

"I went to a bachelor party here about five years ago while you were working in Philly."

"A bachelor party? Who could afford to have it here?" The classy establishment seemed like the last place to hold a bachelor party. She couldn't imagine drunk thirty- and forty-year-old men with beer bongs, loud music, and heaven forbid—strippers.

"My boss at the time could afford it."

Once again, she was reminded that Azad had worked at a five-star Atlantic City casino restaurant. Not for the first time she wondered if he regretted leaving his sous chef job to become head chef at Kebab Kitchen. The Mediterranean restaurant wasn't luxuriously decorated, pricey, or even famous. It was a small and intimate family place, much like Ocean Crest itself.

Lucy's gaze returned to the window. Ocean Crest hadn't changed much over the years. Of course, McMansions had been built on every remaining square inch of available land—which hadn't been much. Beach property in New Jersey continued to climb in value, and her brother-in-law, Max, did well with rentals as the self-professed real estate king in town. But Lucy hadn't seen anything as grand in the small town as Castle of the Sea.

The catering van jostled as they drove over the first of several speed bumps to ensure visitors moved cautiously on the resort grounds. Pots, pans, and trays rattled in the back. The van was old and her father had purchased it from a local Protestant Church that had used it to transport senior citizens to church as well as to weekly outings of bingo, Saturday spaghetti dinners, and ball games. He'd removed all ten seats and converted it to Kebab Kitchen's catering van.

Azad pulled into the service lot and shifted the van into reverse to get close to the service entrance.

Lucy glanced in the rearview mirror. "Be careful. This thing handles like a boat."

With one hand on the wheel and the other stretched

behind Lucy's seat, Azad looked out the rear window as he maneuvered the van. "I know what I'm doing. I want to get closer to the back door to unload."

"I know, but—"

There was a sudden, loud bang and pots and pans crashed to the floor.

Azad jammed on the brake, threw the van into park, and killed the engine. They both hopped out and ran to the back. A dent the size of a softball marred the bumper where it had rammed into a concrete pole. A nearby sign said in big, black letters, Fire Zone, No Parking.

Azad's brows knit together as he surveyed the damage. "You think your dad will notice?"

Lucy looked at him in disbelief, but at his crest-fallen expression she stopped herself from blurting out, "I told you so."

"Don't worry about it," she said. "I'll tell him something hit us."

He opened the rear doors of the van, and his frown deepened. "Damn. One of the baklava trays tipped over."

Lucy came close to peer inside. The floor was littered with walnut and cinnamon pastry. She reached inside to pick up the fallen tray. "It's a good thing we made extra."

"Let me help with that." Azad grabbed a broom mounted on the inside of the van and began sweeping up the mess. "We have to wait for Butch and Katie before we begin unloading anyway."

Lucy used a dustpan to collect the baklava, and disposed of the waste in one of the trash bags they carried in the van. When they were finished, Azad set the broom aside. "Here come Butch and Katie now."

A battered blue 1970 Buick pulled up beside them. Two of the doors were different colors. Butch liked to refurbish "junkers," as he called them, and turn them into classic cars. Once a year Ocean Crest had a car show, and Butch always entered.

Katie stepped out of the car and shielded her eyes from the sun with the back of her hand. "Oh, my gosh! What do you think it costs to have a wedding here?"

"I can't imagine," Lucy said. Even the back of the building appeared welcoming with a striped awning above a wide set of double doors.

"I'm dying to see the ballroom."

Lucy gave Katie a conspiring wink. "Maybe we should ditch the aprons and crash the wedding."

Katie chuckled. "Now you're talking. We can pretend we're back in high school when we snuck into Lois Webster's party when her parents were away."

"Those were the days."

Katie Watson had been Lucy's friend since grade school. They were physical opposites of each other. Katie was tall and slender with poker-straight blond hair and blue eyes, whereas Lucy was petite at five foot three, had brown eyes, and shoulder-length, curly dark hair that never cooperated in the humid Jersey summers. The two also came from vastly different cultural backgrounds. Katie's family tree could be traced back to the Pilgrims while Lucy was a first generation American. Katie's mom had packed peanut butter and jelly sandwiches in her school lunch box, and Lucy had shown up with hummus and pita. None of it made a difference. They'd been best friends forever, and since she'd returned to Ocean Crest, Lucy had been staying with Katie and her husband Bill, an Ocean Crest police officer.

"Everything looks great, Lucy Lou," Butch called out as he peered inside the now tidied van.

Butch had been the line cook at Kebab Kitchen since Lucy was in kindergarten. A large and tall African American man, he had the broadest shoulders and chest of any man she'd ever seen. He always wore a checkered bandana on his head and had a gold front tooth that flashed whenever he smiled. He also had a propensity to call her nicknames, and "Lucy Lou" was his favorite.

"Let's get started," Lucy said.

Together, the four of them unloaded the rolling catering carts and everything else in the van. The food had been packed in air-tight containers stored on the shelves of the carts. The lamb and chicken were marinating in olive oil and spices and would be threaded on shish-kebab skewers and grilled over charcoal. Because of the difference in cooking times, the vegetable skewers would be served separately. The lentil soup was in large tureens and ready to be heated. The remaining hot food would be prepared in the kitchen. The cold items—the tubs of hummus, tabbouleh salad, and sliced vegetables for dipping, had already been prepared and were stored in the refrigerated cart.

Lucy stepped into the kitchen, then stopped short to gaze around in admiration. The kitchen of Castle of the Sea was brand spanking new with stainless-steel appliances, plenty of worktables, top-notch gas ranges, and a full-length hood for maximum ventilation. There wasn't a scratch on the tables, or a dent or smudge of a handprint on the shiny appliances. She couldn't help but compare it with Kebab Kitchen's smaller and older kitchen. She'd only been the restaurant manager for a short while, but she had a running list of tasks to accomplish—from refreshing and updating the decor, to replacing one of the grills, to adding new shelving in the storage room.

She also knew she'd be up against her father for every change. She felt like a boxer preparing for a big Atlantic City fight.

Azad whistled between his teeth. "This is a chef's dream come true."

Lucy set an empty stockpot on the counter. She couldn't help the words that came out of her mouth. "Even an *amateur* like me can appreciate it."

Azad looked at her in surprise, then threw his head back and laughed. "Don't worry. I like our place best."

She felt an unwelcome surge of excitement. *Our place?* Was he flirting with her?

It wouldn't be the first time he'd suggested he'd like to resume romantic relations. A few months ago, things had heated up between them, but she wasn't certain she wanted to take that leap. He'd broken her heart in the past—and even putting aside that they were now working together—she'd sworn she wouldn't be a glutton for punishment and risk heartache again.

Fortunately, she didn't need to contemplate that matter much further. Butch returned from his second trip carrying more stockpots, and Azad turned into a serious chef, clapping his hands to get everyone's attention. "The first thing we have to do is preheat the grills and ovens. Once I assemble the shish kebab skewers, Butch can help me grill. Meanwhile, we need to finish the cold appetizers and—"

"You're late."

All four of them turned to see Victoria Redding standing in the kitchen doorway holding open the doors that led into the ballroom. Dressed in a full-length, dark green, sequined gown with her hair styled in an elaborate chignon, the older woman looked like she should be the mother of the bride rather than the wedding planner.

Lucy glanced at her wristwatch. "We're exactly on time."

Victoria gave her a haughty look, then let the swinging doors close behind her. The clipped sound of her stilettos—dyed the exact shade of green as her gown—echoed across the ceramic floor as she approached. The scent of her floral perfume made Lucy's nose twitch with the need to sneeze. "The ceremony is over and the couple is taking pictures by the gazebo for the next two hours or so," Victoria said. "Cocktail hour is at five sharp."

Lucy straightened her shoulders. "I assure you, Ms. Redding, we're ready."

Victoria ignored her. "Don't forget tables two and thirteen each have a vegetarian and table nineteen has someone who insists on a gluten-free menu."

"We have it covered," Lucy insisted.

"Be sure that you do." Victoria turned on her heel and stormed from the kitchen.

Katie whistled. "She's a piece of work."

"You have no idea. She was harassing me all last week over changes to the menu."

Lucy had modified their initial menu three times over the course of the past seven days. It had been maddening and inefficient. Lucy was no stranger to stress and pressure. She'd had her fair share of demanding clients at the law firm, but this was worse.

No matter how much she'd planned, she feared something could go wrong. Or worse, that she'd never satisfy the finicky wedding planner.

"Did you check out her fancy getup?" Katie sniffed the air and shook her head. "Someone ought to tell her to lighten up with her perfume. She smells like my grandma."

Lucy rubbed her nose. "I don't know what's worse, that I'm allergic to her or that I'm scared of disappointing her."

"Relax," Katie said. "We have your back."

Gratitude welled in Lucy's chest. "Good to know." Her friend was giving up her weekend to help. Lucy had offered to pay Katie, but she'd refused, saying, "No way! What are friends for?"

Next to arrive was the service staff. Each server wore pressed black slacks and a crisp button-down shirt with a gold *C* embroidered on the shirt pocket, for Castle of the Sea. The women had their hair neatly tied back and the men were cleanly shaved. They looked like a well-seasoned regiment, and Lucy was relieved. It was her job to oversee the servers for the cocktail hour and the reception and to make sure the wedding guests were satisfied. She knew a professional waitstaff was essential.

Azad went to work assembling the marinated chicken, lamb, and vegetables on stainless-steel shish kebab skewers. Five hundred skewers to be exact, two for each wedding guest, one for meat and the other for vegetables. Butch started heating the lentil soup, and Katie and Lucy were busy arranging trays of stuffed grape leaves, tabbouleh salad, and hummus from one of the rolling carts. Armenians called these trays *mezze*, and Lucy hoped they'd be a hit. The kitchen soon began to work like a well-oiled machine.

Not long afterward, Victoria notified them that the guests had begun to arrive for the cocktail hour. The bridal party had a private room for their own cocktails before they were announced at the reception, and Lucy made sure the waitstaff checked on the bridal party numerous times to ensure they had everything they needed.

Shortly after she returned to the kitchen, the door leading into the ballroom swung open again, but this time, a man in a tuxedo stumbled into the kitchen. He was of average height with a full head of brown hair sprinkled with gray, and green eyes. His bow tie was askew and his steps were a bit unsteady. He held up an empty bottle of Jack Daniels as he approached. "Is there more whiskey in here?"

"Pardon?" Lucy set down a bin of hummus and stepped forward. The man was clearly intoxicated, with red eyes and a flushed face. He was older, in his midfifties, but fit and attractive.

Still, they didn't have time for a drunk, wandering, wedding guest.

"Hi, sweet pea. I'm the best man in the wedding. You have any more of these?" He waved the empty whiskey bottle back and forth like a pendulum.

Lucy wrinkled her nose at the odor of alcohol wafting from him. "I'm afraid you made a wrong turn, sir. This is the kitchen, not the bar. There's no alcohol here."

"Too bad. I guess I'll be on my way then." His gaze traveled down her white shirt and black slacks before returning to her face. "Save a dance for me, will you?"

Before she could come up with a smart reply, Azad

stepped forward. He was in the middle of assembling the shish kebab, and he held an empty skewer with the sharp tip aimed downward by his side. "Henry Simms?"

The man's bloodshot gaze turned to Azad. "That's right. Do I know you?"

"Damned right you do," Azad said tersely.

A flicker of emotion crossed Azad's face—part incredulous and part furious. Beneath the fluorescent lighting in the kitchen, his dark complexion looked flushed, and Lucy was surprised by his uncharacteristic reaction.

Once again, Henry raised the empty bottle. In his drunken state, he must have missed the tension in Azad's expression and voice. "Good. Be a useful cook and fetch me another one of these."

Azad turned a mottled shade of red. "You don't remember me, do you?"

Henry Simms shrugged. "Sorry."

"I can't believe you don't remember." Azad took another step closer, his fingers tightening on the skewer. "You're the bank president of Ocean Crest Savings and Loan. You assured me that my loan had been approved by *your* bank, only to later tell me there had been a mistake and the loan fell through."

A loan? Lucy turned from the intoxicated best man to Azad. He'd never mentioned a loan to her in the past.

"Sorry. Still don't know who you are or what you're talkin' about," Henry slurred, and wavered on his feet.

Azad's jaw hardened like a lump of granite. "When I went back to the bank and asked other workers, they had no idea what happened. Not one bank employee could explain it to me."

"You must have the wrong person," Henry said.

"No, I don't." Azad's eyes narrowed and he took a step closer. "Whatever you did cost me five grand in attorney's fees and a shot at a great business opportunity."

Lucy knew Azad had planned to buy Kebab Kitchen months ago. He'd told her he changed his mind when she'd decided to stay in Ocean Crest and manage the restaurant. Had he not been entirely truthful? Had he backed off because a bank loan didn't go through?

And even more important, did her parents know about it and not tell her?

Henry laughed. "I think you need a bottle of whiskey more than me."

Azad's nostrils flared. "You messed with my life. I've always wondered, how many others there are."

A cold wave swept through the room, and the busy kitchen grew silent as all eyes focused on Azad and Henry Simms. Butch stopped plating dishes, Katie stopped scooping hummus in bowls, and the liveried servers halted in midstep as all eyes zeroed in on the battle. There was nothing like a fight to quiet a crowd.

Henry Simms set the empty bottle on the counter. "Since you won't help me with the whiskey, I'll go back to the cocktail hour."

After Simms exited the room, Azad raised his skewer and pointed to the still-swinging doors. "Damned drunk. One of these days, that crooked banker is going to get his due."

CHAPTER 3

Azad's altercation with Henry Simms was forgotten as the cocktail hour ended and dinner service began. Tureens of lentil soup were carried out by the waitstaff and ladled into the guests' bowls for the first course. Meanwhile, Azad and Butch were busy in the kitchen plating the main course—shish kebab with sides of bulgur pilaf, eggplant bake, and a delicate spinach salad with lemon and olive oil dressing. Lucy, along with Katie, followed the next wave of servers out of the kitchen.

"Wow!" Katie halted just outside the swinging kitchen doors and nearly caused Lucy to run into her.

Lucy took a quick breath as she caught her first glimpse of Castle of the Sea's ballroom. With its Greek revival architectural, Corinthian columns, and gilded molding, it was magnificent. The walls were covered with beautiful flocked wallpaper, and blue velvet drapes hung on floor-to-ceiling windows overlooking the ocean. The hardwood dance floor was polished and shining. As for the decorations, Victoria Redding had done a fabulous job. Crystal and fine china glittered beneath enormous chandeliers. Centerpieces of creamy white and pink roses graced snowy white linens. Pale pink napkins matched the silk chair covers to create a whimsical atmosphere.

"Check out the wedding cake. Susan Cutie outdid herself this time," Katie said.

Katie was right. A table set up to the side of the dance floor displayed a multi-tiered cake with masses of pink roses. A heart-shaped, porcelain wedding topper of a couple kissing rested on top of the confectionary masterpiece.

"Look at the bride," Katie whispered in awe.

Lucy's attention turned to the head table. Scarlet Westwood looked stunning in a couture wedding gown of silk and gauze. Her blond hair was loose and she wore a delicate tiara of silver beads. Lucy had seen pictures of the groom, Bradford Papadopoulos, who was close to thirty years older than Scarlet. His Mediterranean roots were visible in his olive complexion and dark hair. He wasn't the first wealthy, older man Scarlet had been with, but the first she'd wed. Lucy couldn't help but wonder if Scarlet had married him to help her budding acting career.

The rest of the bridal party was a mix of contrasts. Lucy had read in the gossip columns that the maid of honor, Cressida Connolly, had gone to the same private high school as Scarlet. Cressida was pretty, with red hair styled in a Brigitte Bardot–inspired updo that set off her blue eyes. Unfortunately for Cressida, her escort was the intoxicated, obnoxious, and older Henry Simms.

A few Ocean Crest residents were guests as well. Lucy recognized Edna and Edith Gray, two elderly spinsters and owners of a boardwalk shop; the mayor, Thomas Huckerby; and members of the town council.

The Gray sisters looked up and smiled at Lucy, and she waved back.

Soon, the crackle of the microphone sounded and the band began to play Mediterranean dance music. The guests formed a line, held pinkies, and began a lively line dance. The groom's side knew the steps, and they invited the bride's family to join them. The pounding of the *doumbek*, a goblet-shaped drum played while held under one arm, and the *oud*, a pear-shaped string instrument, had Lucy tapping her feet. She hadn't danced to the traditional songs in years.

From the corner of her eye, Lucy spotted Henry push back his chair, then make his way to the bride and groom, who were sitting at the head table. He was a bit unsteady on his feet, and before he could reach the couple, he was waylaid by Victoria Redding, who grasped his sleeve. She whispered something in his ear, and when he responded, she dropped his sleeve and her face screwed into an unpleasant expression. Henry seized the opportunity and darted away from Victoria as if a team of angry football players were chasing him, then made a beeline for Scarlet and Bradford.

The tensing of Victoria's jaw revealed her extreme disapproval. In some strange way, it was satisfying to Lucy to see that the uptight wedding planner gave others a hard time as well.

The band ceased playing and the singer handed Henry his microphone. Henry tapped the end of the mic, causing a burst of static, then raised his glass. "As the best man, I'd like to pro . . . propose a toast to the bride and groom," Henry slurred. "Brad and I go way back . . . back to college a long time ago, when we were fraternity brothers, and I'm happy my friend met a nice gal like Scarlet."

The guests clapped in approval.

"That explains why Henry Simms is the best man," Lucy said. "College frat brothers. I can just picture both men pumping beer kegs while trying to flirt with sorority girls."

Katie chuckled. "I can see it."

Lucy watched a wave of servers head their way. "We better return to the kitchen." They had gaped enough and they didn't need to stay for the congratulatory speeches. She nudged Katie and they hurried back to the kitchen to check that everything was ready for the dessert course.

Butch set a knife and cake server on the counter. "They're getting ready for the wedding cake, and it will be time for the baklava soon."

Katie counted the trays of baklava on the counter. "We're one short," she said. "Did we leave one in the van?"

Lucy recalled the tray that had tumbled in the van when Azad had hit the pole. "No. We had an accident earlier. I made an extra tray, but forgot to bring it inside. Too much on my mind, I guess. I'll go get it now." She needed a breath of fresh air. The kitchen was hot as Hades and she was sweating from running back and forth from the ballroom to the kitchen.

A sudden thought came to her, and Lucy halted by the back door. "Azad, I need the van key."

She recalled Azad had locked the van after they'd unloaded. Her dad always insisted they lock the van to prevent theft at catering jobs. She doubted it would be a problem at Castle of the Sea, but her father's lessons were ingrained.

Without looking up from his work, Azad pulled the key from his front pocket and tossed it to her.

Lucy hurried outside and headed for the van, but just as she reached the vehicle, voices sounded in the parking lot.

Angry, shouting voices.

Lucy spotted Henry Simms and Victoria Redding four cars away. Victoria's hands were planted on her hips and her gaze was narrowed on Henry. She was talking—no yelling—at Henry. He must have finished his speech and the two were now outside going at it.

Neither of them had noticed her. Impulsively, Lucy ducked behind the van and peeked around the side. Her ears perked up at Victoria's harsh tone, and she strained to hear.

"How could you!" Victoria screeched.

Henry crossed his arms on his chest and leaned against a white Rolls-Royce, the newlyweds' getaway car. White streamers dangled from the trunk and a hand-written sign in the rear window read, JUST MARRIED.

"I don't know what you're talking about," Henry said.

"Don't play dumb with me. I saw you smuggle a cell phone into the reception and sneak shots. I told you, no pictures," Victoria snapped.

Henry looked nonplussed. "What's the harm in a few shots?"

Victoria's eyes narrowed. "I was crystal clear. Scarlet and Bradford said *no* pictures."

"I know what Scarlet said, but the attention will help launch her new perfume line."

"Is money all you think about?" Victoria said.

"I'm a banker, remember? Money is my livelihood," Henry said.

Victoria extended her hand, palm up. "Hand it over."

Henry shook his head. "You can't be serious."

"I'm dead serious. Hand your cell phone over. I'm stashing it where you can't get it until after the reception."

"Where?"

Victoria glanced around the lot until her eyes narrowed in Lucy's direction. "I hired the caterers. I can easily have them lock whatever I want in the catering van."

Lucy's heart jolted in momentary panic, and she shrank lower behind the wheel to be sure she was out of sight. The hot blacktop seared her palms, and the heat seeped through her pants to her knees. She dared not move an inch.

Victoria wasn't heading to the van, was she?

Thankfully, the pair stayed put.

Henry reluctantly turned over his cell phone. "I expected you to be more reasonable. You owe me. I got you this job, remember?"

Victoria widened her stance and glared down at him. With her five-inch heels she was taller than the average-height Simms. "You never let me forget it."

"Then we're even now."

"Even?" Victoria laughed bitterly. "I put everything on the line for you. We're far from even."

"You're acting like a bitter shrew."

Victoria stiffened and sheer hatred crossed her face. "God, I hate you. You'll pay for this if it's the last thing I do." She turned on her heel.

"Wait! Victoria!" Henry shouted after her, but she ignored him and stormed off.

Lucy came to life and scurried farther behind the

van as Victoria kept walking and returned to the building.

Henry shook his head and sagged against the Rolls-Royce. For the first time, he didn't appear like an attractive older man, but rather he looked every bit of his fifty-something years. He scrubbed his hand down his face, and then stumbled back to the wedding.

Lucy stayed where she was, mulling over what she'd witnessed.

First Azad. Now Victoria.

One thing was clear: Henry Simms wasn't liked by many people.

She finally stood from where she had been squatting and stretched her cramped legs. She opened the back doors of the van and fetched the extra baklava tray. Balancing the tray on one hand, she fished for the key in her back pocket, then locked the door.

She wasn't worried about Victoria carrying out her threat and stashing Henry's cell phone in the van. Now that Lucy knew what was up, if Victoria asked her to store anything, Lucy could refuse her request. Victoria didn't have the key and would have to find somewhere else to hide the cell phone until the reception was over. Henry didn't know that, but that didn't matter. If he tried to get in the van, he'd have no luck.

Confident no one had seen her spying, Lucy hurried back to the kitchen.

"Took you long enough. Dessert service is just about to start," Azad mumbled as he cut a tray of baklava in diamond-shaped slices. The pastry smelled delicious, a rich combination of butter, chopped walnuts, cinnamon, and flaky phyllo dough, and Lucy was momentarily distracted. A large jar of simple sugar syrup was on the counter waiting to be poured over the cut baklava. She'd be sure to have a piece as soon as this wedding was finally over.

Azad halted his work to glare at her. "What? You want a piece now?"

With a huff, Lucy slapped the key on the counter and walked away. She wanted to tell him that the wedding had more drama than a soap opera, but decided against it. No sense bringing up the subject of Henry Simms right now. Azad had reacted quite strongly the first time.

Hours later, Lucy had forgotten the argument between Henry and Victoria. After serving twenty trays of baklava and wedding cake, they'd bagged slices of leftover cake and baklava for the guests to take home. When all the work was finished, Lucy let out a big sigh of relief. She pulled a stool up to the work counter and sipped a glass of water. Her lower back ached and her feet throbbed. Now that their catering work was done they could leave. The band was booked for only one more hour, and the staff of Castle of the Sea would remain to clean up the ballroom.

Katie joined her with a plate of leftover wedding cake. She took a bite and shut her eyes. "Hmm. This is good." She set down her fork and patted Lucy on the back. "Congratulations! Your first catering foray was a huge success."

"Thanks, but I couldn't have done it without you, Azad, and Butch."

Katie thrust her plate of cake at Lucy. "Have a bite while I sneak into the ballroom to see if there's extra champagne to celebrate." She pushed back her stool and headed out of the kitchen and into the ballroom.

Butch approached and smiled, his gold tooth

flashing beneath the fluorescent lights. "Your friend is right. You did good, Lucy Lou."

She stood and hugged Butch. Her arms didn't reach halfway around his massive chest.

Azad had a bemused look on his face. "I have to agree. Great job with the servers, Lucy. Butch and I were able to focus entirely on the food while we knew you would handle the rest."

Lucy smiled at the praise. She also knew better than to hug *him*. She'd struggled to shut out any awareness of Azad and it was best to avoid physical contact.

"I meant what I said. You both did the lion's share of the work. I can't cook and you two know it," Lucy said.

It was an opening for Azad to tease her, but he didn't. Instead, he took off his chef's hat, ran his fingers through his dark locks, and said, "We better start packing before that testy wedding planner returns. I'll get the rolling carts from the van." He picked up some clean pots and pans and departed through the back door.

She stared after him with a frown. She knew he was right. Why give Victoria Redding a reason to complain? Then why did she feel an odd twinge of disappointment that he hadn't taken the opportunity to remind her of her lack of culinary talents? Did she actually miss his teasing? Had it become a form of flirting?

Don't go there, Lucy.

Swallowing the lump in her throat, Lucy busied herself by helping Butch gather the soup pots and equipment. But when Azad didn't return after ten minutes, she frowned. How long could it take to roll a cart from the van into the kitchen? Had he been waylaid by Victoria in the parking lot? Was he getting a tongue-lashing as they waited? Or was Victoria retrieving Henry's cell phone from beneath the van's bumper? Lucy wouldn't put anything past the woman.

"I'm going to check on Azad," she told Butch.

She jogged back to the van and slowed as she spotted Azad outside the van's open back doors. One hand clutched the door, his knuckles white.

"Azad?"

No response.

The hair on the nape of her neck stood on end as she came close. "Is everything okay?"

She looked inside and froze. There, splayed on the floor of the van, was Henry Simms, stabbed in the neck with a shish kebab skewer.

CHAPTER 4

Lucy bit back a scream and managed to ask, "Is he dead?"

Azad stood motionless, looking almost as pale as Henry Simms.

"Azad!" she snapped.

He let go of the van door and stumbled back. "I don't know."

Lucy reached out and placed her fingers on Henry's neck, opposite where the deadly skewer had entered.

Nothing. Nada. No pulse. It was what she'd feared. Henry was dead.

She resisted the urge to cross herself. "What happened?"

Azad's gaze remained riveted on the corpse. Afternoon sunlight illuminated the fine lines around his eyes and mouth. "I don't know. He was like that when I opened the doors."

"We need to call the police." When Azad didn't move, she tugged on his arm and pushed him through the service doors. The first person she searched for was Katie. Lucy found her washing a large soup pot.

Her shirt sleeves were rolled up and she was up to her elbows in suds. A half-full bottle of champagne was by the sink.

Katie's eyes lit up as soon as she spotted them. "Hey, Lucy. Look what I found. As soon as I finish up here, we can properly celebrate our—"

"Where's Bill?" Lucy asked.

Katie halted in the middle of scrubbing the pot. "Probably at the police station for the end of his shift. Why?"

"We need to call him. There's a dead body in the van."

The pot slipped from Katie's hands to clatter in the sink. "What?"

Lucy's pulse hammered in her veins as she spoke. "Henry Simms . . . the best man . . . he was stabbed in the neck with a skewer. We found him dead in the van." Lucy turned to Azad, but he had a faraway look in his eyes, probably shock.

Lucy was still in a state of astonishment. Had Henry believed Victoria had stashed his cell phone in the catering van? Had he somehow broken into the van to try to get his phone back?

Was he stabbed inside or killed elsewhere and then dumped in their van?

"Lord!" Katie turned off the water and reached for a dish towel to dry her hands. "I'll call Bill."

Lucy nodded and turned toward the service door leading outside.

"Wait!" Katie grasped her sleeve. "You can't go back out there. You said he was stabbed. What if the killer is still out there?"

Azad finally spoke up. "Katie's right. I didn't see

anyone out there, but that doesn't mean someone isn't watching. It may not be safe."

Lucy's stomach flipped like a fish on a line. She hadn't thought about that possibility. Could Henry's killer be lingering outside?

Katie pulled her cell phone from her back pocket. "Nobody move until the police get here."

The first one through the door into the kitchen was Ocean Crest police officer Bill Watson. He arrived with a young, freckled-faced officer with a crew cut who didn't look old enough to have a driver's license.

Bill headed straight for Katie. "You okay?"

Katie nodded at her husband. Bill was tall, lean, and still had a full head of thick brown hair. He hadn't changed much since the couple had met in high school.

Bill's gaze shifted to Lucy. "How about you? You all right?"

Lucy took a deep breath before answering. She was currently staying with Katie and Bill, and she considered Bill a good friend. But it was the sight of Bill in his uniform that was the most reassuring to her frayed nerves. "I'm fine. Azad was the first to find the body. I checked for a pulse, but there isn't one."

Azad leaned heavily on a worktable, a distinctly green tinge to his face.

"Where's the body?" the young officer asked.

"In the catering van outside," Lucy said.

"All right. Let's see." Bill and the young officer exited through the service door to the parking lot. Lucy, Azad, and Katie trailed behind and halted by the open van doors. Lucy stiffened at the sight of

Henry's body. His eyes were open and unseeing. She hadn't noticed his eyes before. She'd been too focused on the shish kebab skewer in his throat.

Bill pulled out plastic gloves from his belt, snapped them on, and pressed two fingers to Henry's carotid artery. "We need to call in the county coroner." He reached for his walkie-talkie and barked a few orders, just as another police car and the paramedics pulled into the service lot.

Ocean Crest's sole detective, Calvin Clemmons, stepped out of the car. A tall man in his midforties, he was dressed in a dark suit and had straw-colored hair and a bushy mustache. He scanned the crime scene, his expression arrogant, his mouth tight and grim. Then his reptilian gaze caught and held Lucy's, and she struggled not to cringe.

He'd been unfriendly toward her since she got stuck in the middle of a murder case last May. He was probably still bitter that he hadn't been able to pin the poisoning of the health inspector on Lucy. Of course, he didn't care for her family. Not after Lucy's older sister, Emma, had cheated on Clinging Calvin, as she'd called him, with Calvin's best friend in high school. Emma had a tendency to be unfaithful back then, and the fact their parents had never liked Calvin Clemmons hadn't helped matters.

"Well, well. What do we have here?" Clemmons stalked close and crouched down to inspect the body. Lucy heard the strains of the band and the tinkle of laughter from inside the ballroom, and she was relieved the wedding guests hadn't yet learned of the gruesome scene in the parking lot. She cleared her throat. "His name is Henry Simms, and he was the best man in the wedding."

Clemmons stood and his beady eyes focused on her. "Lucy Berberian. Why am I not surprised you're involved in this mess?"

"I'm not involved. We catered the wedding and just happened to find the body in the van."

Clemmons pushed his suit jacket aside to rest his hand on his belt. A shaft of sunlight hit his service weapon. "Hmm. And Mr. Simms was murdered in your catering van with what I'm guessing is a shish kebab skewer from your restaurant."

Lucy's pulse battered erratically through her veins. Detective Clemmons had a knack for making everything sound bad.

"Why was he in your van in the first place?" Clemmons asked.

That was the million-dollar question. "I have no idea."

"Who found the body first?" Clemens asked.

Azad stepped forward. "I did."

Clemmons pulled a notepad from his shirt pocket, flipped it open, and removed a pencil from behind his ear. "And you are?"

"Azad Zakarian. Head chef of Kebab Kitchen."

"Ok, Azad. What time did you find the body?"

"About a half hour ago. We finished the catering job, and I returned to the van to get the rolling carts so that we could pack up our equipment."

Azad's normally olive complexion looked even paler, a feat Lucy didn't think possible. Good grief, she hoped he didn't throw up all over the detective's shoes.

"Were the rear van doors closed when you came out?" Clemmons continued.

"Yes."

"Were they locked?"

Azad frowned, and it was clear he was thinking back. "No. I don't think so."

Lucy spoke up. "They were locked. I locked the van when I went back."

"When was that?" Clemmons asked.

"I had to fetch an extra tray of baklava for the dessert course. I locked the van afterward," Lucy said.

"You sure?"

"Yes."

Clemmons jerked his head toward the younger officer. "Check for signs of tampering." The officer began to circle the van and check the doors. Meanwhile, Clemmons crouched down by the body to examine it more closely. Everyone seemed to hold their breath as he studied the corpse.

"Was he killed in the van or moved inside after he was murdered?" Lucy asked.

A look of annoyance crossed the detective's face. "That's what we'll find out."

The young officer returned and stopped before Clemmons. "It doesn't look as if the locks have been tampered with."

"We'll confirm that for certain at the lab later." Clemmons stood and turned back to Lucy. "What did you do with the key after you locked the van?"

"I returned it to Azad," Lucy said.

Clemmons looked at Azad. "You still have it?"

Azad patted his pocket. "I do."

Clemens nodded once. "Good. I'll take a look at it later. Now tell me what happened after you found the body. Did you move it? Touch anything?"

"No! I was carrying an armful of pots and equipment to the van in order to save a trip, but I dropped everything and had to stop and pick it all up. I set everything down outside the van and fished in my pocket for the key to open the door. That's when I realized the door was unlocked and I found Henry Simms." Azad ran a shaky hand through his dark hair. "Lucy came soon afterward."

Clemmons's stare drilled into her. "What made you come back out if Mr. Zakarian was already fetching the carts?"

"We were in the kitchen waiting for Azad to return. When he didn't come back, I went after him. That's when I saw . . . Mr. Simms."

"I see." Clemmons scrawled in his notepad, and Lucy struggled with the urge to tear it out of his hands to see what he was writing.

Clemmons looked up. "Did any of you know the victim?"

"No," Katie said.

"No," Lucy echoed, before she recalled the argument Azad had with Henry Simms in the kitchen. Her nervousness escalated, and she exchanged a quick glance with Katie. The last thing Lucy wanted to do was bring up Azad's fight with the dead Henry Simms. But surely it would come out? The entire staff of Castle of the Sea had witnessed it.

Clemmons pointed his pencil at Azad. "And you? Did you know the victim?"

Azad opened his mouth to answer just as a woman's scream pierced the air. All heads turned to see Victoria Redding race across the lot as fast as her five-inch heels would allow. "What's going on here?" She came to a screeching halt a few feet from the van and craned her neck to peer inside. "Is that Henry?" she gasped.

Bill intercepted her just as she stepped forward to get a better look. "Calm down, ma'am."

Victoria thrust Bill's hand aside. "Calm down! How

can I calm down when he's been hurt?" One hand flew to her chest, the other to her mouth as her gaze was riveted on the body. "What's that sticking out of his neck? Is he . . . is he dead?"

"Ma'am—" Bill started.

"My Lord, he *is* dead." Victoria's eyes widened. "Poor, poor Henry. Who would do this to him?"

"If you'll step aside and let us do our job—"

Victoria scanned the group, as if noticing them for the first time. Her kohl-lined eyes narrowed as they came to rest on Azad. "You!" she screeched, pointing to Azad. "I just spoke with the waitstaff, who said a fight broke out earlier in the kitchen and you threatened to kill Henry. You were a maniac, yelling and screaming, and brandished a shish kebab skewer at Henry."

The detective's accusing gaze was riveted on Azad. "Is this true? Did you know the victim?"

A shadow of alarm crossed Azad's face. "We had dealt with each other in the past. I had applied for a loan from his bank. It was business, that's all."

"He's lying! Numerous people witnessed him scream at Henry and blame him for denying him a bank loan. They reported the incident to me straightway," Victoria said.

Uh-oh. The kitchen had been full of people when Azad had lost his temper. Even Lucy had been surprised at his uncharacteristic outburst toward the intoxicated best man. She wouldn't be surprised that they'd reported the incident to Victoria. The wedding planner most likely had other weddings at Castle of the Sea, whereas the staff owed Lucy no loyalty.

Lucy had known Azad since she'd been a teenager.

He may have threatened Henry Simms with bodily harm, but he didn't mean *that*.

"I didn't mean it," Azad blurted out.

"So you did threaten to kill Mr. Simms?" Clemmons said.

"That's not what he said," Lucy argued.

Katie piped up. "I can back up Lucy. Ms. Redding is exaggerating. I was there and I don't remember him threatening to kill Mr. Simms."

Victoria's red-glossed lips twisted with distaste. "It's true. All you have to do is ask any of the staff. That man threatened Henry with bodily harm."

"So did she," Lucy blurted out.

Clemmons's stare drilled into Lucy. "What do you mean?"

Lucy raised her chin a notch. "I overheard an argument between Victoria and Henry. It happened just over there," she said, pointing to the spot where the Rolls-Royce was parked. "*She* threatened him."

"When was this?" Clemmons demanded.

"About an hour ago, when I had returned for the baklava tray. They were arguing something fierce. Henry Simms had smuggled a cell phone into the reception, and Ms. Redding told him it wasn't allowed. She took his cell phone and said she'd ask us to lock it in the catering van until after the reception."

"Did she ask you?" Clemmons said.

"Well, no . . . but—"

Victoria huffed. "That's ludicrous. I met Henry outside during the reception to go over the final details of his duties as best man. It's true I took his phone, but I never stored it in the van or asked to do so. I have it right here," she said as she reached inside a dyed emerald handbag that matched her high heels and whipped out a cell phone. "I only requested Henry give it to me and he complied without complaint. He'd forgotten about the rule." Victoria shot Lucy a sidelong glare. "But Ms. Berberian must have misunderstood what she'd heard. It's not surprising since she'd been eavesdropping. God only knows where she was hiding."

Clemmons arched his shaggy eyebrow. "Were you eavesdropping?"

Lucy squirmed. "I didn't plan on it. She was screaming at Henry. I didn't want to get involved so I ducked behind the van until they were finished."

Victoria's eyes flashed. "See. She was eavesdropping, Detective. She couldn't possibly have overheard everything correctly, and she's taking things out of context."

"What did you tell Henry?" Clemmons said.

"Like I said," Victoria continued, "I went over his duties as best man. He was to speak with the chauffeur and arrange for transportation for Scarlet and Bradford to a nearby hotel. The final destination is kept secret to avoid gossip and press. We also talked about how best to avoid paparazzi during the car ride. After he handed over his cell phone, I told him I'd return it at the end of the reception. But I certainly never threatened to kill him."

"She's lying," Lucy said.

Detective Clemmons eyed Lucy speculatively. "So you say, Ms. Berberian."

Lucy breathed in a shallow, quick gasp. "What's that supposed to mean? I'm telling the—"

"Surely you see what's going on, Detective," Victoria said, cutting her off. "Ms. Berberian is making up an elaborate story to protect her head chef. No other witness will verify what she claims she overheard whereas a dozen employees witnessed the fight between her chef and Henry."

Lucy couldn't believe what she was hearing. The woman was an outright liar. But she was telling the truth about one thing: Lucy was the only witness to Victoria's argument with Henry whereas more than half of the crew of Castle of the Sea witnessed Azad's fight with the victim.

Lucy's hands fisted at her sides. She had a strong urge to punch the wedding planner square in the nose.

Victoria Redding wasn't quite done. She leaned an inch closer to stare at Henry's body, then straightened. Her hand fluttered to her chest. "Besides, isn't that your skewer sticking out of Henry's neck?"

Detective Clemmons's chest expanded in his suit, and his mustache twitched with a self-satisfied and arrogant smirk.

Alarm bells went off in Lucy's head, and she struggled to keep her shoulders square. She knew him well enough now to spot the malicious gleam in his gaze. She'd faced it before, when he wanted to arrest her for murder.

Azad was in serious trouble.

Butch, Katie, and the staff of Castle of the Sea were interviewed next. Unlike when he questioned Lucy and Azad, Detective Clemmons was quick with the others. Meanwhile, Henry Simms had already been pronounced legally dead, and the county medical examiner and the other officers continued taking photographs and processing the scene. Lucy cringed as the medical examiner zipped up the body bag and Henry was carried away.

After Detective Clemmons had finished interviewing the others, he approached Lucy. "You're still staying with Officer Watson and his wife?"

Lucy nodded numbly.

"All right. Don't leave town." He pierced Azad with an unfriendly glare. "You either."

"I have no plans to leave," Lucy said. "I'm managing Kebab Kitchen now."

Clemens tapped his pad with a pen. "Your parents retired?"

"Not entirely. They're part-time."

The pen halted. "And Emma?"

Oh, no. She didn't want to go down that path. It was clear Clemmons still held a grudge.

"Emma still works there. Now can we please leave?" Lucy turned to Azad and hoped he'd be of some assistance. But Azad stood still as a statue and stared at the pool of blood on the floor of the van where Henry had lain.

A terrible tenseness filled Lucy's body. How would she ever look at the van and not think of Henry sprawled on its floor? The image of the skewer would be forever imprinted in her mind.

Azad pulled the van key out of his pocket and thrust it at Lucy. "I think you should drive back, Lucy."

Lucy reached out to take the key, but Clemmons stepped in between them. "I'll take that," Clemmons said. He withdrew an evidence bag from a kit and motioned for Azad to drop the key inside.

Lucy blinked. "You're taking the van?"

Clemmons looked at her as if she was an idiot. "Until we examine the vehicle with a fine-tooth comb for evidence, the van is an active crime scene. Same goes for everything in it."

Just great. She should have known. The impounding of the catering van posed all sorts of problems. Never mind that moments ago Lucy was wondering how she would be able to set foot in it. Now she was wondering how they would get back. "If you take the van, then how on earth are we supposed to get all our equipment back to the restaurant?"

The detective's dark eyes impaled her. "That's your problem, Ms. Berberian. If you stayed away from crime scenes and dead bodies, then you wouldn't have to worry about it."

CHAPTER 5

It was well after midnight by the time the four of them drove back in Butch's battered Buick. As soon as the car pulled into a spot in front of Kebab Kitchen, Lucy spotted a pair of glowing green eyes. The car door squealed in protest when she pushed it open.

"Hi, Gadoo." He was the outdoor restaurant cat that her mother had adopted while Lucy was away and working in Philadelphia. The Armenian "Gadoo" translated simply as "cat," and the feline visited twice a day like clockwork to eat. He was exceptional at chasing away the birds and any outdoor rodents who dared cross the parking lot.

The cat came close and she scooped him into her arms and buried her fingers into his soft fur. After the tumultuous events of the evening, his purr was comforting.

Azad placed a hand on her arm. "You can't take him inside. Your mom will have a fit."

Lucy frowned and stepped away. She knew her mother was obsessed with cleanliness in the restaurant and everything had to be bleached at the end of the day, but Lucy wasn't ready to put Gadoo down. "I don't think it's the cat that will make her upset tonight." She walked to the door. "Besides, she's let the cat inside on occasion."

Azad grumbled a response, but opened the door. The group shuffled inside.

Her parents were sitting at a large table waiting for their return. A bottle of Raffi's favorite ouzo—an anise-flavored alcoholic drink—sat unopened on the table to celebrate Lucy's first catering job. Angela stood, her gaze traveling from Lucy's face, to the cat in her arms, back to Lucy.

"What's wrong?" Angela asked.

Lucy let out a sigh and explained the night's events.

"Are you saying a man was murdered? In the catering van?" Her mother looked at her in shock. Her father gazed at her as if she had grown two heads.

Lucy couldn't blame them.

Everyone pulled out chairs and joined her parents at the table. Gadoo jumped off Lucy's lap to rest on the windowsill. Thankfully, her mother didn't comment on the cat. She must truly be in shock. Her father poured everyone a glass of ouzo. But now, instead of toasting their success, they sipped the liquor in silence. Her mother responded the way she always did when bad news hit: she rushed into the kitchen and returned with a *mezze* plate of hummus, olives, feta cheese, and pita.

Lucy cleared her throat. "We couldn't leave until Detective Clemmons finished questioning each of us. The police took the van and we had to leave the equipment behind."

Raffi reached across the table to squeeze her hand.

"Forget the equipment. We can go back and get it tomorrow. All of you are what's most important."

Lucy sipped her drink. She had never been a fan of the anise-flavored alcohol, but she needed something to ease her nerves. "We're fine, Dad. We're all just a little shook up." She wondered if she would be able to sleep tonight.

Angela wrung a cloth napkin. "Finding that man must have been frightening."

"It was, Mrs. Berberian," Azad said. "I panicked. Lucy was the one to think fast, and she ran inside to call the police." Azad finished his ouzo, and Raffi was quick to refill it.

Lucy was surprised by Azad's statement. He *had* frozen, and she had been the one to drag him inside and have Katie call the police, but she hadn't expected him to thank her for it.

"You both received a shock." Her mother placed olives, cheese, and hummus on small plates and passed them out. "Please eat. Food and drink will calm you."

Despite the stress, Lucy smiled. Her mother believed food was the answer to everything—happy times and stressful ones. They all knew better than to refuse her.

"And to think," her mother continued, "we were worried all evening about the catering and whether the guests would enjoy the shish kebab."

"Lucy did a great job overseeing everything, Mr. and Mrs. B," Butch said. "The dinner service went well, too." He took off his checkered bandana and rubbed his bald pate. "But I don't think the guests will be talking about the food after they learn what happened to the best man."

A sudden flash of anger lit Angela's eyes. "I knew

that woman would cause trouble. Drama is Scarlet Westwood's livelihood."

"It wasn't Scarlet's fault." Lucy found herself defending the socialite, then halted. She didn't know whose fault it was, and she'd learned firsthand from the last time someone had been murdered in Ocean Crest that not everyone was who they appeared to be. Who knew if Scarlet had a role in Henry's death?

Victoria Redding was the first person who came to mind. Lucy had overheard her nasty fight with the best man. It didn't matter that she kept Henry's phone and never hid it in the van. All that mattered was if Henry *thought* she had. But how did either Henry or Victoria get into the locked van? And if she killed him somewhere else, how did she move Henry? He outweighed her by at least fifty pounds.

Victoria wanted to pin the murder on Azad, and the next time Lucy crossed the wedding planner's path, she had a few choice words for her.

Azad may not be perfect, especially as a former boyfriend who'd broken her heart years ago, but he wasn't a killer.

So, who else could have done the dirty deed?

The truth was, *anyone* at that wedding could have killed Henry Simms.

"Thank goodness it wasn't from the food. I don't think we could survive that again," her mother said, referring to the death of the health inspector months ago.

"Do they have any idea who would do such a thing to the best man?" Her father looked at Katie. "Does Bill know?"

Katie lowered her fork and set it next to her plate. "It's too soon to tell. They won't know until the investigation is complete."

"Do they have any suspects?"

Other than Azad? Lucy thought.

"Everyone at the wedding is a potential suspect," Katie said. "The investigation will take time."

Raffi nodded. "Azad and Butch, you two go home. You've had a long day. Angela and I will lock up the restaurant."

A flash of relief crossed Azad's face. He finished his drink in one swallow and pushed back his chair. "Thanks. I'll be here in the morning," he said as he went to the door.

Lucy was glad to see the color had returned to Azad's complexion. Maybe it was the drink and the food, but then he turned to wave, and she noticed the tight lines around his eyes and mouth. He was clearly still stressed.

Butch rose and followed Azad out.

Once she was alone with Katie and her parents, Lucy was able to express her concerns. Calvin Clemmons had been on her mind since he'd questioned them. She hadn't missed the glint in his eye. It was almost victorious.

"I'm worried about Azad," Lucy said.

Her mother tilted her head to the side and regarded her. "Azad? Why?"

"Well . . . he found the body."

"So?"

How much to tell? "Azad had bad business dealings with Henry's bank. They fought in the kitchen," Lucy said.

Lucy watched her parents' expressions closely. Did they know about a possible loan? Had they planned for Azad to purchase Kebab Kitchen all along, and never told Lucy after the loan fell through? Was she their second choice to take over the family business?

Azad had claimed he supported her decision to stay in Ocean Crest and manage the restaurant. Had he lied? Was the real reason he'd agreed to work for Lucy as the new head chef because he couldn't get the cash to buy the place?

He'd also led her to believe he wanted to date her again.

Was it all a farce?

"What bad business dealings?" her father asked, interrupting her thoughts.

Lucy pursed her lips. "Something about a loan that never went through. He was pretty upset about it. Azad lost money in attorney fees."

And a business opportunity.

Both Angela and Raffi had blank looks on their faces, like they had no idea what she was talking about. Maybe she was wrong, and they were as clueless as she was.

"The kitchen is a stressful place, Lucy. Chefs are known to be temperamental. It's not uncommon for tempers to flare," Raffi said.

"Well, it flared with the wrong person today," Lucy said tersely.

An uncomfortable silence settled in the room. After several heartbeats, Katie spoke up. "Lucy has reason to be concerned. Detective Clemmons is narrow-minded. It's likely that he'll look for the easiest suspect, even if it's the wrong person."

"That man never liked us, and I haven't forgiven him for thinking it was my hummus that killed the health inspector," Angela said, her color high.

Raffi rubbed his chin with his thumb and forefinger.

"You think Clemmons will try to arrest Azad for the murder?"

"Azad fought with the victim in a kitchen full of impartial witnesses while holding a shish kebab skewer, then he found the dead victim in our catering van. One of our skewers was sticking out of his neck. A dozen or so people saw him fight with the victim in the kitchen. The murder weapon was one of our shish kebab skewers, and everyone saw Azad preparing the shish kebab in the kitchen," Lucy pointed out.

Raffi drew his lips in thoughtfully. "If Detective Clemmons tries to blame Azad, then you have to help him, Lucy."

Surprise coursed through her. "Me?"

"Yes. You have to find the real killer. You did it before, you can do it again," her dad said. "Katie can help you."

He demanded she help as if he was talking about stapling posters to telephone poles to find a lost neighborhood dog, not a murderer. Lucy looked at Katie for help.

But Katie didn't protest.

No help there. Her friend was obsessed with watching crime television shows and detective movies. Lucy suspected it was one of the reasons Katie had been attracted to Bill in high school after learning he planned on attending the police academy. Katie had helped her find a murderer a couple of months ago, and the thought of doing it again, instead of putting her off, seemed to intrigue Katie.

"Of course, Mr. Berberian. I'll do whatever I can to help," Katie said.

"I'm not sure that's a good idea," Lucy said.

"Why not?" Katie said. "We have nothing to lose. Azad on the other hand—"

"No." Her mother slammed a palm on the table. "I don't want Lucy or Katie to get involved. There's too much risk. We're talking about a killer who stabbed a man."

Lucy sat stunned. Of all the people to oppose her father's scheme, her mother was the last person on Lucy's list. Her mother adored Azad. Lucy had thought she'd be first in line to interview potential suspects.

Lucy patted her mother's hand. "Don't worry, Mom. We're not thinking about it. We learned our lesson last time."

But the problem was that Lucy *was* thinking about it, and from the look in Katie's eyes, her friend was, too.

Who had done the banker in?

The following morning, Lucy woke to a cool ocean breeze from her window. Katie and Bill lived in a charming ranch with a white picket fence two blocks from the Atlantic Ocean. The guest bedroom where Lucy had been staying since she'd left her city apartment and returned to Ocean Crest was cozy and comfortable. An iron daybed, painted a glossy white, was tucked in a corner. Sheer curtains embroidered with starfish and shells matched the thick coverlet and throw pillows and allowed for plenty of natural light. Watercolors of beach scenes hung on the pale blue walls, and a white wicker chair with a crab-print chair pad and a wicker chest of drawers occupied the rest of the room.

Lucy was glad she'd slept without memories of

bloody shish kebab skewers or crime scenes. But now that she was awake, thoughts of yesterday returned in a rush.

Who had killed Henry Simms? Despite her father's demands, logic dictated that she stay out of the murder investigation and let the police do their job. But a nagging feeling wouldn't go away: if Detective Clemmons was as quick as last time to point the finger at someone from Kebab Kitchen, she knew he'd overlook other suspects. So how could she stand aside and watch as Azad was arrested for a crime he didn't commit?

Lucy knew she had an inquisitive mind. It was her nature, and three years of law school had honed the tendency. It would be difficult to stay out of any investigation, and Katie would only encourage her involvement. Her friend was currently on a kick of watching every repeat episode of the former hit TV show *CSI: Crime Scene Investigation.*

Sitting up, Lucy slipped her feet into slippers and padded into the kitchen. The aroma of freshly brewed coffee wafted to her. She planned on having a cup, then taking an early morning jog on the boardwalk before heading to the restaurant to prepare for the lunch shift.

Katie was already in the kitchen and standing by the coffeemaker. She was dressed in yoga pants and a tank top, and her blond hair was pulled back in a ponytail. It was Sunday, and Katie worked only weekdays at the Ocean Crest town hall handling everything from marriage licenses to processing real estate taxes to renewing dog tags.

"Good morning," Katie said, handing Lucy a mug of steaming coffee.

Lucy gratefully accepted the coffee. She needed the caffeine more than usual this morning. "Thanks. Where's Bill?"

"He worked the overnight shift at the station. It's not every day there's a murder in Ocean Crest."

The mug halted halfway to Lucy's lips. "You mean until *I* returned to town."

"Neither is your fault." Katie refilled her coffee and added a good amount of cream and two heaping teaspoonfuls of sugar to her mug. Her friend had a sugar addiction whereas Lucy preferred her coffee black.

"I know, but I can't stop thinking about Henry Simms."

Katie sipped from her mug. "Me either. Who do you think killed that obnoxious banker?"

"Two hundred and fifty guests attended the reception, not including the hired help. That's a long list of possible suspects."

"The police can narrow it down, of course, and the employees and most of the guests probably didn't even know Henry or have a reason to kill him," Katie pointed out.

Lucy tapped her foot. "True. Victoria Redding is the first suspect who comes to mind. She was furious at Henry for smuggling a cell phone into the reception and for his plans to sell the pictures to the tabloids. She took his phone and threatened to store it in the van."

"He could have e-mailed or texted the pictures to the newspapers *before* she took his phone," Katie pointed out.

"I didn't think of that," Lucy said. "But what if he'd planned on taking more? The reception wasn't over."

"You think Henry tried to get his phone back and Victoria killed him?"

"Who knows? But the thing is, I'm not sure if a few tabloid pictures are enough motive for murder."

"Maybe Henry had other enemies at the wedding? Azad regarded him as an unethical banker. Victoria clearly viewed him as untrustworthy. Henry didn't strike me as an upstanding person."

Lucy shrugged. "You're right. But still, other than Victoria? I don't have a clue."

"Bill always says the first suspect is the spouse," Katie said. "And in all the crime shows I watch, the detectives interview the wife or husband first."

Lucy looked at Katie in surprise. "Henry Simms was married?"

"Didn't you notice his wedding ring?" Katie asked.

"No. I couldn't look past the skewer in his throat."

The scrape of a key in the front door drew their attention. "Bill's home from his shift. We can ask him." Katie set her mug down on the laminate countertop and smoothed her ponytail.

Bill stepped into the kitchen and halted at the sight of the two women leaning against the counter.

"Good morning." Katie smiled and moved forward to place a kiss on his cheek. "Can I get you a cup of coffee?"

Bill looked from Katie to Lucy, then back to Katie. "I know that expression on your faces."

Katie blinked innocently. "I just asked if you wanted coffee."

"No, you're wondering about the case."

"Hmm. Well, since you brought it up, what's the latest?" Katie poured a mug and handed it to him.

Bill took the mug, eyeing his wife warily. "You know

I'm not supposed to discuss an active investigation. And to make matters worse, you were both at the crime scene. There's a conflict of interest."

Katie shrugged a shoulder. "This is different from last time. Lucy isn't a suspect."

"That's true. But her head chef is—"

"I knew it!" Katie folded her arms across her chest. "Lucy has been worried sick about Azad."

Bill's frown deepened. "There may be good cause for worry."

Anxiety coursed through Lucy. "What about the wedding planner? She had it out with the victim, took his phone, and threatened him. She lied to Clemmons about that, and I'm worried the detective won't believe me."

"I believe you. And from what I've heard at the station, Clemmons will most likely bring Ms. Redding in for further questioning."

"But it still looks bad for Azad, doesn't it?" Lucy asked.

"What can you tell us, Bill?" Katie asked.

Bill frowned, his expression level under drawn brows. "Henry Simms was not killed elsewhere and moved into the catering van."

"You mean he was murdered *inside* the van?"

"That's right. Our crime scene investigators confirmed it."

Lucy recalled the puddle of blood in the van, and gooseflesh rose on her arms. "Henry must have broken into the van to search for his cell phone. He didn't know Victoria still had it."

Bill shook his head. "We inspected the van. No one tampered with the locks or windows. No one broke into the van."

Her heart began to pound. "Then how did Henry and a killer get inside? It doesn't make sense."

"Lucy, are you sure you locked the van after you went back for the baklava tray?" Bill asked.

"Yes." She had a distinct memory of juggling the tray, digging into her pocket for the key, and locking the van. She'd been worried about dropping the extra tray and disappointing her staff.

"And you returned the key to Azad and saw him put it in his pocket?" Bill asked.

Lucy nodded, then thought back. It was the first time anyone asked if she *saw* Azad return the key to his pocket.

Did she?

She'd been anxious after she'd returned from hiding behind the van as Victoria fought with Henry. When Lucy had returned to the kitchen, Azad had grumbled that she'd taken too long. She'd glared at him, slapped the van key on the counter beside him, and stalked away.

Had he returned it to his pocket?

She couldn't remember seeing him do so. The kitchen had been hectic. But Azad must have taken the key because he'd pulled it out of his pocket and given it to Clemmons at the crime scene.

"I'm sure," Lucy said. "And Azad handed the key to Clemmons."

Bill's mouth dipped into an even deeper frown. "From Clemmons's viewpoint, it doesn't look good for Azad. He threatened the victim in a kitchen full of impartial witnesses while brandishing a shish kebab skewer. He had motive and access to the van."

"I've known Azad since middle school. He started working at the restaurant as a dishwasher, then moved on to busboy, and then as a line cook. My mom and dad treated him like their adopted son. He's *not* capable of murder."

Bill lowered his mug. "I'm sorry, Lucy. You've been away for a while. People change."

She shook her head. "Not that much."

Her father's request sprang to mind. "*If Detective Clemmons tries to blame Azad, then you have to help him, Lucy . . . you have to find the real killer. You did it before, you can do it again.*"

She'd already begun thinking about who could have stabbed Henry. She caught Katie's eye, and knew her friend was just as inquisitive.

Bill's gaze darted from Lucy's to Katie's. "Oh, no," he mumbled, wagging a finger at them. "You two stay out of this. You haven't forgotten the last time, have you?"

Lucy hadn't. She knew how dangerous it could be to get involved in police business. She'd almost gotten herself killed by pursuing the last murderer in Ocean Crest. But still . . . this was Azad. Whatever her tumultuous feelings, he didn't deserve to be the fall guy for a horrible crime he didn't commit.

Bill finished his coffee and placed his mug in the sink. "I mean it, ladies. Keep your noses out of it, and let the police do their job."

CHAPTER 6

Lucy breathed in the ocean air as she jogged on Ocean Crest's boardwalk. It was a beautiful June morning and the sunlight shimmered on the Atlantic Ocean. Tourists rode rented bicycles and surreys alongside the joggers. Her running shoes pounded on the boards as she passed a burger joint, a pizza parlor, and a frozen custard stand. She picked up her pace and ran by a tattoo shop and a palm and tarot card reader. A teenage worker stood outside one of the stores hawking T-shirts. The Ocean Crest boardwalk had an eclectic array of shops, and combined with the single pier, which featured an old-fashioned wooden roller coaster, Ferris wheel, and carnival games, there was something for everyone.

"Watch the tramcar, please!" Lucy jumped as a loudspeaker blared behind her, then she moved to the side to let the newest addition pass—a boardwalk tramcar. Bright yellow and blue, the tramcar was a trackless train with twenty seats. It offered tired tourists a ride up and down the boardwalk and stopped at designated spots to pick up riders. Tourists loved the tramcar, especially senior citizens and parents with baby strollers and tired toddlers. Locals put up with the annoying recorded message which repeated every time a pedestrian was in its way.

Lucy jogged to the end of the boardwalk, ran down a wooden ramp, and began making her way across the beach. A few early morning families were already making the trek across the sand with their loaded beach carts and colorful umbrellas. Children sprinted ahead to splash in the surf and search for shells.

She headed for the wooden pier projecting into the sea, and one of her favorite spots overlooking the ocean. Slowing as she approached the pier, she walked down the wooden piles until she reached the end and sat. A cool ocean breeze blew wayward curls that had escaped her ponytail as she drank from her water bottle. Seagulls cried and circled above. A crane looking for its morning meal skimmed the water. The isolation, combined with the vastness of the ocean, made all her problems seem small. It also cleared her head and allowed her to think.

Lucy's thoughts turned back to the wedding. Katie had brought up a good point. If Henry Simms was married, where was his wife during the wedding? The police must have delivered the horrible news by now.

Or had the woman already known because she'd stabbed her own husband?

And what about the rest of the bridal party? For starters there was the pretty, young, red-headed maid of honor, Cressida Connolly. She'd certainly known Henry since he'd been her escort as the best man. And Lucy couldn't overlook the groom, Bradford Papadopoulos. She recalled Henry's speech that he'd known Bradford since college and the two had been fraternity brothers.

Did Cressida or Bradford have a reason to kill the best man?

Lucy sat and took another deep breath of ocean air. She hoped Bill was right and Detective Clemmons would summon Victoria Redding to the police station for further questioning. If not, then Lucy would have to take matters into her own hands.

Again.

A cold knot formed in her stomach. Could she do it? She knew Katie would be on board despite Bill's warning not to get involved. But was she willing to track down a cold-blooded murderer herself?

Yes, if it means saving Azad from hard prison time.

She wasn't sure she wanted to resume romantic relations with Azad, but their past wasn't easily forgotten. Azad Zakarian had been a friend before he'd ever been a boyfriend.

Pushing to her feet, Lucy brushed the sand off her running shorts and jogged back. Sand sprayed the backs of her legs and stuck to her sweaty skin. She'd stop by the restaurant, refill her water bottle with ice water, then jog to Katie's house and shower before she had to return for the dinner shift. Thankfully, her sister, Emma, had volunteered to manage the lunch shift to give Lucy a break after the harrowing wedding.

Just as she cut through the back parking lot of the restaurant, she heard a welcoming meow, then spotted the orange and black cat by the back door.

"Hello there, Gadoo." Lucy squatted down to pet the patchy orange cat. She was rewarded with another meow as the feline rubbed against her legs. "Did Mom leave you enough food and fresh water?" Her gaze went to the bowls by the back door leading into Kebab Kitchen's storage room.

Gadoo had plenty of kibble, and Lucy made a mental note to pick up more of the cat treats he loved at Holloway's grocery store. She had grown quite attached to the cat, and she'd even ordered a new cell phone case online of a picture of herself and Gadoo. Emma had snapped the picture of the two of them on the front lawn of the restaurant. Lucy had been holding Gadoo in her arms and he was looking up at her, his yellow eyes alert.

She refilled the cat's water bowl from what was left of her own water bottle before opening the back door and entering the storage room.

The room was filled with the staples of Mediterranean cuisine—containers of bulgur, rice, jars of tahini to make hummus, and exotic spices. Before Lucy had taken over management of the restaurant, everything was stored on old wooden shelving. She'd wanted to make long-needed changes, starting with installing a computerized ordering and inventory system and replacing the wooden shelves with stainless-steel ones. But any changes meant butting heads with her technology-resistant and fiscally challenged parents.

Especially her father.

She'd finally won a single argument and convinced her father that the investment in steel shelving would be worthwhile. After Raffi Berberian agreed, Lucy ordered the shelves from a restaurant supplier. But her grand plans came to a grinding halt when the new shelving was delayed by a strike at the manufacturer's factory. Meanwhile, the local handyman, Jonathan Hartman, had already dismantled the wooden shelves. Then, a day before the steel shelving finally arrived, Jonathan had thrown out his back installing a hot water heater at the local Sandpiper Bed and Breakfast, and he hadn't been able to finish the job. Finding a handyman during the height of the summer season had been harder than Lucy had anticipated. As a result, all the restaurant's supplies currently rested upon wooden pallets and cheap, temporary plastic shelving.

The room was disorganized and had thrown her father into a fit. Raffi had wagged a finger in her face and said, "I told you not to mess with things. If it isn't broken, don't change it."

This was not how Lucy had envisioned her first attempt at improvements.

Even though it was only a matter of time before the steel shelving would be installed, it was still disconcerting every time Butch or Azad had to rummage through the storage room to find a needed item. Taking inventory also took a lot more time. But Lucy knew she could be just as stubborn as her father, and she still planned to install a computerized inventory and ordering system, and was gearing up for an epic battle with her parents.

As soon as she entered the kitchen, the wonderful smell of Butch's homemade vegetable barley soup, wafted to her.

"Smells great, Butch." Lucy's stomach growled as she came close. All she'd eaten for breakfast was a bowl of cereal, and running made her hungry.

Butch smiled as he stirred an enormous stockpot on the industrial-sized stove. "I'll save you the first bowl, Lucy Lou."

"That sounds—"

"Lucy!"

Lucy whirled to see Emma by a large coffee urn,

her cheeks flushed. "You're not supposed to be here this early."

"I know, Em. Thanks for covering for me. I just stopped by to refill my water bottle." She raised her now empty bottle, then halted when she saw the worried expression on her sister's face. "What's wrong?"

Emma switched the urn to "brew" and wiped her hands on her apron. "Marsha Walsh is here. She gave me her card and asked for you." Emma pulled a business card from her apron and handed it to her sister. "When I told her you weren't expected for at least an hour, she asked for a table and ordered."

Lucy froze at the sight of the raised gold seal of the state of New Jersey on the card. "Oh, no. It's the county prosecutor."

There was only one reason for Marsha Walsh to come to Kebab Kitchen, and it wasn't for the cuisine. *Not again.* The last time the prosecutor had surprised her by showing up at the restaurant, Lucy also had been returning from a run. The woman had impeccable timing.

"Are Mom and Dad here?" Lucy asked.

Emma shook her head. "No. Just Sally and Butch."

Sweaty and sandy after her run, Lucy smoothed her frizzy ponytail. The prosecutor was the last person she wanted to see. "All right. Don't worry. I'll handle this." She hoped she sounded more confident than she felt.

Lucy took a breath and entered the dining room. Marsha Walsh sat checking her smartphone at a table by herself. With her short-cropped hair, navy pantsuit, and leather briefcase, she looked every inch a lawyer. Not long ago, Lucy had dressed similarly and had probably given off the same vibe.

But things were different now, and Lucy felt a jolt

of momentary panic. She'd looked up the prosecutor after her last visit. Walsh was in her late forties and an accomplished prosecutor. From what Lucy had learned, she was careful about what cases she prosecuted and rarely lost a trial.

It was early for lunch and the dining room was empty except for a young couple seated five tables away. By the way they were looking into each other's eyes, Lucy suspected they were lovers or newlyweds and not paying any attention to their surroundings. *Perfect.*

Marsha Walsh lowered her cell phone as Lucy approached. "Hello, Ms. Berberian."

"Hi, Prosecutor Walsh. I was surprised to hear from my sister that you were here, asking to see me."

"I don't blame you. The food here may be exceptional, but I didn't think I'd be back again so soon." Walsh motioned to the chair across from her. "Please join me. I've already ordered."

Lucy pulled out the chair and took a seat. She glanced at the plate before the woman and noticed that she'd made a trip to the hummus bar. Lucy's parents had installed the hummus bar several months ago and it had quickly become popular with the customers. It featured her mother's traditional hummus and a dozen of her unique varieties. Bins of sliced vegetables for dipping were at the end of the bar, and homemade pita bread could be ordered from the kitchen.

Lucy couldn't help but find it odd that Marsha Walsh had helped herself to the hummus. The last time the prosecutor visited, it was because the health inspector had died after eating the hummus.

Walsh dipped a carrot slice into the hummus and

took a bite. "It's very good. I see you've added several different flavors since the last time I was here."

"My mother created different flavors, and we like to change them every week." Lucy eyed her plate. "Roasted red pepper, lemon pucker, and black bean. All good choices."

"You're very perceptive," Walsh said.

Lucy shrugged a shoulder. "It's my business. I have to be able to tell the difference between them all."

Walsh's stare drilled into her. "Perception is a skill that is useful in my profession as well. I wonder if you can use it to guess why I'm here today."

Lucy's fingers twisted beneath the table. "It's not difficult. I assume it has to do with Scarlet Westwood's wedding."

Walsh raised her water glass. "It's not every day a celebrity socialite has a wedding in our county. It's even rarer that there's a murder during the reception."

"I still don't see why you're here. Kebab Kitchen had nothing to do with it."

"That's for law enforcement to decide."

Lucy refused to be waylaid. "I know Detective Clemmons is trying to pin this on our head chef, but he's off."

"Why would you assume that?"

"I was there when he was initially questioned. I also have a feeling Clemmons wants to be quick about making an arrest."

Walsh lowered her glass. "Are you playing investigator again? We're not going to have a repeat of your prior clandestine activities, are we?"

"I don't know what you're talking about."

"You should know me better by now, Ms. Berberian."

Lucy's anxiety rose another notch. Marsha Walsh was much smarter than Calvin Clemmons. That meant she wasn't as narrow-minded. Plus, she didn't have a grudge against Lucy's family.

"I told Detective Clemmons that I'd overheard a fight between the victim and the wedding planner, Victoria Redding."

"We're looking into that."

"Have you questioned her further?" Lucy asked.

Just then, the kitchen doors swung open and Emma arrived. Balancing a plate in one hand and a pitcher of ice water in the other, she set a platter of lamb shish kebab in front of the prosecutor, refilled her water glass, and departed. The aroma of the lamb made Lucy's mouth water. She'd never had a chance to sample Butch's soup. But then she looked at the skewer and her pulse did a double take.

Walsh carefully lifted the shish kebab and removed the meat from the skewer with her fork. The tender lamb came off a piece at a time. She slipped her finger through the loop on one end of the stainless-steel skewer and dangled it in front of Lucy. Sunlight from the window glinted off the sharp tip.

Walsh leveled her gaze on Lucy. "Who would think this handy kitchen utensil could kill someone? But then again, I've seen many household items used to murder. Ingenious really."

Lucy's breath caught in her throat. "Anyone could have had access to one of those skewers during the wedding. We served shish kebab to two hundred and fifty guests."

"Ah, but only one set of fingerprints was found on the murder weapon."

Lucy was afraid to ask, but did anyway. "Azad Zakarian's?"

"That's right."

"But that can be explained. He was in charge of preparing the shish kebab. His fingerprints were probably on *all* the skewers."

"I said *only* his fingerprints. No one else's."

Lucy's mind whirled. There had to be a reasonable explanation. "The murderer could have used gloves." She knew Azad had not used gloves in the kitchen. He was an experienced chef, and he washed his hands before and after handling any food. It wasn't a far stretch to assume the murderer had used gloves, and that explained why the only fingerprints left behind on the murder weapon would be Azad's.

"Perhaps." Walsh picked up her fork and bit into the lamb, then stopped midchew and studied her plate with renewed interest. "This is delicious."

"Thanks." Lucy's attention was no longer on the food, but on what the wily prosecutor had told her.

"What is it seasoned with?"

"It's a marinade of olive oil, garlic, onions, salt, pepper, and other spices." Lucy's frustration rose. One minute the prosecutor was talking about an active murder investigation and the next she wanted to discuss recipes. "Everything you said can be explained. It's not enough to accuse a man of murder."

Walsh paused and took a long sip of water. "By your own admission, Azad had the key to the van and access to the crime scene."

"The van was parked in a public lot. Anyone could have had access to it," Lucy argued.

"Ah, but the van was inspected at the state lab. The

locks and windows weren't tampered with. No one broke into the van."

Lucy knew this information from Bill. Still, it sounded much more incriminating coming from the prosecutor.

"We questioned the staff from Castle of the Sea," Walsh continued. "As an attorney, you are aware that witness testimony is not always reliable, but in this case, we had over a dozen witnesses who said Azad threatened to do Henry Simms bodily harm while wielding a shish kebab skewer."

Crap. This was going from bad to worse. "Are you going to arrest him?"

"I wouldn't share that information with you."

"Then why are you telling me all this?" Lucy asked.

Walsh rested her fork on her plate and leaned forward, her eyes sharp and assessing. "I want to be certain that we have an understanding. I realize Azad Zakarian is your head chef and an important member of your staff. You are to stay out of the police investigation. If Detective Clemmons needs more information from you, he'll ask for you to visit the station."

Lucy fought the urge to squirm in her seat. "All right." What could she say? She knew better than to argue with a state prosecutor.

"Meanwhile, if you happen to remember anything or hear anything, you will report it to the authorities immediately. You have my card."

"Got it. If anything comes to mind, I'll tell the police."

Walsh nodded. "Are you still residing with Officer Bill Watson and his wife?"

"Yes, and I'm behaving like a model citizen." Last time, the prosecutor had warned her that any involvement on her part could jeopardize Bill's position on the force. It was a warning that she took seriously.

"Good. Let's keep it that way."

As soon as the prosecutor left, Emma rushed out of the kitchen and bombarded Lucy with questions. "What did she say?"

Lucy reached for a rag and started wiping down the waitress counter. It was a needless task—the counter was already clean—but she was anxious and restless. "The prosecutor told me to stay out of police business."

Emma took the rag from her and set it aside. "Dad wants you to get involved. Mom doesn't. What are you going to do?"

"I'm not sure." She was sure, but Emma didn't need to know that. The fewer people who knew, the better. Katie was her partner-in-crime, and Lucy didn't want anyone else to get involved.

Emma placed her hands on her hips. "Are they going to make an arrest?"

"Arrest who?"

Lucy and Emma spun around to find Azad standing in the swinging doors that separated the dining room from the kitchen. He wore his chef's coat, but the top two buttons were undone. The fitted white T-shirt beneath revealed the corded muscles of his neck. His dark, wavy hair was disheveled, as if he'd repeatedly run his fingers through it.

Lucy's pulse quickened. "What are you doing here? You're not supposed to work until tonight."

His gaze roved her body and returned to her face. "Neither are you."

Lucy folded her arms across her chest. She was highly conscious of her running outfit, an unflattering T-shirt and shorts, and her messy ponytail. What had possessed her to stop by the restaurant on the way home from a run? First, the prosecutor. Now, Azad. Refilling her water bottle wasn't worth it.

"I just stopped by during a jog. I'm not working," she said.

"Well, I needed a distraction, too, and work is it for me. Plus, your mom recently booked a baby shower and I need to prepare. Now what's going on?"

Emma watched them. "You two should talk about this privately. Go to the office."

"That's fine with me," Azad said.

If she said no, she would look like a coward. Plus, Azad would suspect something was really wrong. "Fine," Lucy mumbled.

Azad followed her through the kitchen and into the storage room where she opened a door that led into the small office her parents had used for years. The metal desk was littered with time sheets and invoices. A shelf crowded with cans and boxes of food samples from restaurant suppliers rested against one wall. A safe was mounted on the opposite wall where she placed the cash from the register until she could make a daily deposit to the Ocean Crest Savings and Loan.

Azad leaned against the desk. "Now, who's getting arrested?"

"Azad, I . . . I don't know."

"It's me, isn't it?"

"That's not what I said."

"You didn't have to. I know you. You have a 'tell' when you're lying."

"What tell?"

"A muscle tics by your left eye." He stepped close to point to a spot at the corner of her eye.

Her pulse quickened at his nearness. She took a quick step back and glared at him. "No one's ever mentioned that I have a tic before."

"Well, maybe they didn't notice. Or they don't know you like I do. So give it to me straight."

"Fine. The county prosecutor was here. Your fingerprints were the only ones on the shish kebab skewer found in Henry Simms's neck."

"So? I prepared all the shish kebabs."

"That's what I told her. But there's more. They interviewed the Castle of the Sea employees, who testified they heard you threaten the victim in the kitchen."

Azad sighed. "I shouldn't have done that, but I just lost it when I saw that crook."

Here was her chance to ask him the question that had plagued her since his outburst at the wedding. "Azad, why were you furious with Henry Simms about a loan that fell through?"

"It doesn't matter now."

"It does to me. Did you apply for a loan to buy the restaurant?" She knew her father had initially planned to be the mortgagee and for Azad to offer a sizable down payment and then make monthly payments until the restaurant was paid in full.

"You know I wanted to buy the place. It was never a secret."

"No, it wasn't, but you said you supported my decision to stay in Ocean Crest and manage the restaurant."

"That's the truth. It still is."

"But only because your loan fell through."

"That loan fell through *before* you returned home. You can't hold that against me."

He was right, but still . . .

What if the loan had gone through? Would they have fought over who would take over the restaurant? Even more disturbing, would her parents have given her the chance, or simply chosen Azad?

She didn't like the thought one bit.

"I can see where this is going, but you should know me better by now. If I wanted to go to a different bank and apply for another loan after you had come home, then I could have. But I didn't."

That much was true.

"Let's not talk about this right now. Other than my fingerprints on the murder weapon and a room full of witnesses who saw me threaten the victim, what else did the prosecutor say?" he asked.

She grudgingly agreed. There were definitely more immediate issues to consider. "We both gave statements saying we locked the van and that you had the key. The police inspected the van and it wasn't tampered with, so how did the murderer get inside?"

"It doesn't look good, does it?" He shook his head. "They want my neck in the noose. So, are they going to arrest me?"

Lucy was more than a little worried. She could only assume Walsh hadn't made a move because the police were still investigating, and the prosecutor wanted a slam-dunk case before going forward. "They would have done it if they had enough evidence."

"You mean at least for now."

Looking into his dark eyes, Lucy felt a sense of

urgency. "Don't worry. Katie and I aren't going to let that happen."

His expression changed from worry to concern. "No way. I don't want you to get involved in this. It's too risky."

"I won't put myself in danger. I'll just plan to ask a few questions around town. Katie knows a lot of people from work and she wants to help."

"I'm not sure. I don't want you or Katie to put yourselves in danger for me."

"We won't," she promised, then hoped that this time it was the truth.

"I mean it, Lucy. Think of your parents."

"My dad wants me to investigate, remember?"

"Your mom doesn't."

"A few questions do not count as a full investigation."

"I don't want your safety on my conscience."

"Azad, I'll be careful—"

"Please, Lucy. I know I hurt you in the past. I was young and stupid and things were progressing way too fast. But you know I care for you. A lot. We have history and I'm asking you not to do anything dangerous."

Wow. The way he looked at her was too serious. So was the racing of her pulse. She had to diffuse the emotions racing through her, and not let him know that her feelings were strong. "I'm more worried about Detective Clemmons. He's looking for an excuse to hurt the family, and even though you're not family, he knows it wouldn't go well for us if you were arrested. The restaurant needs you."

The restaurant, not me. Definitely not me, she repeated to herself.

A shadow crossed his face. "I didn't kill that banker. I'm innocent. I have to believe that's enough."

It may not be.

Her conversation with Prosecutor Walsh wasn't reassuring. No matter how much she hoped Azad was right, Lucy knew better.

CHAPTER 7

Later that afternoon, Lucy greeted Katie outside Lola's Coffee Shop. "I got your voice mail about meeting. I'm glad you called."

"Are you thinking about how to solve the murder?" Katie said.

Lucy halted and lowered her voice. "Let's get some caffeine and an isolated, quiet table."

Katie opened the door to the coffee shop and motioned for Lucy to enter.

The coffee shop had a steady stream of customers and Lucy and Katie stood in line, breathing in the delicious smells of rich coffee and warm pastry. The glass display case featured scones, doughnuts, and muffins freshly baked and delivered daily from Cutie's Cupcakes. Oversized white mugs were stacked against the wall beside coffee and hot water urns. The owner of the shop, Lola Stewart, was busy behind the counter working on a hissing espresso machine as it turned milk into a frothy foam.

Customers sat in wire-back chairs drinking coffee, chatting, working on laptop computers, and reading the *Ocean Crest Town News*. The coffee shop was painted a cheerful yellow color, and framed photographs featuring beach scenes of sunbathers, colorful umbrellas, and sandcastles hung on the walls.

"Hi, ladies. I heard about what happened at Scarlet Westwood's wedding. Who would have thought the best man would be murdered!" Lola said as soon as they approached the counter. She was a tall, thin woman with angular cheekbones and steel-gray hair pulled tightly back into a bun. Her friendly smile softened what others might consider her harsh features.

"It was quite a shock and not what I expected when I agreed to cater the reception," Lucy said.

Lola leaned across the counter. "Are you two all right?"

"As good as can be expected after seeing a dead body," Lucy said.

"Caffeine will help," Katie said.

Lola straightened away from the counter. "Of course. What would you two like?"

"A cappuccino and an orange scone, please," Katie said.

"Ditto," Lucy said. "It smells too good in here to resist."

Lola reached in the display case and placed two scones on plates and handed one to Lucy. "By the way, I saw pictures of the reception at Castle of the Sea. Stunning."

Lucy looked at her in surprise. "You saw pictures?"

"In the tabloids. Scarlet's dress was gorgeous. Despite what happened after the wedding, I'd die to see the bridal party in real life." Lola set two steaming cappuccinos on the counter.

Katie and Lucy took their mugs and plates and chose a spot in the corner. The table was hand painted by a local artist and featured seashells and horseshoe crabs. The closest customer was three tables away and he was occupied working on a laptop computer.

"My gosh! You were right," Lucy said. "Henry must have texted or e-mailed pictures to a reporter."

Katie nodded. "Victoria Redding will be furious."

Lucy's thoughts turned as she stirred her cappuccino with a white rock candy barista stick. The demitasse stirrer had quickly become one of her favorite things about the coffee shop. She took a sip of her cappuccino and promptly burned her tongue. "Be careful. It's really hot." She stirred the drink some more. "Have you heard anything more from Bill?"

Katie took a bite of her scone. "Not much. The police are still investigating. But Bill said Calvin Clemmons is being hardheaded."

All the rock candy had melted into her cappuccino, and Lucy set the stirrer on her plate. "More than usual?"

Katie tested her cappuccino to be sure it had cooled enough before sipping. "Clemmons is pressuring for an arrest. The county prosecutor was called in and Clemmons wants to look good."

"I know about the county prosecutor. Marsha Walsh stopped by the restaurant today."

Katie blinked. "She did? When?"

"During the lunch shift. She ordered shish kebab, dangled the skewer in front of my face, and warned me to stay out of the investigation."

Katie snorted. "You mean as a warning because of last time?"

"I guess you could say so."

"Bill said that Clemmons is hungry for a promotion, and he sees this as an opportunity," Katie said. "It's not every day a celebrity like Scarlet Westwood gets married in town. And for a murder to happen at the reception—well—this is huge."

Lucy carefully sipped her cappuccino. This time it was perfect. "Marsha Walsh said Azad's fingerprints were the only ones on the murder weapon. I told her that this wasn't surprising because Azad was the only one who'd prepared the shish kebab. I don't think my arguments helped."

"That's why I wanted to meet. I asked around about Henry's background and lucked out. Francesca Thompson was recently hired at the town hall. She used to work at Henry's bank as a secretary, and she's a font of information."

Lucy knew her friend better than anyone. Katie was drawn to mysteries, and a murder would be as irresistible to her as Susan Cutie's lemon meringue pie was to Lucy.

Katie reached into her bag and pulled out a file. She took out a handwritten sheet of paper. "Henry Simms was the chief operating officer of the Ocean Crest Savings and Loan. According to Francesca, there were rumors flying around that his position had been in jeopardy over the past year."

"My parents started a business account there long ago. We still bank there. Are they in trouble?" Lucy asked.

Katie shook her head. "Not the bank itself, but their former CEO had been in deep water. Henry was suspected of conducting some shady business practices."

"Like what?"

"Francesca didn't know all the details. But she used the word 'embezzlement.'"

"Embezzlement? That's a serious accusation." Lucy

tapped her fingers on the table. "But it wouldn't be the first time a bank CEO was caught with his hand in the cookie jar. The only thing is that Henry didn't embezzle from Azad. The loan never went through."

"I asked Francesca if she knew about Azad's loan when she worked at the bank. She said Azad's application was for one hundred grand and he put up his parents' house that he'd inherited as collateral."

A hundred thousand dollars wouldn't be enough to purchase the family business, but if her parents had planned to hold the mortgage, then that amount of money would have been a sizable down payment.

"What happened to the loan?" Lucy asked.

"Francesca couldn't say. The collateral was sufficient and the initial loan paperwork was approved, but at the last minute the final loan was denied."

"Why?"

"Who knows? Maybe Simms was in financial trouble and the bank couldn't make the loan," Katie said.

Azad still had his house, but he was furious about the way he'd been treated by Henry, that he'd still had to pay his attorney, and because he'd missed out on a unique business opportunity.

Lucy cradled her mug. "That's theft and a big breach of Henry's fiduciary responsibilities. Why wasn't he fired?"

Katie shrugged. "Maybe they couldn't prove it and put him on probation."

"If Henry was desperate enough for money to risk his job by stealing from the bank, we need to find out why. Was he a drug user, a gambler, or was he just outright greedy and living a life of luxury?"

"All good questions."

"I'm going to ask around," Lucy said. "I make daily

deposits at the bank for the restaurant, and I know the teller, Betty."

Katie sipped her coffee. "Good idea. I'll try to pump Francesca Thompson for more information."

Lucy snapped her fingers. "I thought of something else. When Victoria was arguing with Henry, he mentioned something about Scarlet's new perfume line. Henry wanted to leak news of Scarlet's wedding to the press in order to boost the launch."

"You mean Scarlet's Passion?" Katie set down her mug.

Scarlet's Passion? That sounded cheesy to Lucy and certainly not something she'd buy for herself. Maybe teenagers would go for it.

"You've heard of it?" Lucy asked.

"It's been in the tabloids for months, and there's been talk around town about it, too. Scarlet is preparing to start her own line of fragrances, body wash, and lotions. Her husband, Bradford, is backing her with a hefty sum of his own cash and a loan from Henry's bank."

"I never heard."

"That's because you keep your head buried in the sand when it comes to gossip."

"That's not entirely true," Lucy argued. "I heard Scarlet planned to film a scene on the Ocean Crest beach."

"That's because I told you."

Lucy ignored the barb, even if it was true, and steered the conversation back on track. "Maybe Francesca's right. What if Henry embezzled funds from Bradford's and Scarlet's accounts, and they found out?"

"It's possible. Better yet, what if Henry had money

problems, and he 'borrowed' the money and failed to return it?" Katie asked.

"It would make both Bradford and Scarlet suspects. Money and greed are always good motives for murder," Lucy said.

"Then the million-dollar question is: who was angry enough to kill? Victoria, Scarlet, or Bradford?" Katie asked.

"I don't know." Lucy nibbled her scone. "Victoria was pretty upset. Henry mentioned that he got her the job as wedding planner because of his friendship with the groom. That set her off. But I still can't help but wonder, is that reason enough to kill someone?"

"Who knows? All I do know is that the list of suspects is growing. If Clemmons is smart he'll look into all of them. But I don't have much faith in the detective," Katie said.

Lucy leaned back in her chair. "My father wants us to help Azad. My mother is dead set against it."

"What do you think?" Katie asked.

"I think it doesn't look good for Azad, but he doesn't want me to get involved either."

"He doesn't?"

Lucy frowned as she recalled their conversation. "He says there's a killer out there and he's worried that I could get hurt." Azad had said more than that— he'd brought up their past and said he still cared for her.

A lot.

The trouble was, she wasn't sure she wanted to go down that path again. Especially now that they were working together.

"So what are you going to do?" Katie asked.

"It's not in my nature to sit back while someone I care for gets arrested for a crime he didn't commit."

"You still care for Azad?"

"I didn't mean it *that* way. I meant that I care for him as a friend and a coworker only."

"Hmm," Katie said in a way that suggested she didn't believe a word Lucy said. "Well, I'm glad you're committed to solving this crime, because I have a plan."

"Why am I not surprised?"

Katie ignored her teasing tone and pulled out a second sheet of paper from the folder. "Other than digging into Henry's past and why he needed cash, we can start with the obvious suspect."

"Victoria Redding?"

"The wedding planner, yes. But I was thinking of Holly."

"Who?"

"Holly Simms is Henry's wife. She owns a McMansion in the new development on the edge of town. Scarlet and Bradford recently purchased a shore house nearby when they decided to film in Ocean Crest. Victoria is staying at the Sandpiper Bed and Breakfast."

"I'm surprised everyone hasn't hightailed it out of town," Lucy said.

"They can't. Clemmons requested the entire bridal party to stay in Ocean Crest until the investigation is complete. If any one of them flees, they'll look guilty."

"How convenient for us," Lucy said.

"We can talk to Victoria first, but then we need to interrogate Holly."

"What about Bill?"

Katie looked at her blankly. "What about him?"

"Don't act dumb. Aren't you worried about what he'll say? He warned us to keep our noses out of this one."

Katie shook her head. "I'm not worried. Bill was removed from the case because there's a conflict of interest. I was at the wedding and Detective Clemmons questioned me at the scene."

Lucy drew in a deep breath, held it for a few seconds, then slowly let it out. "Prosecutor Walsh scares me. The first time we met, she warned me that any involvement on my part could harm Bill's career in the police department."

"We'll be careful. What should scare you more than that prosecutor is if your longtime 'friend' and current head chef gets arrested for a murder he didn't commit."

"Fine," Lucy said. "We approach Victoria and Holly. But why would they even talk to us? We can't just knock on their doors and ask to interrogate them like the police."

"You're right. We can't. So what do we do?"

Lucy grinned as a thought occurred to her. "We get creative, just like we did during our last murder investigation."

CHAPTER 8

Lucy left Lola's Coffee Shop and returned to the restaurant. She found Sally in the kitchen standing by the industrial-sized coffee urn. The scent of freshly brewing coffee wafted to her and made her mouth water. Ridiculous. She'd just had a cappuccino.

How much coffee could one person drink in a day?

"Hey, Lucy. Your mother had to step out to run an errand. She said she'd be right back," Sally said.

Tall and skinny with short dark hair, Sally looked like Olive Oyl from the Popeye cartoon. Chatty and friendly, she'd been a waitress at Kebab Kitchen for years, and customers loved her. Her parents often joked that Sally was a walking directory of local folk and should run for mayor. Sally had also become a good friend to Lucy since her return home.

Lucy eyed the long prep table. An array of ingredients and herbs was already spread out—finely chopped parsley, eggs, blocks of butter on a tray, a mound of grated cheese she couldn't name, and phyllo dough. "What's all this?"

"Angela has a catering job. They ordered six dozen cheese *boeregs*."

"Six dozen?" Lucy knew the flaky phyllo pastry with cheese filling was a popular appetizer on their menu. They could be made into bite-size pieces and served on platters carried around by liveried servers and offered as hors d'oeuvres to guests at parties. But six dozen sounded like a lot to Lucy.

"It's for a baby shower," Sally added.

Lucy reached for the butter tray. "Azad mentioned a baby shower. It's a big order, and my mom's only supposed to work part-time. I can help. I just learned how to clarify butter."

"I'm sure she'd be grateful," Sally said.

Lucy looked up. "Thanks. You're the only person here that doesn't crack jokes about my lack of culinary talent. Even Emma teases me sometimes."

Sally grinned. "That would be the pot calling the kettle black. I can serve the food, but I can't cook worth a damn. Besides, how will you learn if you don't get your hands dirty?"

Lucy nodded. "My point exactly."

Her mother had been teaching her, albeit slowly, how to cook Armenian, Lebanese, and Greek dishes and pastries. Lucy knew she'd never replace Azad or Butch, but if she was going to successfully manage Kebab Kitchen she should at least have an understanding of how to make the food.

Lucy had surprised herself over the past months. So far, she'd already learned how to make baklava and hummus. Both had their own challenges. The sheets of paper-thin phyllo dough used to make baklava tore easily. The measurements of garlic, lemon, and tahini for the hummus could be tricky when made in large batches.

While Lucy was growing up, everyone in her family

knew how to cook, but Lucy would have rather had a bikini wax than turn on the oven. Angela was a perfectionist, and Lucy had never lived up to her mother's expectations in the kitchen in the past.

But things had changed. She was still anxious in the kitchen, but she'd learned not to panic and flee at the sight and smell of burnt baklava.

"Any luck figuring out who killed the best man at Scarlet's wedding?" Sally asked.

The butter tray slipped from Lucy's fingers to land on the prep table with a thud. Another form of anxiety trickled down her spine that had nothing to do with cooking. "What do you mean? You know my mom forbid me to get involved."

Sally winked. "But I know you. And Katie, too." She leaned across the table and placed a forefinger across her lips. "Mum's the word about it. Good luck." The coffee urn hissed as it finished brewing, and Sally straightened. "I'd better get back to my tables. Mr. Krutcher insists on freshly brewed coffee and gets crankier by the minute until he gets his caffeine." Sally filled a pot and waved on her way out of the kitchen.

Lucy turned her attention back to the ingredients spread out before her. She had no idea how to make cheese *boereg*. If only her mother kept a recipe book. But Angela knew every recipe by heart and never bothered to write them down.

Lucy reached for a saucepan. She may not know how to make it, but she could start on one of the few tasks she did know how to do until her mother returned.

Lucy slipped on a white apron embroidered with KEBAB KITCHEN in green letters, tied it at her waist, and spent the next fifteen minutes clarifying the butter.

She heated the butter in the saucepan until it melted, then removed the white foam on the surface with a spoon. Her mother had told her that the foam contained the salt and it should be discarded. Once the butter cooled, Lucy poured it into another saucepan, discarded any excess solids left behind, and headed for the prep table.

"Lucy! What are you doing?"

Lucy started and turned to see her mother standing behind her.

Angela's hands were planted on her hips. Her signature beehive was perfect, even this late in the afternoon. Anyone who didn't know better might think it was a wig.

"Sally said you have a catering order for a baby shower. I already started with the butter."

Angela's gaze lowered to the saucepan in Lucy's hands, and a satisfied look crossed her face. "Good. You can learn some more." She washed her hands and put on her own apron. It was long on her petite frame, but somehow, she still managed to give off the vibe of a general . . . or a dictator depending on your perspective.

Lucy assumed her mother would double check her work, and she steeled herself for a critical comment about her lack of technique. But Angela picked up a remote, aimed it at a corner-mounted television, and turned it on.

"Cooking Kurt comes on soon. I like to watch his show when I work."

Seconds later, a familiar jingle of the food channel sounded and a handsome blond man in a chef's coat standing in an ultramodern kitchen with sleek, stainless-steel appliances and a quartz countertop appeared on the screen. He flashed a white smile that had to be bleached and bent down to pick up a roasting pan. His muscles bunched beneath his tight chef's coat, and Lucy couldn't help but wonder if the entire maneuver wasn't planned to show off his masculinity and tight rear.

A corner of Lucy's mouth twisted upward. "You like his recipes?"

"Of course." Her mother was too preoccupied with watching the hot chef to catch the mocking tone in Lucy's voice.

Lucy had no doubt that her mother could outcook the celebrity chef any day. Taught by her mother and mother-in-law, Angela created dishes that melted in your mouth.

"What makes your *boereg* so good, Mom?"

Her mother reluctantly tore her gaze away from the TV and reached for a large mixing bowl. "The trick is the Muenster cheese. I don't use cottage cheese or mozzarella, only Muenster. It's my secret. Now help me mix the cheese, eggs, and chopped parsley."

"Got it." Lucy cracked and beat the eggs, then combined all the ingredients and mixed them together.

"The trickiest part is the phyllo dough. We want miniature cheese-filled pastries, so we must cut each sheet into thirds."

The sight of the phyllo dough still made Lucy's pulse pound in trepidation. Each sheet was as thin as newspaper and could tear and dry out quickly. She'd learned how to use it to make baklava, but preparing the miniature *boereg* seemed much more difficult because they were so small.

"Butter the dough, and add a teaspoon of the cheese mixture."

Lucy copied her mother and dipped a pastry brush in the saucepan, buttered a phyllo strip, then added a teaspoonful of cheese mixture to the edge of the dough. "Sally said you need six dozen."

Angela continued working. "I did. I don't need that many now."

Something in her mother's tone made Lucy raise her head to look at her. A gleam of anxiety flashed across Angela's face, but it was gone so quickly Lucy imagined it was a quirk of sunlight from an overhead window reflecting off the stainless-steel oven.

"What do you mean you *did*, but no longer?"

Her mother shrugged a skinny shoulder as she buttered pastry. "I told the customer we couldn't provide as much food."

Lucy didn't get it. Her mother had never said no to a customer or limited orders. She'd taken immense pride in the business and worked tirelessly in the past to increase the catering arm of the restaurant.

A sudden thought occurred to Lucy. "Did you limit the order because you're working part-time hours now? You know I'm willing to step in and help."

"Fold the cheese-filled phyllo into triangles, just like an American flag," Angela instructed.

Lucy glared at her, frowning. "Don't ignore me, Mom."

Her mother's lips thinned in irritation. "Then don't interrupt while I'm teaching you."

"Fine. Fold it like a flag, right?" Lucy's first attempt to fold the cheese-filled phyllo was messy and the edges didn't quite match.

"Press your fingers at the corners to seal the dough and keep the cheese from oozing out while they bake.

Then brush the ends with butter before placing them on a baking sheet."

Lucy did as her mother instructed, and after a dozen or so attempts, her folded triangles looked better.

Angela placed her first tray in the oven and moved on to her second. Lucy looked down at her work. She hadn't even come close to filling her first tray.

How did her mother work so quickly?

Lucy's thoughts returned to her unanswered question. Her mother was avoiding answering it, but why? Something was clearly up, and Lucy could be just as mulish as her mother when she wanted the truth.

"Now tell me the truth," Lucy said. "Why'd you limit the catering order?"

Angela sighed in exasperation. "It has nothing to do with my work hours. It's because we have no way to get all the food there without the van. Our catering profit margin isn't big to begin with and it will cost us too much money to rent another van. The catering equipment, especially the two tall, rolling carts, won't fit in any of our cars."

Damn. Lucy should have thought of that. The murder had more consequences than she'd initially thought. First Azad, now their future catering jobs. What was next?

She straightened as a thought occurred to her. "I'll talk to Bill."

Angela waved her pastry brush. "Why? What can he do? You said Detective Clemmons took the van as evidence."

It was true. Plus, Bill wasn't technically assigned to the case. If she wanted to get the van back, she'd have to deal with Clemmons. And what chance did she have against the biased detective? Not to mention the fact that the murder was unsolved, and the van was a key piece of evidence.

What a mess.

"Mom, promise me you won't tell any of our future catering customers that you have to limit their orders," Lucy said.

Angela eyed her with a critical squint. "Why? You're not getting involved in this murder business, are you?"

Lucy's nerves tensed. She had no choice but to lie. Her mother would blow a gasket if she knew Lucy and Katie were investigating on their own.

"Of course not," Lucy said, "but I can ask. If the police refuse, then Azad and I will make as many trips as necessary with the food. He has a pickup truck, not a car, and we'll tie down the two catering carts with a dozen bungee cords if we have to."

Lucy wasn't even sure that would work. The rolling carts had large Dutch doors and were heavy. Would they even fit in the back of Azad's pickup?

Angela's eyes lit. "You and Azad. Why didn't I think of that?"

Oh, no. She recognized that matchmaking gleam in her mother's eyes.

"Mom," she whined. "Stop trying to hook us up."

"Why not? You're not getting any younger, Lucy. You're wasting all your childbearing years. You spent years away working, and you still have no marriage prospects. I want grandchildren."

Lucy clenched her jaw as a primitive warning sounded in her brain. Arguing about men and her biological clock with her mother was maddening and a subject Lucy did her best to avoid. "I was building my career as a lawyer. And now, I'm working in the family business. Neither was or is a waste of time."

Her mother glared at her. "Don't be stubborn. What's wrong with Azad? You liked him in the past."

"We're now working together, remember? He's my head chef."

"So? I'm married to your father and we owned a successful business together for thirty years."

That didn't reassure Lucy. Her parents may love each other, but they were two hotheads who bickered on a daily basis.

It was *not* the type of relationship Lucy wanted for herself.

The music coming from the television changed from the cooking show to a commercial for acne cream. Pictures of pimple-riddled teenagers who'd miraculously morphed into clear-skinned girls and boys flashed across the screen.

Angela glanced at the TV, made a face, and then turned back to Lucy. "Granted your father's not perfect, but he's loyal. Although I'm currently upset with him because he won't take me to Cooking Kurt's book signing."

Despite being fiercely independent, her mother didn't drive. Her father had once hired a driving school to try to teach her, but she'd lasted one lesson behind the wheel, then insisted the teacher was a fool and didn't know what he was doing. Lucy didn't know who was more stubborn—Angela or Raffi Berberian.

"Dad won't take you because he dislikes the celebrity chef," Lucy pointed out.

"What does that matter? I dislike the nights his friends from church come to our house for back-gammon. They're too loud, drink too much raki, and smoke their stinky cigars in the house. But I still allow them to come, don't I?"

Lucy burst out laughing. "Fine. I promise to take you to the book signing."

Her mother smiled. "Good girl. Now, let's finish cooking."

Thank heaven for that. No more talk of men. No Azad, or Cooking Kurt, or her father.

Lucy went back to buttering, adding dollops of cheese mixture and folding phyllo into small triangles. After her third tray, her muscles were protesting. Her mother showed no signs of slowing down, and Lucy was amazed at her stamina.

The first trays were done baking and the delicious smell of buttered, cheese-filled pastry filled the kitchen. Lucy's stomach grumbled.

Angela used a spatula to transfer one from the baking sheet to a plate and held it out to Lucy. "Taste it. I need to make sure it's right."

Lucy was more than happy to oblige her. She bit into the buttered, flaky pastry, and the Muenster cheese filling melted like heaven in her mouth. "Mmm. It's delicious, Mom."

"Good. We're almost finished. I'm stopping at three dozen," Angela said.

"Why not prepare the entire six dozen?"

Angela sighed in exasperation. "I already told you why."

"And I told you that I don't want you to cut back on orders. We'll make it work, I promise."

"Are you going to use your lawyering skills to get our van back?"

"If I have to, yes."

Angela pursed her lips and eyed her. "Fine. But I still don't want you getting involved in that murder. I want you to stay safe, Lucy."

"I will." That was a promise Lucy intended to keep. She'd had enough risky business from the last murder she'd gotten involved in, months ago. She still had bad dreams of dark and shadowy alleyways and her narrow escape from death.

But she couldn't stop herself from wondering. The faster she solved the case, the sooner Detective Clemmons would have to return the van, wouldn't he?

CHAPTER 9

Katie was waiting for Lucy in the restaurant's back parking lot the next day. Close to three o'clock, it was after the lunch rush and right before dinner service, when the restaurant was slow. Lucy left Emma in charge of the dining room and Azad in the kitchen.

Katie leaned against her jeep and smiled when Lucy stepped outside. Gadoo was sitting at her feet and Katie was scratching the orange and black cat beneath his chin.

Gadoo purred. "He likes you," Lucy said.

"You sound surprised." Katie continued to pet the cat.

"He doesn't approach many people. Only family. He hides behind the Dumpster for everyone else."

"I guess I'm family to him."

Lucy cocked her head to the side and smiled. "Yes. You are. To me too."

"Aww. Thanks, Lucy." Katie turned her attention back to the cat. "Gadoo's getting fat."

"That's because my mom keeps feeding him liver treats."

Katie chuckled. "Please tell your mom that I love her baklava. It's the best I've ever tasted."

"Don't encourage her. She'll try to feed you more than just baklava. Mom thinks everyone who crosses her path needs a good meal." Lucy had been trying to watch her weight since returning to Ocean Crest, but running a restaurant and having Angela Berberian as her mother was a bad combination. She needed to double the number of times she jogged up and down the boardwalk.

Katie pushed away from the car. "Great. Tell your mom Bill and I would be happy to come to her house for a meal."

"I'll do that. But make sure you don't eat that entire day," Lucy said.

Katie laughed as she pulled her keys from her jeans pocket. "Are you ready to question Victoria Redding?"

"Don't you have to get back to work?" Lucy asked.

"Nope. I worked through lunch and took an hour of personal time. I wouldn't want to miss this."

Lucy eyed the jeep. "Maybe I should drive?"

"Why?"

"No offense, but you have a tendency to drive like you're racing in the Indy Five Hundred."

"Hey. Watch it. You tend to be a backseat driver."

"Don't get your lashes in a knot. If you try to obey all the local speed laws, I promise to zip it." Lucy made a motion across her lips with her thumb and forefinger.

Katie grinned. "Deal. Now, do you have what we need?"

Lucy showed her a large manila envelope she'd tucked under her arm. "These are all the catering bills and invoices for Scarlet and Bradford's wedding. I added a few items, and I hope it's good enough to get us through Victoria's door. I already received a down payment for the catering job, and everything else was handled through the mail. Victoria is bound to wonder why I'm hand delivering the final bill."

Katie winked. "You're a lawyer. I have faith in your ability to talk and charm."

Lucy rolled her eyes. "It's been months since I left the firm. I'm getting rusty."

Katie opened the car door. "Nonsense. Lawyers are like sharks. You can take them out of the ocean and stuff them in an aquarium tank, but they still have razor-sharp teeth and a scent for blood."

Lucy burst out laughing. Katie always had a way with words.

But some shark she was. She was still nervous about approaching Victoria. Lucy clutched the envelope as she opened the passenger side door and stepped inside Katie's jeep.

"If all else fails, you can tell her you're hand delivering it because you wanted to save a stamp," Katie said as she started the engine.

Lucy buckled her seat belt, and Katie drove past the town's mile-long main strip. They passed Holloway's Grocery, Magic's Family Apothecary, and Cutie's Cupcakes. Soon Lucy spotted the twisted red and white barber pole of Ben's Barber Shop as they neared the end of the strip and drove closer to the ocean. Sand dunes and dune fences came into view, and she knew they were important natural barriers that protected the coastline. The dunes were a fixture and without them it wouldn't look like the Jersey shore.

The air from the open window was warm, a typical June day in Ocean Crest, and Lucy loved the heat despite the high humidity that could feel like a wet blanket against your skin.

True to her word, Katie kept the jeep's speedometer to a legal thirty-five miles per hour, but the pedestrian traffic made that a necessity. Katie yielded for a family of four heading to the beach. The father pulled a loaded beach cart with protruding boogie boards and a mesh bag of sand toys tied to the side of the cart. The mother held the hands of her two young daughters in pigtails who wore matching rash guards and flip-flops. Memories returned in a rush, of Lucy and Emma with their parents spending lazy summer days at the beach building sand castles and boogieboarding in the surf. The Jersey shore was in her blood and the pull back home had been strong.

Katie turned onto a side street and the Sandpiper Bed and Breakfast came into view—a Victorian-style home that resembled a dollhouse with elaborate wood trim, bright blue and orange paint, and a wraparound porch. White rocking chairs and lanterns resting on end tables completed the picture, with guests reclining on a summer afternoon while sipping iced tea and waving to passersby strolling down the street. It was a throwback to another time, and the only modern item was a lit neon sign that blinked No VACANCY every three seconds. The summer season was in full swing and a tourist would be hard pressed to find a place to stay in Ocean Crest without a reservation made months ago.

Katie parked in a spot labeled VISITORS ONLY, and they stepped out of the car. Opening the front door, they entered a sitting room tastefully decorated with a red velvet settee and antique end tables and lamps.

A woman in her midsixties with dyed blond hair wearing a yellow dress with printed daisies and a starched white apron walked into the room.

"Hello, Katie. What a nice surprise."

Katie smiled at the older woman. "Hi, Hannah. This is my friend, Lucy Berberian. Lucy, this is Hannah Smith. She owns the Sandpiper."

"Of course!" Hannah said as she shook Lucy's hand. "Your parents are lovely people. How are Angela and Raffi?"

"They are doing well, thank you," Lucy said.

Hannah cupped Lucy's hand. "A while back your mother asked if I could go to a book-signing at Pages Bookstore with her to get a signed copy of Cooking Kurt's latest cookbook. Unfortunately, I had to decline because I have to work that day. But you know who he is, don't you?"

Lucy smiled. "I've seen him on TV once or twice." The image of the two older women fawning over the hot celebrity chef was amusing.

"I'm afraid I finished cleaning up from brunch, but I can always put on a fresh pot of coffee. Or do you ladies prefer tea?" Hannah asked.

"Thank you, but we don't want to put you to any trouble. We're here to speak with one of your guests," Katie said.

"Which one?" Hannah asked. "I have a full house this week."

"Victoria Redding."

Hannah's eyes grew large, and she leaned close and lowered her voice. "Does your visit have anything to do with that socialite's wedding? It was awful what happened to Mr. Simms at the reception. He was a fixture at the town bank."

Gossip traveled as fast as the Internet in Ocean Crest, and Lucy didn't want to start another stint. She especially didn't want their visit to get back to Detective Clemmons or Prosecutor Walsh. "It was a tragedy, but the restaurant catered the wedding and we are here today just to go over the final bill with Ms. Redding." Lucy held up her manila envelope as if that would back up her story. If by chance Clemmons heard about their visit, she had a good excuse.

"I usually don't like to bother my guests. The Sandpiper is quiet and my guests expect a level of privacy, but since I know you both, I think it would be fine. Ms. Redding is in room number five. Upstairs. First door on your left."

"Thank you," Lucy and Katie said in unison.

Halfway up the winding wooden staircase, Katie whispered, "See. I knew you could do it."

"Don't congratulate me just yet. I'm more nervous than before. I didn't know Hannah Smith was friends with my mother. I hope our visit doesn't get back to her. My mom will know we're getting involved with this murder business." Lucy was almost as wary of her mother as she was of Prosecutor Walsh.

They reached the top of the stairs and turned right. Lucy rapped on the first door.

Seconds later, footsteps sounded inside the room and the door opened. Victoria stood in the doorway dressed in black slacks, a red silk blouse, stilettos, and a full face of makeup. She held her purse in one hand and car keys in another. Clearly, she was on her way out.

"May I help you?" she asked tersely.

Lucy took a small step forward. "Hello, Ms. Redding.

You remember my friend, Katie Watson, from the wedding reception."

Victoria's kohl-lined eyes narrowed. "I remember. What do you both want?"

"There are some last-minute additions to the catering bill, and I thought it would be best to go over everything in person," Lucy said as she shifted the envelope from one hand to the other.

"What last minute additions? We went over everything beforehand. There was a contract," Victoria said.

"Yes, I know. But things came up. Can we come inside and go over everything before I send the final bill? That way there won't be any surprises or conflicts," Lucy said.

Victoria huffed, and Lucy could tell she was contemplating slamming the door in her face, but business won out. "Fine. But we have to make it quick. I was on my way out to visit Scarlet." She held the door open, and Lucy and Katie stepped inside. The room was decorated in lovely Victorian style with flocked wallpaper and antique cherry bedroom furniture.

Victoria motioned for Lucy and Katie to seat themselves on a blue settee situated beneath the window. Lucy set out her paperwork on a coffee table, and Victoria sat in an armchair across from them. Her strong floral perfume made Lucy's nose itch. It was the same perfume she had smelled on the day of the wedding, only fainter.

Lucy cleared her throat and looked Victoria in the eye. "I'm sorry about what happened to Henry. It was a true tragedy."

"Yes, it was. Shocking and upsetting to everyone at that wedding." Victoria eyed her. "But I'm surprised *you* of all people would mention it. Isn't your chef a prime suspect?"

Lucy expected hostility from Victoria. The memory of Detective Clemmons questioning Azad and Lucy while Henry's body was sprawled in the back of the van wasn't something she could easily forget. "The police have not made any arrests. They are still investigating."

Victoria's lips narrowed. "But *you* tried to blame me."

Lucy straightened. "No. I was just telling them what I'd heard."

Victoria huffed. "I can tell you this much. Henry had been a longtime friend of the groom since college, and Henry recommended me as the wedding planner. I was *grateful* to him."

She hadn't sounded grateful to Lucy in the parking lot of Castle of the Sea. Henry had accused her of acting like a shrew. "I heard you argue," Lucy retorted.

"So? Weddings are stressful events. I was responsible for making sure Scarlet and Bradford had a perfect day. Henry had a tendency to drink too much and do and say stupid things."

That much was true. Lucy had witnessed Henry's drunken behavior firsthand when he'd burst into the kitchen and demanded whiskey.

Victoria looked Lucy directly in the eye. "I may have yelled at him in the parking lot and taken his cell phone, but I did it to get his attention. I did *not* murder the man."

Kate leaned forward in her seat. "Do you know of anyone who would have wanted to hurt Henry?"

Victoria waved a hand. "Ha! I could give you a long list of people who disliked Henry."

"Can you limit it to those who'd want to kill him?" Lucy asked.

Victoria smoothed her hair before answering. "His wife, Holly Simms. Their marriage wasn't amicable."

"Amicable is one thing," Lucy said, "but murder is something else entirely. Why would Holly want to kill her husband?"

"Because she recently found out Henry was having an affair," Victoria said.

Lucy dropped the envelope on the table in surprise. "An affair? With whom?"

Victoria made a disgusted face. "Cressida."

Lucy's jaw went slack. "Cressida Connolly? Scarlet's maid of honor?"

"That's right."

"But Cressida must be . . ." Lucy hesitated as her mind made the calculation.

"Almost thirty years younger," Victoria finished the math for her. At Lucy's amazed look, Victoria scoffed. "Not only is she young enough to be his daughter, but she is Scarlet's best friend. The two girls went to private high school together."

"Did Scarlet know?" Katie asked.

"It wouldn't surprise me. Scarlet once told me that they both wanted to snag older, rich men. Sugar daddies, they'd call them," Victoria said, her expression one of disgust.

Sugar daddies? Lucy found it hard to believe that in today's day and age, that would be a woman's goal.

"The fact is that Henry had been a cheater, and his wife Holly was humiliated when she discovered the truth," Victoria said.

"How do you know Holly found out?" Katie asked.

"It happened at the rehearsal," Victoria said. "I was organizing the progression of the bridal party in the church. Bradford was waiting by the altar, and the best man was nowhere to be found. Neither was the maid of honor. I went in search of them and found them alone in one of the dressing rooms. Cressida was in Henry's arms. When they heard me come in the two jumped apart looking as guilty as burglars fleeing a convenience store with a bag of cash. When I turned around to leave, I ran straight into Holly. She'd been right behind me the entire time."

"What did Holly do?" Katie asked.

"Nothing. She just walked away. But I caught a glimpse of her face. She was livid."

"You believe Holly was mad enough to kill her husband?" Lucy asked.

Victoria looked at her like she was a simpleton. "Her husband had cheated with a much younger woman. The maid of honor, no less. It was like a slap in the face."

"Did you ever overhear Holly and Henry fight?"

"No. Holly was surprisingly quiet for the rest of the wedding rehearsal." Victoria crossed her legs and leaned forward in her chair. "But if it turns out the murderer wasn't Holly, then I'd put my money on that hotheaded chef of yours."

Lucy's voice was adamant. "Azad didn't kill Henry Simms."

"So you say."

Lucy stood. There was no sense arguing with her. They had a new lead and that's what they'd hoped for. "Thank you for your time," Lucy said. "I'll leave the catering bill for you to review before you send it to Scarlet and Bradford." Lucy reached into her purse and pulled out a business card. She'd had cards printed with the restaurant's name, her title as manager, and her cell phone number at the top. "If you have any questions about the bill, please call." They hurried from the room and out the front door of the bed and breakfast.

Once back in the jeep, Lucy turned to Katie. "What do you think?"

"Holly could very well be the murderer. Spouses are first on the suspect list."

"You think Detective Clemmons is thinking the same thing?" Lucy asked.

"Who knows? The truth is I wouldn't be surprised if Clemmons overlooks Holly Simms as a suspect. Less is more for him. He has his eye on Azad."

CHAPTER 10

After leaving the bed and breakfast and returning to Katie's house, Lucy received a cell phone call from Emma notifying her that the restaurant was almost out of cream, and their dairy supplier wasn't scheduled to make a delivery until three days from now. Lucy estimated that they needed eight pints of cream for the restaurant's coffee and tea drinkers, and she told Emma that she would make a quick stop at Holloway's Grocery on her way to work. Her father would have made the trip, but Raffi Berberian was only working part-time now, and the duty fell to Lucy.

Walking into Holloway's was like walking into the past. Holloway's had been the sole supermarket in Ocean Crest since Lucy was a little girl. The owner, Edgar Holloway, had started the business and had long since retired. His three sons, who now ran the store, had made an effort to keep it a small, hometown grocery. The baked goods were fresh, the produce seasonally local, and the milk delivered from local dairy farms whose farmers fed their cows organic grain. The workers wore green aprons and greeted customers with a smile. The only change had been the teenage stock boys. They looked a lot younger.

Or had Lucy just gotten older?

She was in the refrigerated food section loading up her cart when she spotted Mae Bancroft farther down the aisle. Mae was the head teller at Ocean Crest Savings and Loan, and Lucy saw Mae every day when she made her daily bank deposit for the restaurant. Heavyset with dyed auburn hair, Mae dressed in bright colors and owned an array of interesting costume jewelry. Today she wore a bright orange sundress with a print of blue and green parrots and dangling orange earrings to match. Mae knew almost all the town locals and she liked to gossip.

Lucy pushed her shopping cart close by. "Hi, Mae."

Mae turned and her orange earrings swayed as she moved. It took a moment for Lucy to realize they were miniature parrots that complemented the pattern of Mae's dress.

"Hello, Lucy!" Mae smiled brightly. "Fancy bumping into you here. I don't think I've ever seen you outside the bank."

"The restaurant ran out of a few things before our suppliers can make a delivery," Lucy said.

Mae's gaze swept Lucy's cart. "Ah, cream. I suppose that's important enough to make a supermarket run."

Lucy may not have planned this encounter with Mae, but it was the perfect opportunity to ask about her dead boss. "Mae, I never had the chance to say how sorry I am about Henry Simms."

A sad look passed over Mae's face. "We were all

shocked. And to have it happen the way it did . . . well, Henry didn't deserve that."

"How long did you work for him?"

"Twenty-two years, to be exact."

"Wow. That's a long time."

Mae sniffled. "He was a good man. A good boss."

Lucy tilted her head to the side and regarded her. "Mae, I need to ask you something about Henry."

Mae played with the strap of her handbag in the front of the shopping cart. "You don't need to worry about the bank. Your account is secure."

Lucy shook her head. "That's not what I'm worried about."

"Then what?"

"I want to ask you about some rumors I've heard about Henry's personal difficulties at the bank. Gossip says he'd been on probation."

Mae, who always liked to talk, looked suddenly taken aback. She twisted the handle of her purse. "I don't think I should discuss bank business."

"You won't get in trouble. I promise not to tell anyone, and Henry is gone."

"Still, I—"

"It is important that I know. I'm living with Officer Watson and his wife. If there's any information that can help find Henry's killer, wouldn't you want to share it? You don't have to worry about having your name dragged into it, because I'd never reveal my sources."

"Well . . . I suppose you're right. Nothing I say can harm poor Henry now, and I want to see his killer arrested. But I don't think I know anything that can help."

"You never know."

"All right." Mae lowered her voice. "But not here." Mae pushed her shopping cart out of the refrigerated foods aisle and into the pasta aisle. Lucy followed and they halted by jars of spaghetti sauce. Mae looked both ways to ensure they were alone. "I picked up the phone one day and happened to overhear one of Henry's conversations. It was by chance, you see."

"Of course." Lucy didn't believe Mae had just happened to pick up the phone and eavesdrop on her boss's conversation. Mae was too nosy.

"Henry was a huge sports fan, especially the Philadelphia teams. He rarely missed a Flyers, Eagles, or Sixers game. And he went nuts over the Phillies."

Lucy knew South Jersey residents tended to be fans of the closer Philadelphia sports teams rather than the North Jersey or New York teams. "My dad is a Phillies fan, too, but not me. I like football and try never to miss an Eagles game," Lucy said.

"Well, Henry also liked the boxing matches. You know, the big ones held in Atlantic City. But he could never attend them or bet on a fight because his wife frowned upon it. Holly kept Henry on a tight leash."

Lucy tucked this interesting fact away, but something else Mae had said caught Lucy's interest. "You said he couldn't bet on the fights. Are you saying Henry gambled on the sports teams and boxing matches?"

Mae glanced around once more before nodding. "I overheard Henry place sports bets with a man over the phone that day."

"A sports bookie?"

"I guess so."

It would explain a lot if Henry had a fondness for illegal sports betting. A person could rack up debt

fast that way and find himself desperate for cash.
Desperate enough to risk his job at the bank by "bor-
rowing" loan money from the accounts of unsuspecting customers and hoping to replace it after his next
big win.

But what if he failed to win?

Katie had said Bradford and Scarlet had an account
with Henry's bank for the launch of Scarlet's Passion.
Had Henry taken some of their cash? Lucy looked at
Mae. "Do you recall the name of the sports bookie?"

Mae shrugged. "Well, I wasn't listening for long—"

Lucy's patience was at an end. This was a lead that
couldn't be overlooked. "Think, Mae. It's important."

"I believe he said his name was Sam."

"Just Sam? Any last name?"

Mae shook her head.

"Anything else you can remember?"

Mae pursed her lips. "Sam told Henry to meet him,
with cash, at this country bar, Denim and Spurs. Henry
agreed, then hung up."

Lucy had heard of Denim and Spurs, but she'd
never been inside the place, which was just outside
town. Country music and line dancing weren't her
thing. But she now planned on making her first trip
to the place. "Thanks, Mae. You were a big help. And
don't worry, my lips are sealed. I'd never reveal your
name."

"Glad I could help. You'll be sure to tell me what
Officer Watson finds when you visit the bank?"

*Only if I want the entire town to know the news within
two hours.* "Of course."

Lucy turned her cart around. "I'm headed to
check out."

"Me too." Mae chatted about the current tourist season as they pushed their carts toward the cashiers. Lucy was behind Mae, but that didn't stop her from continuing to talk as she removed items from her cart to place them on the conveyer belt. Mae dug in her handbag, removed a handful of coupons, handed them to the cashier, then froze.

"Would you look at that!" Mae pointed to one of the tabloid magazines on a display rack next to the cashier. The front cover was splashed with images of Scarlet Westwood in her couture wedding gown with Bradford by her side. The couple both looked shocked, and the headline read: *SOCIALITE'S WEDDING TURNS DEADLY.*

Beneath the text were smaller pictures of the paramedics wheeling Henry's corpse into the coroner's van.

"What a disgrace!" Mae's color was high, and her parrot earrings swayed from side to side as she shook her head. "How could the tabloids make money off such a tragedy as a man's murder?" Mae reached for the magazine and flipped it open to reveal pictures of the reception and the guests at Castle of the Sea.

Only someone who had been at the reception could have taken those pictures and sold them to the tabloids. Lucy's bet was on Henry. If he needed funds, and fast, what better way to get them than to smuggle a cell phone inside the reception, text or e-mail the pictures directly to a gossip paper, and make a quick buck?

Hadn't Victoria accused Henry of doing just that at the wedding? Henry must have sent the pics before Victoria had snatched his cell phone.

Mae dropped the paper on the conveyer belt along

with her groceries. "I want to read the entire article and see exactly what that magazine claims."

It was clear Mae's outrage didn't outweigh her penchant for gossip.

This time Lucy would join her. She plucked another copy from the rack and dropped it into her cart.

That night, Lucy tugged on her seat belt as Katie sped down Ocean Avenue.

"I haven't been to Denim and Spurs in years," Katie said.

Lucy reached up and grabbed the little handle above the door as Katie zipped past another car. "I've never been, and if you don't slow down, I may never make it."

Katie chuckled. "You're still not used to my driving?"

"Will I ever get used to it?"

They passed the center of town and drove by the sand dunes and the dune fences. It was close to eight-thirty in the evening, but the sun didn't set until late during the long summer days. The dune grasses danced beneath a strong breeze. In the distance, the ocean waves were rough and only a few brave people were walking on the beach. The weather channel had said it was going to rain, and although they were accurate only half the time, Lucy believed their prediction today. As they passed a sign that read LEAVING OCEAN CREST, THANK YOU FOR VISITING OUR BEACH, Katie slowed down.

"Are you worried you might get a speeding ticket now that you've left Bill's jurisdiction?" Lucy couldn't help but ask.

Katie cracked a grin. "It would be unethical for me

to take advantage of my husband's job, but I admit the thought had crossed my mind years ago when Bill had just been hired by the township police department and we'd tied the knot."

"No longer?"

"No. I wouldn't want to put him in that position."

"But you're okay with helping me investigate a murder behind his back?"

"That's different. I like Azad and want to help him. And like I said, Bill isn't involved in this investigation. But Calvin Clemmons is, and I don't have much faith in that man, do you?"

No, she didn't. And if she was truthful to herself, Lucy was grateful for Katie's help. "Thank you for coming along with me today."

Katie shrugged. "You're my best friend. You can't get rid of me that easily."

Lucy was reminded of how much she'd gained since leaving Philadelphia and returning home. Friendship, family, and a new career as manager of a family restaurant.

"Do you think this bookie will talk about Henry?" Katie asked, interrupting Lucy's thoughts.

"I'm not sure, but it's worth a try. If Henry owes the guy money, then I'd think he'd want to get paid."

Ten minutes later, Katie turned down a graveled drive and a rustic-looking wood building came into view. It was designed to look like a throwback in time, and it would have achieved that effect, except for the glowing neon cowboy boot sign that flashed the name DENIM AND SPURS. A couple dressed in jeans, cowboy boots, and Stetsons strolled arm in arm inside the front door.

Katie pulled into a parking spot and put the jeep in

park. "Check this place out. It hasn't changed since the last time Bill and I were invited for happy hour years ago." She reached in the backseat and pulled out a cowboy hat.

Lucy's eyes widened at the brown faux leather hat with a black hat band. "Where'd you get that?"

"I've had it for years. Do you think it will help us blend in?"

"Only at a costume party dressed as Annie Oakley."

"That bad?"

"Let's just go inside first and check the place out, okay?"

Katie tossed the hat onto the backseat. They got out of the car and opened the club's front door to the sound of loud country music from a live band. Men and women dressed in cowboy boots and Stetsons crowded the bar and the tables. A dozen dancers were burning it up on the dance floor, doing some type of intricate country line dance. The band's lead singer removed the mic from the stand and called out, "Let's all now get movin' to 'Boot Scootin' Boogie,' by Brooks and Dunn!" The dancers whooped and began stomping their boots, clapping their hands, and shuffling across the wooden dance floor. Lucy could barely keep up with their steps—it reminded her of a high-intensity Zumba class she'd taken in the past.

"Wow," Lucy said. "This place is hopping."

Katie stared wide-eyed. "I don't remember it being this busy."

"Let's head to the bar and ask questions." Lucy spotted a couple leave their bar stools and walk to the dance floor. She nudged Katie and the pair hurried over and slid onto the empty seats.

Men and women talked and tapped their boots to

the lively music. The bartender was busy serving drinks to a group of thirty-year-olds at the far end of the bar. A blonde with big hair and a Garth Brooks T-shirt was flirting with a man in an oversized cowboy hat.

"Look at that!" Katie pointed to a corner of the club. "Two mechanical bulls. Last time I was here, they had only one."

Lucy watched, fascinated, as a man with worn jeans, a large silver belt buckle, and a wide-brimmed cowboy hat rode one of the bulls. One of his hands held the bull's horn and the other waved in the air like a professional rodeo rider. He lasted ten seconds before the mechanical bull bucked him off, and he landed on his backside. People standing on the sidelines burst into cheers.

"Jeeze. I wonder how he stayed on the bull for that long," Katie said.

Lucy smiled. "You want to try?"

Katie poked Lucy in the arm. "Not unless you plan on calling nine-one-one tonight."

Lucy sobered as the bartender finished serving drinks to the group. "Here he comes. Let's ask him if he knows of a Sam."

The bartender wiped the bar before them with a clean cloth, then grinned at them. "What can I get you two?"

Lucy leaned forward and rested her elbows on the bar. "We're looking for a man named Sam."

"Sam, huh? You two pretty ladies want to talk with him?"

Lucy held his gaze. "You bet."

The bartender chuckled. "If I didn't know better, I'd almost be jealous of Sam Turner." He turned to the dance floor. "He's over there."

Lucy and Katie swiveled on their stools to see a man sliding across the dance floor doing the two-step with a woman. He appeared to be in his late sixties with a leathery, wrinkled face. He was dressed in dark jeans, a white button-down shirt embroidered with a country pattern, and a bolo tie of leather shoestring. His cowboy boots were well worn. The large hat made it impossible to tell if he had hair.

"That's Sam Turner?" Lucy wasn't sure what she'd expected the bookie to look like, but a senior citizen, country line dancer wasn't it.

"That's right. Sam is our resident dancing instructor. On weekdays at two and four, you can stop by and schedule a lesson. Sam can teach you any country dance, from the two-step to the Cotton-Eyed Joe."

Katie lowered her voice to whisper in Lucy's ear. "Looks like fun. Maybe we should schedule lessons. We can pump him for information as we learn how to line dance."

It wasn't a bad thought, but just then, the dance ended, and Sam grinned and tipped his hat at his partner.

"You're in luck," the bartender said. "The band's taking a break and Sam will be heading this way for a drink."

As if on cue, the DJ took over and a Garth Brooks song came over the speakers. Sam sidled up to the bar, and the bartender popped the cap of a domestic beer and slid it across the worn, wooden bar. Sam tipped his hat again and took a long swig.

Lucy knew she wouldn't have a better opportunity. She slid off her stool and sidled up to him. Katie trailed behind. "Mr. Turner?"

He lowered his beer to look at Lucy and Katie. His

face creased in a wide grin. "To what do I owe the pleasure, ladies?"

"We'd like to ask you a few questions," Katie said.

"Ah, y'all lookin' to learn how to line dance? I'm a great teacher, and y'll learn the 'Achy Breaky Heart' on our first lesson."

Up close, Lucy noticed his leather string bolo tie was decorated with a silver and turquoise grizzly claw. "Thanks, but that's not why we're looking for you."

Sam winked. "Oh? I'd be happy to oblige y'all in any other way."

Oh, brother. "Not that either, Mr. Turner."

"Please call me Sam. No dancin'? No datin'? So, what can I help ya with?"

"Henry Simms. We understand you helped him place sports bets," Katie said.

All humor vanished from Sam's expression. His face shuttered and he looked away. Lucy glared at Katie. Her friend had never learned the fine art of subtlety. They needed Sam Turner to speak up, not clam up.

Sam cleared his throat. "Now, I don't know what he told you, but—"

"He didn't tell us anything. Henry Simms is dead," Lucy said.

Sam's eyes darted to her in shock. "Henry's dead?"

"You haven't heard?" Lucy lowered her voice.

He shrugged. "I don't live in town, and it's not like we are . . . were best friends. I helped him with his entertainment." All trace of his country accent vanished.

"You mean his sports bets?" Katie said.

Sam took a swig of his beer and swallowed. "Henry had a fondness for the Philadelphia teams. He also loved boxing. Why are you asking?"

"Don't worry. We're not undercover police or the Gaming Commission," Lucy said.

"Then who are you? And what do you care about Henry?"

"We are friends of his wife, Holly," Lucy said. "We want to settle his debts quietly before his affliction for gambling gets out." It was a small lie, but they needed to know the truth about Henry Simms's risky behavior at the bank. Lucy looked him square in the eye as she waited for his response. Investigating murders had one result: she was definitely getting better at deception.

Sam rotated the kinks out of his neck and took another drink of beer before continuing. "I get it. You want to hide his problem from the rest of the family before people like me start crawling out of the woodwork to knock on his door and demand our cash."

"Exactly," Katie said.

Sam's eyes darted back and forth between them. "Perfect. Henry owed me two hundred and fifty."

"Two hundred and fifty dollars?" Katie asked.

"No. Two hundred and fifty *thousand.*"

Lucy's and Katie's jaws dropped.

"He owed you that much cash just from betting on sports teams?" Lucy gripped the back of a bar stool.

"Sure. A couple bad bets can add up fast."

"And you didn't require payment up front?"

"I've placed bets for Henry for years. There's a matter of trust involved between a bookie and a long-time customer. We conducted business over the phone. Henry always pays up. Or, I guess I should say he always paid up."

"When was he going to pay you?" Katie asked.

"Next week. I would have shown up at his home if

he failed to meet me. I take it you ladies will speak with his wife and meet me instead?" Sam said.

Lucy wasn't surprised he still expected a huge lump cash payment after he'd learned Henry was dead. Bookies weren't ethical—they operated illegal cash businesses. He probably expected Henry's widow to pay. But what if Holly never knew Henry had gambled? Would Sam begin threatening tactics? Looking at the old geezer, he didn't seem that intimidating, but what did she know? Maybe he'd hire a few of the muscular cowboys in the club to do his dirty work for him?

Lucy's pulse skittered as a disturbing thought occurred to her. Now that they'd gotten involved, what if Sam expected her or Katie to make good on Henry's debt? Would his "muscle men" show up at Katie's doorstep looking for cash?

Holy crap.

"We'll talk with Henry's widow." Lucy did plan to have a conversation with Holly. They needed to learn what the widow knew about her late husband.

Sam tipped his Stetson. "Much obliged. It will save me a hassle." The band returned from a short break and began playing another lively tune. "Are you sure you two ladies don't want to learn the two-step?"

"We're sure, but thank you anyway," Lucy said.

Sam shrugged. "Suit yourselves." He hopped off the stool and strode toward the dance floor, took the hand of a middle-aged brunette as he passed by, and twirled her onto the hardwood.

"He's smooth for his age," Lucy said.

Katie nodded. "I guess it comes with his occupation."

They left the country bar and sat in Katie's jeep. Katie started the engine, but kept the car in park and gripped the steering wheel. "I still can't believe the amount of debt Henry had racked up."

"Sam will want payment. Either from Holly or someone else," Lucy said.

"By someone else you don't mean us, do you?" Katie asked.

Lucy stirred uneasily in her seat. "I sure hope not. But what if he shows up at your doorstep?"

Katie's fingers tightened on the steering wheel. "I'll set Bill on him."

"It must be nice to have a husband who's a cop."

Katie offered a big smile. "I won't lie. It comes in handy at times."

For a moment, Lucy felt a stab of jealousy. Katie and Bill had been together since after high school. No matter what Katie did, Bill would always be there for her and vice versa. Lucy wondered if she'd ever find that kind of devotion in a man.

"Let's not worry about Sam's money-collecting efforts for now. We need to focus on Henry's gambling."

Lucy nodded. "You're right."

"Henry's debt was considerable. No wonder he was taking risks with the loans at his bank. He was probably living week by week, paying off lost bets, then turning around and doing it all over again. How'd Henry get away with it?" Katie asked.

Lucy pulled her seat belt across her lap and clicked it into place. "I don't think he did, entirely. You said Henry was on probation. I can only guess he wasn't fired because he was the CEO. He must have had friends in high places." It may not be ethical, but it wouldn't be the first time big banks had gotten away with fraudulent activity. Lucy had read law school cases where bank executives had stolen millions . . .

sometimes billions . . . from unsuspecting customers by charging wrongful bank fees or questionable loan practices.

Katie pulled out of the parking spot and headed back to Ocean Crest. She drove below the speed limit, and this time Lucy suspected it was because she was thinking about all they had learned. They both were.

"It explains a lot," Katie said.

It did. If Henry was always strapped for cash, then he'd do anything to get it. "We already suspect he'd stolen bank funds from clients. And chances are he also sold pictures of Scarlet and Bradford's wedding to the paparazzi. When I ran into Mae Bancroft earlier today at Holloway's, I saw photos of the wedding reception in one of the tabloids by the checkout aisle. Victoria had taken Henry's cell phone, but I think she was too late, and Henry had already sold them for cash."

Katie whistled. "What if Henry had dealt with more than one bookie?"

"It's possible." Lucy drew her lips in thoughtfully. "And if he did, then more people had motive to want Henry Simms dead."

CHAPTER 11

When Lucy walked into the restaurant the next day, both Azad and Butch were hard at work in the kitchen. Emma read from a slip of paper taped to the back of her order pad. "Tonight's specials are baba ghanoush for an appetizer, a *fattoush* salad of mixed greens, vegetables, and pita chips, and main entrees of chicken kebab and stuffed peppers and zucchini with meat and rice."

Lucy licked her lips. Baba ghanoush, the eggplant and sesame seed dip, was a popular item on the menu. "Sounds delicious."

Emma tucked the pad into the front pocket of her waitress apron. "It's a full staff tonight. Mom and Dad are helping. Sally and I are waitressing."

Lucy entered the dining room through the swinging doors and was happy to see that half of the tables and booths were already occupied. Her father was at the hostess stand greeting and seating customers as they entered. Her mother was behind the register. Working part-time had been good for her parents and was easing them into retirement. Her father was teaching Lucy how to manage the books, inventory, and the payroll, and her mother was teaching her how to cook. Lucy was quickly mastering the books and paperwork, but the cooking lessons were an entirely different challenge and were taking more time and effort.

"We're booked for tonight, Lucy." Her father patted the weathered, black reservation book.

Lucy eyed the book speculatively. "Have you thought about a computerized reservation system? I left quotes from a couple vendors in the office for you to review."

"Your mother and I have thought about it and decided against it," Raffi said.

"Dad, change is nothing to be afraid of," she argued.

"Tell that to the storage room."

Lucy cringed. The haphazard status of the storage room kept returning to haunt her. "That's different, Dad. I had no control over the strike at the shelving manufacturer, and I certainly couldn't help that our handyman injured his back."

"Who's to say something similar won't happen if you install an expensive computer system?" Raffi asked. "My method has worked for thirty years without a hitch. If it isn't broken, don't fix it."

Lucy frowned. There was no doubt that Raffi Berberian was mulish.

But she was learning from the best. *One step at a time, Lucy,* she thought. She remained confident that she would wear her parents down.

Her father stepped close and touched her cheek. "You know we are proud of you."

Lucy could never stay mad at her father for long. He could be gruff and he never minced words, but he was affectionate with his daughters. "Thanks, Dad. But you know I won't give up."

He broke into a wide, open smile. "You wouldn't be a Berberian if you did." The front door opened and Raffi gathered menus to seat a family of five.

A steady stream of hungry customers was in line for the hummus bar. "It's been a good tourist season so far," her mother said. "I came up with new hummus recipes of Greek olive, edamame, and spicy jalapeño hummus. Customers like the flavors."

"Sounds delicious. Make sure you wrap some hummus and baklava for Katie and Bill. They've been asking."

Her mother's face lit up whenever anyone complimented her cooking. "Of course. I'll include tonight's special."

"They'd like that, Mom," Lucy said.

After making the rounds and chatting with customers, Lucy returned to the kitchen to find Azad plating one of the dinner specials. He set the dish on the stainless-steel counter beneath the heat lamps and called out number three. Each waitress had a specific number, and when the chef called it out, the waitress knew one of her orders was ready. Sally was number three. Lucy had always been number six when she'd waitressed. It was another one of the old systems that Lucy wanted to computerize.

Azad waved her over as soon as he saw her. "Hey, Lucy. Can I talk with you in private?"

"Sure."

He wiped his hands on a towel and motioned for her to follow him to an isolated corner of the kitchen. His features were tense and a trickle of anxiety ran down her spine.

"What's wrong?" Lucy asked.

"Detective Clemmons wants me to go to the station for questioning tomorrow."

Her anxiety heightened. Had Clemmons come up with more evidence against Azad? And if he had, then why ask for Azad to come to the station for questioning? Wouldn't Clemmons have shown up at the restaurant with a warrant for his arrest?

Her reasoning should reassure her, but it didn't. "You need a lawyer," Lucy said.

"You think I need one?"

"I know you do."

"Can you do it?"

She sighed in exasperation. "Azad, I'm not a criminal attorney. I practiced patent law. I could patent Detective Clemmons's handcuffs—if they hadn't already been patented—but I can't defend you. Plus, I'm your employer and I was present at the wedding. It's a huge conflict of interest."

He sighed. "All right."

"Call Clyde Winters. He's local and handles criminal matters like municipal court cases and DUIs. Municipal court can get pretty busy during tourist season."

Azad's head snapped up. "He's like a hundred years old!"

She hadn't seen the town's lawyer in a decade. Was it true? The only criminal defense lawyers she knew were in Philadelphia. "Then I'll give you a good recommendation for—"

Her cell phone rang and cut her off. Lucy pulled it out of her back pocket and caught a glimpse of the cell phone case with a picture of her holding Gadoo. "Hello?"

"It's Katie. Can you talk?"

"I'm with Azad in the kitchen. What's up?"

"Ditch him."

"Hold on." Lucy covered the receiver and looked at Azad. He was watching her with a hopeful expression. "I need to take this privately."

She hurried into the small office in the corner of the storage room, shut the door, and sat on the chair in front of a desk littered with order forms, invoices, and payroll sheets. "I'm alone. What's wrong?"

"I did some digging while I was at work. It turns out there was a million-dollar life insurance policy on Henry Simms."

Lucy's pulse leaped. "A million dollars is a boatload of money."

"No kidding. It gets better. Holly Simms is the beneficiary, and the policy was purchased only three months ago," Katie said.

"Can someone collect life insurance benefits if the insured is murdered?" Lucy asked.

"Yes, as long as the beneficiary isn't the murderer."

Lucy processed this information. She'd thought Henry's murder had been a spur of the moment killing. It's not like anyone would have known the catering van would be in the parking lot and shish kebab skewers would be available inside.

But what if she was wrong and the murder had been premeditated? What if the skewer just happened to be convenient, but the killer would have murdered Henry by another method anyway?

"You're awfully quiet," Katie said. "What are you thinking?"

Lucy fidgeted with the paperwork on the desk. "What if Holly knew about Henry's affair with Cressida earlier than we thought?"

"You mean before the wedding rehearsal?" Katie asked.

"Victoria said Holly didn't say a word when she saw Cressida Connolly in Henry's arms at the church rehearsal. Only that Holly looked furious. Victoria assumed Holly had just learned of the affair, but what if Holly had already known about it?"

"You think she knew her husband was cheating, and as a result, she took out a million-dollar life insurance policy on him?" Katie asked.

"What if, and she gets away with it?"

"Then I'd say Holly had motive, time, *and* means to plan her husband's murder. We need to talk with her," Katie said.

Lucy's palm grew sweaty as she clutched the phone. She hadn't forgotten about Azad's scheduled meeting with Detective Clemmons. "I agree. But there's something else I need to do first."

The Ocean Crest police station was located in the center of town in a redbrick building across from the library. The station also housed the town hall and municipal court, but had its own separate entrance. The same young, freckle-faced officer who had accompanied Bill Watson to the crime scene at Castle of the Sea sat behind the desk when Lucy entered the vestibule. He looked up from a sports magazine as Lucy approached the counter.

She rested her hands on the counter and smiled. "I'm here to see Detective Clemmons."

"Is he expecting you?"

"Yes," she fibbed. "I'm Lucy Berberian and it's about what happened at Scarlet Westwood's wedding."

"I remember you." He pointed to one of the closed doors at the back of the station. "That's the detective's office."

Lucy didn't have to strain to read the nameplate. She already knew which office belonged to Clemmons. The detective had summoned her here for questioning a few months ago for a different murder.

She made sure to smile at the young officer again, then walked farther into the station. Cops in uniform were busy typing up reports on their computers, talking on the telephone, cracking wise jokes at each other across their desks, and tossing balled-up pieces of paper into overfilled wastepaper baskets. Ever since Lucy was a kid, the town hired extra officers during the busy summer months, the locals referring to them as "rent-a-cops."

She glanced down to see a handful of carbon copies of traffic tickets on an officer's desk. Fines from expired parking meters issued to tourists during the summer provided a solid source of revenue for the small shore town. Of course, the tickets also meant a busy municipal court season. Once again, she thought of Clyde Winters and hoped Azad had contacted him or another attorney.

She rapped on Detective Clemmons's office door.

"What?" a voice grumbled from behind the door.

Lucy opened the door. Clemmons sat behind his desk holding a cup of coffee. A white, powdered doughnut rested on a napkin in front of him.

Really? she thought. Doughnuts and cops were the ultimate cliché.

He lowered his cup and glared. "Ms. Berberian, to what do I owe the pleasure?"

Lucy stepped into his office. Clemmons wore a

white shirt and solid blue tie, and his shirtsleeves were rolled up. His jacket hung on a coatrack in the corner. The air-conditioning was blasting from the overhead vent, and the room was frigid.

Gooseflesh rose on her arms under her light-weight running jacket. "I understand Azad Zakarian is coming in today for further questioning."

"Why am I not surprised you know?" A cold, congested expression settled on his face.

"I'm sure you remember that we work together. He told me."

The detective's smile didn't reach his eyes. "I see. I didn't realize I needed your approval to summon a suspect."

Katie's comment that he was hungry for a promotion and that he believed solving the murder quickly would help him achieve that goal made Lucy uneasy. It also justified today's visit. If the detective was focused on Azad as the main suspect, then she needed to inform him what they'd learned and have him consider other suspects. But how to tell him without admitting that she and Katie had been investigating on their own?

Clemmons motioned for her to sit in a faux leather chair across from his desk, and Lucy took a seat. The office was just as she remembered. It was spacious, twice as big as her tiny office in the corner of the restaurant's cramped storage room. A picture of Clemmons on a fishing boat holding up a large fish hung on the wall behind his desk. She recalled from her last visit that he liked to mount stuffed fish on his office walls, and she counted four taxidermied fish, one more than last time. An openedmouthed flounder had joined the bluefish, salmon, and trout.

Folding her hands in her lap, she kept her voice level. "You're wasting your time. Azad's innocent."

"A couple months back in town and you're an expert investigator," he said, his voice laced with sarcasm.

"I've known Azad for years. So have my parents. We can testify to his character."

"He's also the person who threatened my murder victim with bodily harm in a kitchen full of *impartial* witnesses."

Lucy ignored the emphasis on the word "impartial."

"I also looked into the loan Azad Zakarian attempted to obtain through the victim's bank, Ocean Crest Savings and Loan. The initial application was approved, only to have the final loan denied. He paid a nice chunk of change to his attorney in wasted fees. It would make me spitting mad, too," Clemmons said.

"I get all that, Detective. I just want to make sure you're not overlooking other people with motive to kill Henry Simms."

"What other people?" He leaned forward in his chair, his nostrils slightly flaring. "Are you sticking your nose in an active investigation again?"

"Prosecutor Walsh paid me a visit. She told me to come forward immediately with anything I remember or heard about the murder." That much was true, and she met his glare with one of her own.

Clemmons took a bite of his doughnut and powdered sugar fell on his blue tie. He swiped at it, but only managed to smear it on the dark blue fabric. "All right. Shoot."

"A tabloid printed pictures of the reception." Lucy fished the tabloid paper that she'd purchased at Holloway's Grocery out of her purse. She set the paper on the desk and opened it to the relevant page. Several shots of Scarlet in her wedding gown were displayed on the glossy pages.

Clemmons flipped the page. "So?"

"Take a closer look. The pictures are of *inside* Castle of the Sea. Phones and cameras were prohibited at the reception. Someone smuggled a phone inside and took these pictures and sold them to the tabloid. The wedding planner, Victoria Redding, was fighting about this very thing with Henry and took his phone."

"You believe Simms took these pictures?"

"I do."

"How? You just said Ms. Redding took his phone."

"Henry could have texted or e-mailed the pictures to the paper from the reception in exchange for payment *before* Victoria took his phone."

"How is this useful to me? I already summoned Ms. Redding for questioning," he said. "She admitted to fighting with the victim, but denies killing him."

That was what Victoria had told her. The trouble was Lucy didn't think Victoria was lying. The temperamental wedding planner may have been mad, but were a few pictures enough motive to kill someone?

"I looked into the newspaper claim. I didn't find any evidence that Henry sold pictures of the wedding. A paper won't reveal its source, even a tabloid." He took a sip of his coffee. "I'm busy today, so is there anything else you'd like to share, Ms. Berberian?"

How much to tell and how? If she told him they'd questioned Victoria on their own and learned that

Henry was cheating on his wife, then he'd know they'd been snooping around. Plus, Katie had discovered the million-dollar life insurance policy for the victim, and that could also be a big motive. Still, she had to push him in that direction.

"What about the victim's wife?" she asked.

"What about her?"

Was he being purposely obtuse or was he testing her? How would Katie phrase it? "The television crime shows I watch always suspect the spouse. Adultery and money were two motives on a recent episode."

He rolled his eyes. "Good to know. I wouldn't want to alter your perception of TV."

"Detective—"

He raised a hand. "I appreciate you taking Prosecutor Walsh's advice seriously and coming here even if your amateurish suggestions are obvious and not helpful. Leave the investigating to the pros. Anything else?"

"As a matter of fact, there is. When will we get our catering van back?"

"I told you before, it's a crime scene."

"I understand. But haven't the crime scene investigators completed their inspection?" she asked.

"Why do you want it back so badly? Is there something incriminating in the van that you're not telling me about?"

What a jerk. Lucy's heartbeat throbbed in her ears. "No. We need it for future catering jobs."

His mustache twitched. "I'll take that under consideration."

Well, that didn't go well. She doubted she'd get the van back until Henry's killer was brought to justice.

Katie was right. If they wanted to help clear Azad's name and solve the murder and get the van back, then they'd have to do it all on their own. She was stuffing the tabloid back in her purse as a knock on the door made her jump.

"If you'll excuse me, this is my appointment." He stood, and Lucy pushed back her chair.

Clemmons opened the door, and Lucy stepped outside the office.

And ran smack into Azad.

"Lucy! What are you doing here?" Azad stared, clearly surprised.

"I . . . I was just following up with Detective Clemmons." An older gentleman stood behind Azad, and Lucy shifted to get a better look.

Azad noticed her interest. "I took your advice. This is Mr. Winters."

Clyde Winters was in his early seventies with a swath of wrinkles and brown spots on his neck and hands. The man's face broke into a smile as he looked at her. "Hello there, Lucy. Last time I saw you was at your parents' restaurant years ago. You were thinking about going to law school."

"I did, but I'm back now."

"Good for you. I'd like to hear more about your adventures, but at another time. We have a meeting with the detective."

Lucy had almost forgotten about Clemmons standing behind her. She turned and glanced up at him. Clemmons looked like he'd just sucked on a sour lemon as he stared at Mr. Winters. A thrill of satisfaction coursed through her.

Perfect.

Azad was in good hands. Clyde may be old, but it was clear that he still had an edge.

"Thank you for showing up on such short notice, Mr. Winters," she said. "Please stop by the restaurant for dinner whenever you're free. It's on the house."

Clyde winked and tipped his hat. "Now that's a type of payment I look forward to."

CHAPTER 12

Lucy poured a bowl of cat food and carried it out the back door of the restaurant. Dinner service had been busy and exhausting, and she was relieved when the last customer departed and she could close the place for the night. Her visit to Detective Clemmons's office had taken a toll. Even though she'd been relieved when Azad had shown up with an attorney in tow, she was more convinced than before that she needed to solve the murder of Henry Simms, and fast.

Gadoo meowed, sashayed close to sniff the bowl, then looked up as if to say, "That's it? No liver treats?"

"Spoiled kitty," she said, then reached into her apron pocket to pull out a few cat treats shaped like tunas and offer them in her outstretched hand. Gadoo approached and quickly ate the treats, then turned his attention to the bowl of cat food. She looked forward to feeding him, and not for the first time, she understood her mother's affection for the outdoor orange and black cat.

She let out a long breath as she watched Gadoo. She didn't feel she was any closer to solving the murder, but at least Azad's interrogation at the police station had gone well. He'd returned to work with a smile and had thanked her for recommending Mr. Winters. Clemmons had been forced to follow all the rules.

Gadoo's bright yellow eyes twinkled at her. Just as she reached down to scratch him beneath his chin, a loud rumble pierced the quiet night air. The cat abandoned his bowl in a flash and flew across the parking lot to hide behind the Dumpster.

Lucy had an entirely different reaction. Her heart thumped in anticipation.

Smoothing her hair, she walked the length of the white fence separating the restaurant from the business next door. Anthony's Bike Shop rented bicycles, trikes, and surreys to tourists to ride on Ocean Crest's boardwalk and streets. The shop would be long closed by now, but the owner's son was just warming up.

It was dark out, but the shop's garage door was open and brightly lit. Bicycles were parked in neat rows, spare tires hung from hooks on the walls, and the shelves were full of new and used bicycle parts and tire pumps. A chrome and black Harley-Davidson motorcycle was in the driveway, its engine purring like a large contented beast. A tall, good-looking, dark-haired man wearing faded jeans and a leather jacket walked out of the garage and halted by the Harley. Lucy couldn't see his eyes from this distance, but she knew they were as bright blue as the sky on a sultry, summer day at the beach.

She made her way to the sidewalk, then walked up the shop's driveway.

The man grinned, motorcycle helmet in hand. "Hey, Lucy. What took you so long?"

Her pulse skipped a beat. "I have a business to run, remember?" she teased.

His grin widened. "How can I forget? We're both in charge now."

Michael Citteroni ran his father's bicycle rental shop. They'd become fast friends when she'd returned home. His father was a bit shady, and she'd grown up thinking Mr. Citteroni was a mobster who used his many businesses—bike rentals, laundering services, and trash trucks—to launder money from his illegal activities in the neighboring town of Atlantic City. But Michael was different. He hadn't always gotten along with his father in the past. His sister, on the other hand, was eager to follow in their father's footsteps. As a result, Michael had been roped into managing the bicycle rental shop, and Lucy had commiserated with him in the past about the guilt of family responsibility.

She'd been surprised at how much she'd enjoyed his company. Michael had a great sense of humor, was hot, and had introduced her to the thrill of motorcycle riding.

He handed her a helmet. "Do you want a ride home?"

"I'd love one."

His leather jacket creaked as he leaned forward to help her fasten the strap of a spare helmet beneath her chin. His fingers brushed hers, and the faint scent of his cologne wafted to her. Her heart skipped a beat, and she mentally shook herself.

Life had been complicated enough since returning home, and an attraction to two dark-haired men made it downright dangerous. Still, a part of her couldn't believe it. Her love life during her law firm days had been as dry as the Sahara, and now she had two handsome men express interest in her.

She was no closer to picking one, but who said she had to? Katie believed it was time for Lucy to enjoy herself and see how things naturally progressed. Her mother, on the other hand, kept telling her that her biological clock was ticking away like a time bomb waiting to detonate, and that she better get married and pop out a grandchild soon.

Lucy tended to favor Katie's advice.

"Let's take the long way home," she told Michael.

His perfect lips curled in a smile. "Your wish is my command."

Oh, my. She was asking for trouble.

Lucy climbed on the bike behind him and held on to his leather-clad sides. The bike roared to life, and he turned down Ocean Avenue. The night air caressed her face and blew the tendrils of curls at her nape. The faint smell of the ocean tickled her senses, and the shops on the main strip were a colorful blur of light as they sped by. Soon, they were zooming past cars and trucks making late night deliveries. She closed her eyes and let all her stress and inner turmoil blow away along with the night breeze.

Michael slowed down for tourists dashing across the street to a crowded custard stand. The bike rumbled beneath her again as they rode by the boardwalk. Lucy could make out the cries from the old-fashioned wooden roller coaster and the bright lights of the Ferris wheel. The ride was thrilling and exciting and she couldn't fathom how she'd initially feared riding on the back of the Harley just months ago.

He turned down a side street. "Do you want to stop on the boards?"

"You bet."

He parked the bike and helped her unclasp her helmet. Offering his arm, they made their way up the ramp to the end of the boardwalk. It was less crowded here, and Michael always seemed to know where to go to escape the throng of tourists. They sat on a wood bench and watched the night sky and listened to the sound of the ocean in the distance. It was high tide, but the waves hadn't yet reached beneath the boardwalk.

"So, what's troubling you?" he asked, breaking the silence.

The moonlight illuminated his chiseled profile, and her heart kicked up a notch. "Am I that readable?"

"Maybe not to everyone. But we're kindred spirits, remember?"

How could she forget? Michael had an overbearing and controlling Italian father. Raffi Berberian could be overbearing and overprotective, too. Their ethnicities may be different, but they did have a lot in common.

She sighed. "Managing the restaurant is harder than I initially thought it would be. My attempts to change the shelving in the storage room haven't gone exactly as I'd planned. I want to update to a computerized system, but my parents insist on staying in the Dark Ages. Plus, there's the payroll, the labor, the ordering, and my not-so-successful attempts to learn how to cook from my mother."

He whistled through his teeth. "It's a lot to take on. The restaurant business is tough."

"The catering end is not all peaches and cream either. The food at Scarlet Westwood's wedding may have been good, but the entire affair turned out to be a disaster."

"I know. I was there."

Her gaze flew to his. "You were?"

"My father was invited, but he had a last-minute business conflict and asked me to go in his place. I arrived late to the reception. I saw you, but you were busy running back and forth from the ballroom to the kitchen and I didn't want to distract you from your work. I planned on slipping into the kitchen to say a quick hello at some point, but I noticed that head chef of yours and I decided to stay away."

Lucy wasn't sure how to respond. It wasn't a secret that Azad and Michael had disliked each other from the first moment she'd introduced them.

Two big male egos could really clash.

In a strange way, Lucy was flattered by the attention. What did that say about her?

"You should have flagged me down in the ballroom," she admonished.

"Yeah, well, I encountered another obstacle. The best man's wife was as clingy as a vine."

"You mean Holly?"

"I couldn't get away from her. I told her straight out that married women weren't my thing, not to mention that if my mom was alive they'd be the same age, but even that didn't deter her."

No woman wanted to be reminded of her age. What was Holly thinking? Her husband had been the best man at the wedding. But then again, his young lover, Cressida Connolly, had been the maid of honor. No wonder Holly had been hitting on Michael. Seeing

Henry escort Cressida at the wedding and then later at the reception must have sent her overboard.

"What did Holly say?" she asked.

Michael shrugged. "She didn't seem fazed by it at all. She told me that her husband was a jerk cheating with a woman my age and that he deserved everything he got. 'Tit for tat,' she said."

"Did Holly pursue you all night?"

"Almost. She left me alone for a bit at the reception. She said she had to freshen up her lipstick and went to the ladies' room. Thankfully, she took her sweet time. It was the only chance I had to truly enjoy the food. The meal was excellent, by the way."

"Thanks," Lucy said as her mind was churning to digest this information. "You said she was gone for a while. Do you remember when and for how long?"

"About a half hour near the end of the reception."

A half hour at the end.

It would have been possible for Holly to follow Henry outside, witness the argument between Henry and Victoria, and hide until Victoria returned to the wedding. Holly could have then stabbed Henry and returned to the reception. But how did she manage to get Henry in the van? It was a question that continued to plague Lucy.

"Don't worry. If anyone can figure out who killed that best man, it's you," Michael said.

She looked at him in surprise. "I never said I was trying to solve the murder."

His smile hitched up a notch. "You didn't have to. I've gotten to know you, Lucy Berberian. You want to help others. Plus, I've also heard rumors that your new head chef is a prime suspect."

"Where'd you hear that?"

"Do I have to remind you that gossip travels as fast as wildfire in Ocean Crest?"

No. He didn't. News of the murder and Detective Calvin Clemmons's prime suspect had probably spread within six hours after Henry's body was found in the catering van.

A sudden explosion made Lucy jerk. A flash of colorful light burst in the night sky above the Ferris wheel.

"Fireworks!" she gasped.

"Every weekend in the summer. Did you forget?"

She had. The neighboring Jersey beach towns were larger than Ocean Crest and had a bigger budget—which included fireworks on the summer weekends. Another burst of red, blue, and white lights crackled above and illuminated the dark sky for shining, glimmering moments.

"I remember the first time I saw the fireworks in the summer. I must have been five. My dad put me on his shoulders and I watched from the boardwalk. It was one of my earliest memories," Lucy said.

"I remember watching with my mom and sister. My dad spent his weekends at the Atlantic City casinos," Michael said.

She glanced at Michael beneath lowered lashes. He didn't seem saddened by his recollection, but deep down she wondered if he had regrets. In Lucy's opinion, Mr. Citteroni should have lots of them.

"Ready to go back?" he asked.

She nodded. "Thanks. I needed this." The bike ride, the ocean breeze, and the company had eased her tense shoulders. Not to mention she'd learned about

Holly Simms and the opportunity she'd had to slip away and stab her adulterous husband. Add a million-dollar life insurance policy, and the motive grew.

"My pleasure. Any time you want to go for a bike ride, all you have to do is ask." He offered his hand.

Oh, he was tempting. He helped her to her feet and together they walked back to the Harley. Twenty minutes later, they were in Katie's driveway.

She dismounted the bike and handed him her helmet. From the corner of her eye, Lucy spotted curtains fluttering at the window, and she knew Katie had seen the motorcycle. She expected to be peppered with questions as soon she stepped foot inside.

"I'll walk you to the door." Despite the leather and the Harley, Michael was a perfect gentleman.

Lucy halted on the porch. Katie was probably burning with curiosity and she wouldn't be surprised if her friend's ear was plastered to the door.

"Thanks again. I'll see you around," Lucy said.

"Wait." He reached out to touch her sleeve.

She froze as his gaze dropped to her mouth. He wasn't going to kiss her, was he?

"I admire you for wanting to help your friend by finding out who got rid of the best man, but be careful, Lucy. Not everyone is as innocent as they may appear."

Lucy found Katie inside dressed in workout capris and a faded "Hard Rock Philadelphia" T-shirt. A kickboxing DVD was on the TV screen. Katie picked up the remote, pressed mute, and patted the couch for Lucy. "Sit. I want all the juicy details."

Lucy collapsed on the sofa. "There's not much to tell. Michael Citteroni gave me a ride home on his Harley."

Katie looked at Lucy in disbelief. "That's it?"

There was no sense fighting it. Katie could be persistent. "We went the long way home and watched the fireworks on the boardwalk."

"First, Azad. Now, Michael. You're on a roll."

Lucy held up a hand. "Don't jump to conclusions. I'm not sure about either of them."

"Who says you have to pick?"

"My parents. They'd be thrilled if I picked Azad. They've wanted us together since college."

Katie chuckled. "You'd get to keep everything in the family business."

Lucy rolled her eyes. "As if that's a reason."

"Well, if you do decide to date Azad again, you'd best clear his name of murder first."

Lucy sat upright. "Talking about murder, you wouldn't believe what I learned tonight. Michael was at Scarlet's wedding reception."

Katie scooched forward on the couch. "He was? I didn't see him."

"That's because he came late and he was busy dodging Holly's amorous advances all night."

"Holly Simms? The victim's wife?"

"Yup. She stuck to him like super glue, and when Michael tried to tell her he didn't mess with married women, she shot back that her husband was a cheating jerk."

"That's more proof that Holly knew of Henry's affair," Katie said.

"That's not all. Michael said Holly wouldn't leave

him alone, except for about half an hour near the end of the reception when she said she needed to use the ladies' room."

Katie rubbed her chin. "Hmm. A half hour is a suspiciously long time to spend in the ladies' room. It would definitely be enough time to sneak outside and stab her husband, and it fits the timeline of Henry's death."

"I'm thinking she's a scorned wife who wanted to get back at her husband. Plus, there's the big life insurance policy. Holly has more motive than Victoria."

"I wouldn't be surprised if Holly was the murderer," Katie said. "Except there is one small problem to that theory."

"What?"

"Both you and Azad claim that you locked the van, and Bill said there was no sign of forced entry. So, how'd Holly get inside?"

Lucy had been asking herself the same question. Still, there had to be an explanation. "The catering van is old as dirt and it doesn't have power locks, power windows, or an alarm. Maybe Holly used the old-fashioned method of a simple coat hanger?"

"No way. The crime scene investigators combed through the van with a magnifying glass. They also looked inside the door compartment. A coat hanger would leave scratches. There weren't any," Katie said.

"Then how did the murderer get in the van?" A thought crossed Lucy's mind. "I placed the key on the counter beside Azad where he was working. He said he put it in his pocket. Maybe it sat on the counter in plain sight for anyone to snatch. The kitchen was a hubbub of activity that day. Anyone could have snuck in to take the key. They could have returned it just as easily."

"It's possible. But I also think it's time to talk to Holly. I was at the Big Tease Salon today and overheard the owner, Beatrice Tretola, mention that Holly comes in for a facial and manicure every other Thursday at noon. That's two days from now."

"Her husband was just killed. Do you really think she'll show up for a regular spa day?"

"According to Beatrice, Holly's super-high maintenance and swears the facials make her appear a decade younger. She wouldn't miss a manicure either." Katie glanced at Lucy's short nails.

Lucy curled her fingers to hide them from view. "Hey," she said defensively. "Restaurant work is hard on the nails. I've also been trying to learn how to cook. My mom will have a fit if I show up with long, fake nails."

"Tough. You definitely need the manicure more than me. Besides, I'll be at work. Make an appointment."

CHAPTER 13

"Oh, my gosh," said Lucy, as soon as she arrived at the restaurant the following afternoon. "You put tables on the sidewalk."

"We didn't have a choice." Emma met her at the door, looking flustered. "We got a lot more calls this morning asking for reservations, and Azad helped me carry all the extra tables and chairs outside." Azad came up behind Emma.

"The place was booked?" Lucy asked.

Azad nodded. "Booked solid."

"That's wonderful!" said Lucy. "And I never had a chance to place an ad in the *Ocean Crest Town News.*"

"People must be talking. The hummus bar is a huge hit." Azad was busy buttoning his chef's coat.

"It's not just the hummus, Azad. Your specials have been fabulous, too," Lucy said.

Azad's fingers halted on his coat, and his coffee-brown eyes held an intimate warmth. "Thanks. That means a lot."

Her heart thumped uncomfortably. Lucy shifted her feet, suddenly nervous. "Are your dinner entrees ready for tonight?"

"Yes."

"How about the dining room tables?" Lucy peeked inside the dining room to see pressed white linens, lit candles, and silverware settings.

"After our last lunch customer paid a half hour ago, we rushed to get everything ready," Emma said.

Gratitude welled in Lucy's chest. "Everything looks great. Thank you both."

Emma slipped her waitress apron around her neck and tied it at the waist. "Excuse me. I still have to stock the waitress station and prepare the coffee." Emma departed and left Lucy alone with Azad.

"Do you really like the outdoor tables? Emma added hurricane candles, vases with a single rose, and folded the napkins into swans," Azad said.

"It looks fabulous." It was a lovely summer evening, and a pleasant ocean breeze felt wonderful on her skin. Azad held the front door open and placed a hand on her lower back as he followed her into the dining room. The simple touch made her knees weak and a quiver surge through her veins. "Azad, I—"

Just then a flash of white caught her eye out the front bay window.

Oh, no.

Her heart hammered as a white van pulled up and brazenly parked in the handicapped space. Bold, black letters screamed across the side of the van: *Ocean Crest Town News.* A short, stocky man with black-rimmed glasses hopped out and headed for the front door.

"What's Stan Slade doing here?" Azad said.

"Whatever it is, it can't be good," Lucy said.

Stan Slade was the town's sole reporter. A New York City native, he'd relocated to Ocean Crest a few years

ago for reasons unknown. Her mother had told her
Slade had left a prestigious reporting job at a national
newspaper to run Ocean Crest's small-town paper.
Lucy's first experience with the reporter months ago
hadn't been good, and she doubted it would be better
today.

The front door swung open and Stan strode inside.
"Lucy Berberian," he said in a nasally voice that grated
on her nerves like nails on a chalkboard. "I heard you
catered that socialite's wedding."

She shrugged a shoulder as if she didn't have a care
in the world. "Catering isn't big news."

He huffed. "No. But a murder is. Seems like you
attract dead bodies like flowers attract bees."

Slade's brusque manner had rubbed her the wrong
way in the past and it hadn't changed.

"That's unfair. There were two hundred and fifty
people at that wedding," Azad said, coming to her
defense.

"Then how convenient for me that the two people
who found the body are standing in front of me."
Slade pulled out a digital recorder from his coat
pocket. "Care to be interviewed for the paper?"

"No," Lucy and Azad said in unison.

Stan Slade's gaze zeroed in on Azad. "Too bad.
You'd make a great interview, Mr. Zakarian. Rumor
has it you were more involved than just finding the
best man stuck like a pig."

The reporter was downright rude. Lucy placed her
hands on her hips. "Where did you hear that?"

"I can't divulge my sources. All I can say is that
Mr. Zakarian has quite an extensive history with the
bridal party. A kitchen brawl over a denied loan with
the victim's bank would make for a gripping exclusive."

Things were going south, and fast. "The police know all about that. I wouldn't call that a gripping exclusive," she said.

"I'm not just talking about a fight or a failed loan," Slade said.

"There's nothing else," Azad said tersely.

A smug look crossed Slade's face. "You haven't told her, have you, Mr. Zakarian?"

"Told her what?" Azad retorted.

"Your connection to the bridal party goes deeper." Slade pulled out a newspaper from his briefcase and slapped it on the nearest table. It was the front page of the *Ocean Crest Town News* showing a homecoming parade. The homecoming king and queen were waving from the top of a float that looked like a multilayered frosted cake. The queen's frilly gown and the large bow in her hair combined with the king's ruffled tuxedo shirt dated the picture, and Lucy glanced at the date at the top of the paper.

"This paper is at least a decade old. I don't see anything but a crowd of people and a big pink float," Lucy said.

"Right here." Slade stabbed a finger smack in the middle of the picture. Lucy bent closer to get a better look. Her eyes widened. There, in the thick of the crowd, was Azad with Cressida Connolly. She was wrapped in his arms, her face tilted to his, and they were lip-locked.

Shock swept through Lucy, and made her limbs feel as sturdy as jelly. Somehow, she managed to stay upright and keep her composure. She pulled back her shoulders, but didn't . . . couldn't look into Azad's eyes.

Lucy's gaze returned to the date at the top of the page. Her mind whirled as it did the calculation. A little over ten years ago. Right after they'd graduated from college. Azad had said that he wasn't ready to commit—to take their relationship to the next level. He'd sworn that their break-up *wasn't* because of another woman.

Azad's voice was strained. "Lucy, I can explain."

"How sweet," Slade said sarcastically.

Azad glared at the reporter. "This paper has nothing to do with Henry Simms's murder."

"Maybe, but don't you think it's a coincidence that Cressida Connolly was Henry's mistress?" Slade said.

Whoa. Lucy's eyes rose to Stan Slade's. "Where did you hear that?" She may have known the truth, but how the hell did the reporter know?

Slade smirked. "Like I said, I have my sources." He pointed a stubby finger at Azad. "Maybe you still had feelings for Cressida and decided to stick a skewer in her lover's neck."

A tense silence enveloped the dining room. "You should leave," Lucy said to Slade before Azad could respond.

The reporter shrugged. "Fine, but if you decide to give an interview, you know where to find me."

"Lucy?"

It took a full thirty seconds before Lucy could look Azad in the eye. She felt light-headed for fifteen of those seconds, then raving mad for the following fifteen.

"Lucy?" Azad asked again. "Are you ever going to speak to me again?"

"Since you are the head chef, I suppose I have

to. It would be difficult to run the restaurant without talking."

Azad's expression was strained. "It was a long time ago, and a brief fling *after* you and I broke up. I haven't seen Cressida since then."

"It's none of my business."

"I know you better than anyone. I owe you an explanation."

She gripped the hostess stand. Should she just leave? Come back when her head was clear? Would she even make it to her car without grabbing the nearest knife and throwing it at his head?

She turned to face him head on. "You're right. You *do* owe me an explanation."

He let out a breath. "I never lied to you."

"Oh, really? I'm a lawyer. I consider omission as lying."

"Fine. What I told you after college was true. I panicked. I wasn't ready to get engaged. Your father was clear about his expectations for us and I just wasn't ready to buy an engagement ring at twenty-one."

Lucy acknowledged what he said about her father was true. Raffi Berberian was old-fashioned and his expectations had been crystal clear. Azad had worked for her parents at the restaurant since he was fifteen, and he'd started dating Lucy a year later. It was no secret that her parents would have been thrilled for them to marry. When Raffi had sat them both down at the kitchen table at her home, Lucy had known it was serious. All serious business was conducted at that table. For the first time, Lucy hadn't protested at her parents' meddling. She'd been head over heels for Azad.

But looking back, she knew the heartbreak she'd

experienced when Azad had ended their relationship had been for the best. Marrying at an early age would have changed *everything*. She would never have gone to law school. She would never have experienced living on her own in Philadelphia, or acquired the inquisitive skills that had already helped her solve one murder. She would never have left Ocean Crest only to return and realize the true value of friends and family, and that the restaurant was where she wanted to be.

She sighed. "Okay. I believe that you didn't date Cressida until after we broke up, but that's not what's upsetting. You should have told me about your relationship with her in the first place, preferably as soon as Henry Simms was murdered."

"You're right."

"Where did you meet her?" she asked.

"At an Atlantic City nightclub. There was a popular cover band that night. We started talking and went on a few dates. It only lasted a couple of months."

"Why didn't you tell me?"

Lucy experienced a stab of satisfaction when Azad appeared even more uncomfortable. "I know that I should have said something. I didn't because I knew how it would look."

"With me? Or with the police?"

"With you. We only recently started working together and I didn't want to rock the boat."

"It's too late for that," she retorted. "Did you know about Cressida and Henry?"

"No! The truth is, I find it hard to believe. He was old . . . not her type. But no matter whom she was sleeping with, my prior relationship with Cressida has nothing to do with Henry's murder."

"If what Stan Slade said about Cressida being Henry's lover is true, then Detective Clemmons won't see it that way."

Azad's normally dark complexion paled a shade. "It's looking worse and worse for me. I know I asked you to listen to your mom, not your dad, and to stay out of the investigation, but I've changed my mind. Will you try to find out whatever you can?"

Lucy hesitated. She was already investigating with Katie and they'd made some progress. She'd wanted to aid Azad, and she was still convinced of his innocence. But now, she was also angry at him. Angry—and hell—even a little jealous.

But jealous of what?

A relationship he'd had over ten years ago after they'd broken up? Or was she mad that he'd lied and kept the truth from her?

Which led to an entirely different question: what else was he hiding?

He stood still, waiting for her answer. "I told you I would ask around and see what I can find out," she said. "I haven't changed my mind."

"Thanks, Lucy." She turned to leave, but he touched her arm. "Wait. One more thing. What about us?"

Her pulse skipped a beat. The depth in his eyes told her *exactly* what he meant. "Let's keep it strictly business between us."

He shoved his hands into his pockets. "Business?"

Her mouth felt like dry paper. What could she say? She needed time to think about the past and see if she was ready to move on to the future. "That's right. I should focus on the murder. Everything else is a distraction."

CHAPTER 14

Thursday afternoon rolled around quickly, and Lucy found herself waiting in her Toyota Corolla outside the Big Tease Salon. The place was located in the center of town across from Cutie's Cupcakes, Ben's Barber Shop, and next to a small park with a man-made lake. She was anxious and changed radio stations every few minutes.

At last a fancy, blue Mercedes turned into the salon's parking lot. The high-end vehicle matched the description of Holly Simms's car that Katie had given her. The car door opened and the tall, slim, fifty-something brunette who stepped out also looked just as Katie had described Holly. Dressed in a black skirt with high heels, she sauntered past and opened the door of the salon. Lucy waited ten minutes, then stepped out of her car and followed.

The salon was busy and ladies occupied many of the chairs. Beatrice Tretola, the salon's owner, was teasing a blond woman's hair and spraying each section with a good amount of Aqua Net. The customer must have had her makeup done as well. Her eyelash extensions reached just shy of her eyebrows, and her lips were lined with a dark cherry shade.

Beatrice was a slender, middle-aged woman who wore a bohemian-style red dress with vivid orange flowers, chunky turquoise bracelets and rings, and gladiator sandals. She was chewing gum and talking nonstop as she worked. The last time Lucy had a scheduled haircut appointment, Beatrice had told her that she'd given up smoking and had started chewing gum to help with the nicotine cravings.

"Lucy! Good to see you." Beatrice waved as soon as she spotted Lucy by the front door. "I've been meaning to make it to the restaurant now that you're the new manager and that hunk is the new head chef." She winked. "But the salon's been super busy."

Lucy approached and smiled. "Hi, Beatrice. Good to see the place so crowded. How about I have lunch delivered here tomorrow instead?"

"That would be great!" Beatrice's excitement subsided as she scrutinized Lucy's hair up close. "Are you here for a blow out or a straightening treatment? You'd look very nice with straight hair. Wouldn't even recognize yourself."

Lucy stifled a groan. Every time Beatrice visited the restaurant or ran into Lucy in town, she commented about straightening Lucy's hair. Of course, it seemed every time Beatrice saw Lucy her hair was frizzy from the hot kitchen or the Jersey shore humidity.

"Not today, Beatrice."

"You want a trim?"

Lucy shook her head and held up her hands for inspection. "No. I'm here for a manicure."

Beatrice's eyes lit up like Christmas trees. "Well, it's about time. Do you have a date with the chef?"

Goodness. First, her mother. Now, Beatrice. Did everyone want her to date Azad?

"No. Katie suggested that I take care of my nails."

"Katie's right." Beatrice set down the can of hairspray and whipped the drape off her customer. "I'm just finishing up here. Have a seat by one of the nail stations and I'll be right with you."

Lucy chose one of the padded black seats beside Holly Simms. Holly's right hand was already soaking in a bowl of bubbly pink liquid, and a pretty Asian manicurist was laying out her tools.

Holly glanced her way, and Lucy smiled. Holly's makeup was expertly applied, but heavy. She knew Holly was in her late fifties, but her makeup made her appear a decade younger. Katie had said that Holly never skipped her biweekly salon visit and that she was obsessed with looking younger.

Up close, her outfit appeared to be costly—a silk blouse, black pencil skirt, and leather boots. Her designer bag hung from a hook on the side of the manicure table. Her shoulder-length chestnut hair had the perfect tint of highlights.

It was obvious that Holly took great pains with her appearance. Not for the first time, Lucy wondered how she'd taken her husband's affair with a much younger woman.

Time to find out.

"Good afternoon," Lucy said. "Are you Holly Simms?"

Holly arched her pencil-thin brows into triangles. "Yes. Do I know you?"

"Not personally. But Henry assisted me with a loan a while back at the bank, and he was very helpful," she fibbed. "My condolences."

"Thank you. The funeral is Friday."

Beatrice came over with a bowl of pink suds. She took Lucy's hands, turned them this way and that, and frowned in obvious disapproval. "When was your last manicure?"

Lucy squirmed in her seat. "A while. I haven't had much time lately."

Beatrice clucked her tongue. "A lady needs to treat herself on a regular basis."

"Amen to that advice," said Holly as the manicurist lifted Holly's hand out of the bowl and set it on a towel on the table.

The manicurist mumbled in Korean, and Beatrice looked over. "Good grief, Holly. What happened to you? Did you get your hand caught in a car door?"

Lucy glanced over. Three of Holly's long nails on her right hand were jagged and broken.

Interesting.

Forget the car door. What if she broke her nails while stabbing her husband in the neck with a shish kebab skewer?

"Lin can fix those in no time," Beatrice said as the manicurist produced a nail file and began filing down Holly's jagged nails.

Beatrice reached in a drawer and laid out her own instruments. One looked like a small wire trimmer, and Lucy didn't like the ominous look of the tool one bit. Beatrice lifted her hand from the bowl to pat it dry with a warm towel. "Put your other hand in the bowl," she instructed, then picked up the scary-looking instrument and began trimming away at Lucy's cuticles.

"Ouch!"

"No whining." Beatrice popped a bubble. "Did you pick a color?"

"How about you choose for me?"

A pleased expression crossed Beatrice's face, and she pushed back her chair and sashayed to a wall-mounted rack of nail polishes in the front of the salon. Lucy took the opportunity to turn to Holly.

"Pardon my asking, but do the police have any leads?" Lucy asked.

"Not that I know of, and there haven't been any arrests," Holly said as the manicurist began painting her nails with a red polish that looked like . . . well . . . blood.

"I'm sorry to hear that. I still can't believe it." She leaned forward in the pink chair. "After all, who would want to harm him?"

Holly's lips parted, but she was stopped from answering as the door opened and the salon's bells tinkled.

Lucy looked up to see who had stepped inside and was stunned to recognize Cressida Connolly. Her long red hair was pulled back from her face with small jeweled clips and fell in loose curls down her back. The style emphasized her flawless complexion and blue eyes. She wore a miniskirt and tight top, and she looked like she was plucked right from a college campus. She didn't look at the salon's occupants, but went straight to the rack of displayed nail polishes.

Lucy swiveled in her seat to glance at Holly and froze. Sheer hatred crossed the woman's face. Her entire body had stiffened and the unpainted nails on her left hand curled like talons on the towel.

Whoa! If looks could kill, Cressida would have dropped dead on sight.

Beatrice returned, carrying two bottles of nail polish—one a bubblegum pink that matched what she was chewing and the other a bright green. Neither was something Lucy would have picked.

"Which one do you like?" Beatrice vigorously shook both bottles.

"I'm not sure either, especially the green." Her mother would have a fit if she showed up for cooking lessons with green nails. She'd think Lucy had forgotten to clean out the walk-in refrigerator and found something moldy.

"Nonsense," Beatrice said. "This is called Sea Green and it's fashionable, but if you're dead set against it, then we can go with the pink."

Beatrice smeared a pink streak down Lucy's finger. "See? That's pretty." Lucy wasn't so sure. Now it looked like she'd accidentally popped Beatrice's bubble and was left with a wad on her finger. But pretty nails weren't the purpose of her visit to the salon. Getting Holly Simms to talk was her ultimate goal.

Beatrice kept painting and talking, oblivious to the tension radiating from Holly. Meanwhile, the manicurist had finished Holly's nails and left her to dry.

"Holly, you need to keep your fingers straight or you'll smudge your polish," Beatrice chided. "If you want, you can move to the nail dryers or sit in a chair over there," she said, pointing to a reclining chair beside a table with numerous bottles and jars of what Lucy assumed were facial scrubs, "and I'll start your facial when I'm finished with Lucy."

"Forget the facial." Holly's eyes narrowed to unattractive little slits as she glared at Cressida's back. "I just remembered I have somewhere I have to be."

Confusion crossed Beatrice's face. "Are you sure? It won't take me long to finish here. And if you're worried there will be a wait, my afternoon appointment canceled."

"I'm sure. And by the way, something smells rotten in here."

"Rotten?" Beatrice set the bottle of nail polish aside and turned to another stylist, who was cutting hair. "Billy Jean, did you bring leftover fish for lunch again?"

Billy Jean froze. "No. I learned my lesson the last time I tried to microwave leftover salmon."

Beatrice sniffed the air and then turned back to Holly. "I don't smell anything."

Just then, Cressida plucked a bottle of nail polish from the shelf and headed their way. Her step faltered the moment her eyes settled on Holly and recognition dawned. The two women's gazes clashed and the air crackled with tension.

Lucy looked from the young woman to the older one, then back to the younger. What were the chances Cressida would show up at the salon at the same time as Holly?

Maybe Lucy should drive straight to Holloway's and buy herself a lottery ticket.

"I'm positive." Holly's voice was tense. "Something reeks in here." Oblivious to her wet nails, Holly hooked her arm through the handle of her designer bag, lifted it from the little hook mounted on the manicure table, and stood. For a brief moment, Lucy wondered if a fight was about to happen.

Cressida opened her mouth, must have thought better of it, then shut it as Holly swept by her and shot her a black look as she passed, then sailed out of the salon.

"Don't touch anything else until they dry!" Beatrice shouted at Holly as the door swung closed.

The ladies in the salon remained silent. Even Cressida stood frozen with the bottles of nail polish in her hand.

Making a snap decision, Lucy rose. "I'm sorry, but I need to leave, too."

"But you're not dry yet either," Beatrice protested, then sniffed the air. "Is it the smell?"

"No. Please don't worry about that. There's no odor. I just forgot I have a restaurant delivery." At least she could put poor Beatrice at ease. She didn't want her to close the salon and cancel her remaining appointments for the day because of a fictitious odor. "I promise I'll send you lunch tomorrow. How about shish kebab and baklava?"

Beatrice cracked a smile. "That sounds delicious."

"Great. Now, please excuse me. I really have to get back." She gave a jaunty wave as she rushed out the door.

Once outside, Lucy shielded her face with her hand from the bright sunlight and scanned the parking lot for Holly's Mercedes. She spotted her opening the driver side door. "Mrs. Simms!" Lucy called out, then hurried toward her.

Holly halted. "What is it?"

"Are you okay?" Lucy asked. "You seemed really upset in the salon."

Annoyance flashed on Holly's face. "I'm fine. I just forgot an appointment."

"Are you sure? The young redhead that walked in the salon—it's clear that she upset you."

"I don't know what you're talking about," she said, her words cold and clipped.

Lucy took a deep breath, then let it out slowly. "I was there the day of the wedding."

"Oh? I don't remember seeing you."

"That's because I wasn't a guest. I was working in the kitchen."

Holly's brown eyes sharpened. "I thought you looked familiar. I must have seen you with the wait-staff."

"Most likely. I was supervising them that day."

"Supervising? You must be from that Mediterranean restaurant that catered the food."

"Yes, Kebab Kitchen."

Holly's vexation was evident. "You never received a loan with my husband's bank, did you?"

"No."

"But your head chef attempted to in the past?"

At Lucy's silence, Holly huffed. "He's the man the police consider a prime suspect."

So, Holly did know that Azad was on the top of Detective Clemmons's list. "He didn't do it."

"What makes you think so?"

Lucy decided it was time to raise the stakes and press Holly for answers. "I spoke with the wedding planner, Ms. Redding. She claims the woman who just walked into the salon, Cressida Connolly, was involved with your husband."

Holly's voice was heavy with sarcasm. "Involved? Is that what they're calling it these days?"

Lucy remained silent, and Holly huffed. "Her little flirtation with my husband didn't matter. Henry would never have left me for a light skirt like her. He needed me."

"By 'need' are you referring to the life insurance policy you took out on your husband?"

"How do you know about that?"

"It's not difficult to find that information." Actually, it was. But Katie was gifted when it came to computer searches. "A million-dollar policy is a lot of money."

Holly placed her hands on her hips. "You think I murdered my husband because he was cheating? Or because of a life insurance policy?"

"They are both good motives." Lucy held her ground. The woman seethed with anger, not grief over losing her spouse.

"No, they're not," she insisted, her tone hard. "Like I said, Henry would never have left me for a young tramp like her." She jabbed a still-wet, red nail at the Big Tease Salon. "As for the measly life insurance policy, I don't need the money. I have a trust fund worth five times more. It was Henry who needed *me* for my money. Not the other way around."

Lucy pressed on. "You don't seem upset that he's gone."

"Go to hell." With those final words, Holly swiveled on her heel and hightailed it to her car.

CHAPTER 15

Well, that went splendidly.

Lucy watched Holly's Mercedes tear out of the parking lot. She tapped her foot and thought about what she'd learned. Holly knew about her husband's affair, and from the bad vibes and hostility radiating from her when she spotted Cressida enter the salon, it was clear she knew exactly who Henry's lover had been.

Lucy needed to fill Katie in. Crossing the parking lot, she came up to her car just as the salon door opened and Cressida stepped outside.

Her first thought was, that was one fast manicure. Her second was, where was Cressida going in such a rush?

Pretending to fish through her purse for her keys, Lucy kept an eye on the redhead. Cressida slipped her purse strap across her body, walked swiftly through the parking lot, and headed for the park. Lucy followed, careful to dodge behind trees and playground equipment to avoid being noticed. Cressida walked for a while, and Lucy thought she would exit the park, but at the last minute she paused by a park bench occupied by a woman wearing a trench coat and dark sunglasses.

Lucy immediately recognized Scarlet Westwood. The socialite wore the same disguise the first day she'd walked into Kebab Kitchen and hired Lucy to cater her wedding. She'd thought it had been a ridiculous disguise then, and it was no better now.

On impulse, Lucy stooped low behind a hedge and strained to hear their conversation. She couldn't believe she was eavesdropping like this. Hiding in the bushes in a public park wasn't something she did every day, and she felt a moment of indecision, but then she pushed it away. If the two women had information, she needed to learn what they knew.

"Thanks for meeting me," Cressida said as she sat beside Scarlet on the bench.

"I came as soon as you called," Scarlet said. "What's wrong?"

"I ran into Holly at the salon. The woman hates me."

Scarlet waved a hand, and her large diamond flashed in the afternoon sunlight. "So? I don't know why you care about her, Cressida. Especially now that the man is dead."

Cressida's voice was hoarse. "His name was Henry."

"Okay." Scarlet's big lips pursed in annoyance. "You shouldn't give a damn if Holly Simms hates you. If it was me, I would have publicly confronted her. You had the perfect opportunity at the salon."

The prickly bush scraped Lucy's cheek as she parted it to get a better look at the women.

"Confront her?" Cressida shook her head. "No way."

"Why not?"

"Because what happened between Henry and me was private."

Scarlet scoffed. "All my personal business is out there for the world to see and it doesn't bother me."

"What about your wedding?" Cressida countered. "You wanted it kept private, and you had a fit when the tabloids published those pictures."

Scarlet's mouth took on an unpleasant twist. "All right. You got me there. I was screaming mad, but only because I told that incompetent wedding planner to take every precaution to prevent cell phones and cameras at the reception."

"Without frisking every guest, that was an impossible task."

"Whatever." Scarlet adjusted her oversized sunglasses. "Let's go back to your problem. I still would have confronted Holly Simms. The *rest* of my personal life has always been splashed across the front pages, and it hasn't harmed me."

"That's because it helps your fame. I don't want this getting out. Henry wouldn't have wanted it known," Cressida said.

"You're being too sensitive," Scarlet argued.

The tensing of Cressida's jaw betrayed her frustration. "What we had was special. I won't betray Henry by having it out with that bitch. She was bad for him. Mean and cruel. I finally got him to agree to leave her."

Lucy shifted. Her foot was growing numb, and pins and needles were traveling up her leg from her uncomfortable position. But she wasn't willing to risk moving and making a sound that could alert the two women to her presence.

A single question arose in her mind: had Cressida convinced Henry to leave his wife?

Holly had been certain that her husband would never abandon her. She'd claimed he needed her money. Was Holly lying? Did she suspect Henry was planning on dumping her for the much younger Cressida? It would be humiliating and a huge blow to Holly's ego.

"I still don't see what the big deal is. It's not like they were happily married," Scarlet said.

"I don't want to give her the satisfaction of turning herself into a wronged woman. She's already faking the grieving widow, and it makes me sick," Cressida said.

"Well, I suppose that's a good reason." Scarlet reached out to squeeze Cressida's hand. For several seconds, the two women were silent. Lucy shifted again and tried to stretch her muscles. If she crawled away, would the two women notice her?

"You okay now?" Scarlet asked.

Cressida nodded. "Yeah. Thanks. I needed to talk to someone."

"What are friends for?" Scarlet stood first, then Cressida. "I'll talk to you tomorrow." Scarlet raised the collar of her coat, then walked away.

Lucy's thoughts spun as she waited for Cressida to head back to her car. Holly had more motive than she'd initially thought. If Holly suspected Henry was going to walk out, then why not get rid of him and cash in the million-dollar life insurance policy? If she was never convicted of the murder, the insurance company would have to pay out. Even with a large trust fund, another million dollars couldn't hurt, could it? Plus, she'd be a sympathetic widow rather than the older wife who was abandoned for a younger model.

"What are you doing, Ms. Berberian?"

Lucy spun to find Stan Slade hovering above her.

His beady eyes sparked behind thick lenses and his gaze darted to the park bench to see Cressida walk away.

"You're eavesdropping now?" he asked.

Lucy's heart jumped in her chest. *Of all the rotten luck!* She stood—her stiff muscles protesting—and brushed dirt and leaves from her jeans. "No, of course not. I just dropped my keys and was searching for them."

He looked at her in disbelief. "What were your keys doing in the bush?"

"I accidentally kicked them." Lucy moved past Stan. "Sorry I can't stay and chat, but I have to get back to the restaurant. Summer is the busiest time of year for us." She hurried across the park and prayed he wouldn't follow.

But Stan Slade wasn't easily deterred. He ran after her like a hound chasing a fox. "I saw Scarlet Westwood walking away from that bench minutes before. Her ridiculous disguise doesn't fool anyone in town."

"Really? I didn't notice. Must have fooled me."

"Uh-huh. I'd say you were listening to Scarlet and Cressida. Why? Did you hear anything interesting about the murder?"

A cold knot formed in Lucy's stomach. "No. I wasn't spying, remember?"

"Tsk. Tsk. Lying doesn't suit you, Ms. Berberian."

Lucy ignored the barb and quickened her pace as she passed the playground. Mothers pushing their young children on swings and kids climbing a rock wall were a blur as she rushed out of the park with the reporter on her heels. She needed a distraction, and fast. Her gaze zoomed in on Cutie's Cupcakes across the street from the Big Tease Salon.

Would bulldog Stan follow her inside and make a scene?

Luck was with Lucy. Just as she stepped foot out of the park, a man called out and gained their attention. "Hey, Stan!" Ben Hawkins, the owner of the barber shop, stood beside the twisted red and white barber pole outside his store and waved his hands above his head. "Can you spare a minute? I want to go over my ad for next week's *Town News*."

Stan paused, conflict flashing in his dark eyes behind his glasses. He was clearly torn between chasing down Lucy and responding to Ben. Lucky for Lucy, business won out, and the reporter headed toward the barber shop and disappeared inside.

Saved by a newspaper ad.

Lucy opened the door of the bakery and the delicious scent of baking doughnuts, cookies, and pastries wafted to her. It smelled like heaven. Susan Cutie was behind the dessert case, sliding enormous cupcakes onto refrigerated shelves. Each shelf was labeled with her specialty flavors: salted caramel, chocolate delight, red velvet, killer carrot cake, banana peanut butter, and cookies and cream.

A second refrigerated case displayed her homemade pies, and Lucy's gaze immediately went to the lemon meringue. The combination of the tart lemon and sweet meringue made her mouth water.

"Hey, Lucy. I take it you want one lemon meringue pie," Susan said, motioning toward the pie case. She was pretty, with a shoulder-length bob and a quick smile, and spent many of her waking hours in her bakery.

Lucy shook her head. "Not the entire pie. Just a slice."

"You sure? I baked them all fresh this morning."

Lucy groaned. "You're right. I'll take a slice for me and the rest of the pie for Katie and her coworkers at the town hall."

"How nice. Tell Katie I said hello."

Lucy watched as Susan finished displaying the cupcakes. "How do you stay so slim, Susan?"

Susan slid the glass door closed and set down the empty baking sheet. "Baking is hard work. And when you make it all day you're not as tempted to eat it."

"I don't believe it," Lucy said. "I'm at the restaurant all day and it hasn't killed my appetite. Emma's the lucky one."

"The firstborn has all the luck." Susan went to the pie case and took out a lemon meringue pie. "But if you ask me, Emma's too thin. You're in great shape, Lucy. I'm also jealous of your hair. Mine's limp and won't hold a curl even with a piping hot curling iron."

"Thanks, Susan." Lucy liked the bakery owner. She was another friend that Lucy had discovered since returning home.

Lucy's gaze returned to the shiny glass doors with new interest. "Hey. Is that a new refrigerated case?"

"It is. I took out a business loan and used the money to buy some new equipment. Business has been good, and interest rates were low at the Ocean Crest Savings and Loan."

"Henry Simms's bank?"

Susan tsked. "Poor guy. He handled my loan. The bank has to find a new president now."

Lucy hesitated, not sure how to ask about Susan's business dealings, then decided just to be forthright. "Did you have any problems getting the loan?"

Susan looked up. "You mean with the collateral?"

"With any part of it?"

"Well, I have a lot of equity in this building, so I had collateral. That part of the loan went smoothly enough. But dealing with Henry Simms was a bit odd. I remember going in to sign some paperwork and Bradford Papadopoulos was in his office. They were arguing something fierce."

"Arguing? Do you remember over what?"

"I do. It made me a little nervous because they were fighting over an account at the bank, and I hadn't signed my final loan paperwork yet. Bradford claimed that checks he'd written had bounced—payroll checks and bills that he'd paid from his account. He said there were more than sufficient funds in the account, but he'd received complaints from employees and vendors that the checks were bad. Bradford blamed Henry, and accused him of fishy business practices. Bradford was furious and said it put his business with his fiancée, Scarlet Westwood, at risk."

"Wow. I don't blame you for being nervous."

Everything Susan said confirmed what Lucy and Katie had suspected. Bradford and Scarlet had a business account at Henry's bank that they'd planned to use to launch Scarlet's perfume line. Henry must have embezzled money from their account and caused the pair to write bad checks. The two men may have been college fraternity brothers and good friends in the past, but that friendship could have quickly deteriorated after Henry had stolen that money.

"Everything turned out okay," Susan said as she

took a meringue pie out of the case and set it on the counter to cut a large piece. "I never had a problem with my loan. Henry always treated me professionally and was kind. I feel horrible about what happened to him. His wife must be devastated."

Not really. Holly had expressed a lot of emotions during her short manicure, but grief hadn't been one of them.

Susan wrapped the slice of lemon meringue, put the rest of the pie in a box, and handed both containers to Lucy. When Lucy opened her purse to pay, Susan shook her head. "It's on the house. Your mom gave me a take-out container of her famous traditional hummus last time I was at the restaurant. Tell her I said hello."

CHAPTER 16

When the lunch rush had finally dwindled down, Lucy sat at a table across from Katie. Her friend had taken a late lunch hour from work to hear the scoop on Lucy's escapade at the salon. As soon as Lucy's mother had spotted Katie, she'd hurried into the kitchen and come out to set a platter of grilled halibut kebabs in a lemon dill sauce in front of her. Katie's face had lit up like a thousand-watt bulb, and she'd thanked her mother. Lucy had waited until her friend had dug into the food and her mother disappeared into the kitchen before summarizing the day's events.

Katie's fork froze in midair. "Stan Slade did you a favor."

Lucy scowled. "How? By showing me the old newspaper of Cressida and Azad together?"

"I wasn't thinking of that, but yes. How else would you have learned?"

"You're right," Lucy said, a note of bitterness in her voice. "It's not like Azad would have told me." Things were still awkward between them, and they hadn't spoken more than a few words since the incident. Lucy had avoided him as much as possible.

Katie reached out to squeeze Lucy's hand. "I'm sorry that newspaper upset you, but look on the bright side. If Stan hadn't caught you eavesdropping in the park, then you would never have rushed into Cutie's Cupcake and learned what you did."

Lucy rubbed her temples. "I know you're right. But I also hope I don't run into that aggressive reporter again anytime soon." He made her nervous and it would be a good while before she forgot the image of the newspaper picture showing Cressida in Azad's arms.

"Hopefully, you won't." Katie picked up her fork and pointed it at Lucy. "But we were right. Henry's gambling problem led him to embezzle from bank customers. Bradford's and Scarlet's account could have been one of many. If you ask me, I think what Henry did to Bradford was even worse. Bradford was Henry's longtime friend, and he took advantage of that friendship."

Lucy's thoughts turned back to what she'd learned. It was much better to concentrate on that rather than her strained relationship with Azad. "Henry probably believed he could replace the money in time with his gambling winnings, but he couldn't come up with the cash fast enough. Instead Bradford's and Scarlet's employee paychecks and creditor payments bounced. Henry's actions put their business endeavor, Scarlet's Passion, at risk before it ever launched. It's a reason to want to kill Henry."

Katie took a bite of the halibut and chewed. "Something doesn't make sense. Why ask Henry to be the best man if you hate him?"

Lucy sat forward in her seat. "What if they'd asked

him to be the best man just to have a chance to murder him and blame it on someone else? After all, who would believe a bride or groom would kill the best man at their own wedding?"

"In a perverse sense, it's the perfect crime." Katie set her fork down. "But what about Holly? Do you think she told you the truth?"

"If she has a large trust fund, then that would eliminate one of the motives. Money."

"There's still jealousy. You said hatred radiated off Holly when Cressida walked into the salon."

"Yup," Lucy said. "I wouldn't have been surprised if Holly jumped up from her manicure, grabbed the nail clippers, and went after Cressida."

Katie's nose scrunched. "Holly's old enough to be Cressida's mother. It must eat her alive."

"I bet. But the thing is, Holly swore Henry would never leave her for Cressida . . . that he needed her for her money. As far as I could tell, Holly really believed it."

"It's convenient for Holly that her husband will never be able to confirm that fact."

"True." Lucy sipped a glass of ice water as she mulled this over. Something else bothered her, something about Cressida Connolly. "When I overheard Cressida talking to Scarlet in the park, Cressida claimed she'd finally convinced Henry to leave his wife. She sounded certain to me, too. Which one is telling the truth? Cressida or Holly?"

"Maybe both. It wouldn't be the first time a man lied to two women. Especially a cheater like Henry Simms."

* * *

Early the following morning, Lucy found her mother in the restaurant kitchen.

"I've been waiting for you," Angela said.

Lucy set a coffee cup on the kitchen worktable. "It's barely six o'clock. Aren't you supposed to sleep late in your retirement?"

"Bah! Early risers get more done. Your father is a perfect example. He sleeps late, then is up all night worrying about the invoices and payroll he never finished."

"He's not supposed to do that. I'm handling the paperwork now," Lucy said.

"It's hard for him to let go entirely."

As if it wasn't just as hard for her mother.

Lucy eyed the three large pots on the stove. "What's today's lesson?"

Not long ago, Lucy would rather have visited Doctor Frank, Ocean Crest's sole practicing dentist, and had a cavity drilled and filled than spend time in the kitchen learning how to cook from her mother. But now, surprisingly, she had come to enjoy the lessons as well as their private conversations during their time together.

Angela busied herself by setting a bowl of onions on the worktable, then putting on an apron. "I want to teach you how to make *derevee dolma.*"

Stuffed grape leaves.

Lucy sucked in a breath. "Shouldn't we pick something easier?"

"It is easy." Her mother took a large bin of fresh grape leaves that she'd picked from her own garden and dumped them on the worktable.

Lucy eyed the grape leaves with trepidation. "Mom,

isn't this a time-consuming and difficult dish? I'm not
sure I can learn—"

"Nonsense. You helped me pick the grape leaves.
Why not learn how to make the filling, wrap the
leaves, and cook them?"

Her parents had their own special grapevine in the
backyard of their home. The grapes were bitter and
not good for making jelly or wine, but the leaves were
especially tender. In the summer months, the grapevine thrived and produced thousands of leaves, and
picking the grape leaves was a daily task during the
season. Her father could easily order jars of grape
leaves in brine for the restaurant from his ethnic food
supplier, but the homegrown leaves melted in your
mouth, whereas the jarred leaves could be tough.

"Go grab an apron and stop complaining," Angela
said.

Lucy picked a white apron and covered her Philadelphia Eagles T-shirt. She always wore the football
shirt whenever she had the cooking lessons, and she
felt as if it gave her good luck. She'd especially need
it this morning.

"First, we have to cut the stems from each leaf.
Then we soak them in boiling water to sterilize them,"
Angela instructed.

That didn't sound too hard. Lucy took a sharp
paring knife and went to work alongside her mother.

"I know you've been looking in to that man's
murder," her mother said.

Startled, Lucy ripped a grape leaf. Damn. She
should have known her mother would suspect. The
woman had a knack for ferreting out lies. Lucy and
Emma had never been able to sneak out of the house
as teenagers and meet boys on the beach, smuggle a

bottle of wine or ouzo from the family liquor cabinet, or pilfer a five-dollar bill from her purse.

Lucy went on the defensive. "Dad asked me to investigate, remember? He's worried about Azad." Her voice lacked conviction this morning. She'd spent a sleepless night thinking about the newspaper that Stan Slade had shoved beneath her nose yesterday. Azad and Cressida had looked so happy. Ugh.

"Your father is right," her mom said.

Lucy blinked. "Really?"

Angela didn't hesitate in her work of efficiently cutting and removing the stems from the leaves. "I know. I don't like to admit it, but he is right in this. Azad is innocent and that Detective Clemmons doesn't like our family."

"No, he doesn't."

Her mother finished with her batch of grape leaves, set down her knife, and studied Lucy. "What's wrong with you? You don't seem very happy about helping Azad."

How much to admit? Despite what Azad had told her, Lucy couldn't help but wonder if he still had feelings for Cressida. And why did that thought bother her so much now? She hated that she was feeling like a crushed teenager pining after her first puppy love.

Lucy grew aware of her mother's attention and she scrambled for an excuse. "Azad tried to take out a loan to buy Kebab Kitchen, but it fell through. If it hadn't, he'd be the owner, not just the head chef. I'd be out of luck."

"So?" Angela shrugged a slender shoulder. "He never lied to you about wanting to buy the place."

"True. But he told me he supported my decision. He never mentioned the loan."

Angela wagged a finger at her. "Lucy, it was before you expressed an interest in the place. You can't hold him responsible for that."

Lucy mulled this over as they finished prepping the grape leaves and boiled them.

"Pay close attention," her mom said. "Now we have to make the filling. For every pound of ground beef, I add two finely chopped onions, the rice, parsley, and tomato. Then I season it."

"How much seasoning?"

"A little bit of crushed mint. A pinch of salt and pepper. I don't measure. I just know."

Lucy's lips turned downward. "That doesn't help me at all."

"Watch and learn."

They worked side by side, making the filling, then began the tedious task of filling each individual grape leaf. "Lay the grape leaf shiny side down, add a teaspoon of filling by the stem end, fold the sides, then roll the tip of the leaf to form a cigar-shaped cylinder."

Lucy looked at the massive pile of filling, then at the dozens and dozens of grape leaves. If each only took a teaspoonful of filling, it would take *forever*. At least her mother had dropped the subject of Azad.

"It's not just the bank loan. What else is troubling you?" Angela asked.

So much for that. Lucy should have known better than to think her mother would let the subject go. Her maternal instincts were on high alert. Lucy sighed and stopped rolling. "Azad lied again, Mom. He dated the maid of honor in the wedding, a woman named Cressida Connolly. I saw the picture in the paper."

"That was a long time ago."

Lucy dropped her teaspoon on the worktable and stared at her mother. "You knew about Cressida?"

"Azad's always been like a son to us. He never really left the restaurant and worked part-time shifts if Butch was on vacation. You didn't know about that woman because you left."

Frustration made her voice harsh. "I didn't *leave* you. I was working."

Angela waved a hand as if there was no difference. "He dated that redhead briefly. They never were a good match."

"Why? Because you want me to be with Azad?"

Her mother's eyes flashed in a familiar display of impatience. "No, because they didn't fit."

What does that mean? A part of Lucy wanted to know. Needed to know. Who would Azad fit with?

Her mother continued to wrap the grape leaves with remarkable dexterity and speed. Her leaves looked like tightly wrapped miniature Cuban cigars, whereas Lucy's weren't wrapped as neatly. Plus, her mother's pot was almost half full, and Lucy hadn't even managed to cover the bottom of her pot.

"It was a long time ago," Angela said as she wrapped two at a time. "You need to forget the past."

Lucy's voice was hoarse with frustration. "It's not just the past. He never even mentioned he'd dated Cressida, and it's important to the murder case. The murder that *I'm* trying to solve in order to clear his name."

Angela sighed with exasperation. "I love you, Lucy, and I'm proud to have you as a daughter. But you are very stubborn."

"What's that supposed to mean?"

"It means you should give him another chance."

"You've always wanted us to be together. You just want to keep the restaurant in the family."

"Don't be ridiculous."

"I'm not being ridiculous!"

Her mother stopped working, and her gaze bore into Lucy. "Open your eyes. Every time you walk in the room, he notices you. And every time he comes near, you become nervous and run away. Why is that?"

Why indeed?

Lucy was honest enough with herself to admit she was still attracted to Azad. He was as entwined in her past as her parents' grapevine in her childhood home. Now, he was in her future as well.

But what about motorcycle-riding Michael Citteroni? She was drawn to him, too.

The truth was that she wasn't ready to commit to either.

But that didn't mean she couldn't forgive Azad. Her mother's words rang true. The past was the past. She couldn't hold a grudge for whom Azad dated after they'd broken up. And she couldn't be mad at him for wanting to buy the restaurant before she even returned to Ocean Crest.

"Help him, Lucy," her mother said. "Find out who killed that man. Then do yourself a favor and find out how *you* feel."

Two hours later, Lucy was tired from standing and rolling dozens of grape leaves. Three large pots were simmering on the stove and the smell was a delicious distraction.

"Hey, Mrs. Berberian. What are you cooking?"

Lucy turned to see Azad enter the kitchen. He lifted

a lid on one of the pots and smelled the simmering grape leaves.

"Lucy made that pot," her mother said.

"It smells great. I'm impressed."

His dark gaze sought hers, and he studied her with a curious intensity. The way he looked at her suggested it wasn't just her cooking that impressed him. Her pulse skittered alarmingly.

Get a grip, Lucy.

She'd been careful to avoid him in the kitchen. The only path from the dining room into the storage room and her office was through the kitchen, and she'd wait to race by when Azad was occupied at the worktable or at the stove and his back was to her. It may have been childish, but she didn't want to face him just yet.

Her mother took off her apron and set it on a peg on the wall. "I need to get back home and wake your father."

"It's past nine o'clock. He can't still be sleeping," Lucy said. Her mother was simply trying to get her and Azad to spend some time alone together before the rest of the staff showed up.

"You don't know your father." Angela motioned to the pots. "Let them simmer for an hour." Then she turned and waved on her way out the door.

"She keeps doing that, doesn't she?" Azad asked.

Lucy didn't try to feign ignorance. "She wants us to talk."

"I think it's a good idea. All we've talked about lately is restaurant business."

That's because I wanted it that way. Or so she thought. Her mother's words came back to her.

"How'd it go with your mom today?" he asked.

"She's convinced she'll make a chef out of me yet."
He chuckled. "Is my job in jeopardy?"

"Hardly. You have nothing to worry about."

He looked at her strangely, then asked, "Hey, Lucy, do you want to go to dinner Sunday night? I know a quaint Italian place out of town."

Surprise coursed through her. Was he asking her out on a date?

"Azad, I don't know if—"

"We can discuss the investigation."

Oh, that. She wanted to smack her forehead. Of course, it wasn't a date. Had a simple conversation with her mother changed her perception of him completely?

"Sunday's good."

He flashed a charming grin. "Great. I'll pick you up at six." He placed the lid back on the simmering pot. "By the way, I meant what I said. Good job wrapping all of these. And they smell great, too."

With that, he left her in the kitchen.

CHAPTER 17

By the time Lucy finished hunting for supplies on the wooden pallets in the storage room in order to finish inventory that night, it was almost ten o'clock. What a mess. If the steel shelving wasn't installed soon, she'd bust out her father's old drill in her parents' garage and attempt to do it herself.

She contemplated going home to Katie's, dressing in comfortable sweats, and collapsing in front of the TV to watch repeats of *CSI* with her friend, but then guilt won out. She'd eaten more than one slice of lemon meringue pie, as well as two pieces of baklava straight from the oven. There was no time to work out tomorrow since she'd promised her mother that she'd take her to Pages Bookstore, and she'd told Emma she'd babysit her niece in the evening. If she didn't watch it, she'd have to lie down on the bed to zip up her jeans in the morning.

Lucy trudged to her office where she kept workout clothes and a spare pair of running shoes. After changing into shorts and a T-shirt and refilling Gadoo's food and water bowls, she locked the back door of the restaurant. She didn't normally jog this late at night, but a full moon, combined with the streetlights, illuminated her path. The leaves of tall oak and sycamore trees shimmered and danced as she jogged down Ocean Avenue.

The exercise cleared her mind and she was able to sort through what she'd learned so far about the murder. Numerous people had reason to want Henry Simms dead. Henry's embezzlement and reckless behavior as bank president provided plenty of motive for both Bradford and Scarlet. Then there was Henry's infidelity. His wife, Holly, not only knew about the affair, but she knew the identity of her husband's lover and hated Cressida Connolly with a vengeance. Holly may have a trust fund and not be desperate for the cash from the life insurance policy, but an angry, betrayed spouse could be deadly. Last, there was Cressida, and if Henry had lied to her about leaving his wife, then she too may have decided to get rid of her lover.

The suspects were mounting, but Lucy was no closer to solving the murder.

Crickets chirped and sang as Lucy passed cottages and small rental homes where lights twinkled in the windows and adults gathered around flat screen televisions after the children had gone to bed. Tricycles, beach carts, and beach toys were scattered across freshly cut lawns. Beach towels slung over second-floor railings to dry blew in the night breeze like colorful flags.

She turned down Oyster Street and ran by the new McMansions that were recently constructed at the edge of town. Sprawling white stone facades, towering pillars, gabled roofs, and replicas of seminude Roman statues on well-tended lawns competed with each other. Holly lived in one of these houses, and Bradford and Scarlet in another. For all their luxury, Lucy disliked the garish and ostentatious homes and thought their seven-figure price tags outrageous, but she also knew it was the ocean-front views that truly made the houses worth a small fortune. Still, she much preferred Katie and Bill's cozy ranch home.

Soon she was on the stretch of road by the ocean and sweat beaded on her brow. A refreshing breeze cooled her skin and carried the scent of salt, sand dunes, and the sea. Her pace slowed as she passed the Sandpiper Bed and Breakfast and returned to the smaller homes.

A dark sedan drove by slowly as she came to the end of the street, then accelerated. Lucy kept going. If tourists thought they could get a room, then they would be disappointed. The orange neon No Vacancy sign flashed in the Sandpiper's front window.

When she came upon Ocean Avenue, Lucy stopped jogging and started walking to cool down and catch her breath. Traffic was light on the street, and for a long stretch she saw no one. Then, out of the corner of her eye, she saw a car slide by. She wasn't sure, but she thought it was the same dark sedan she'd seen before. The hair on the back of her neck rose. For the first time, she wondered why she'd left her cell phone behind. She'd decided not to listen to music tonight, preferring the night sounds of the crickets and the ocean waves.

Not such a brilliant idea, Lucy.

She was close to the restaurant, and her Toyota sat beneath the parking light.

Just as she decided to sprint the rest of the way, the

dark car made a sharp right, veered into the parking lot, and stopped next to her car.

What the heck?

The driver's side door opened and a figure stepped out. The woman's long blond hair, flawless profile, and curvaceous figure were unmistakable.

Scarlet Westwood.

Scarlet's heels echoed off the blacktop as she shut the car door and halted by the hood. The socialite was dressed in a short, skintight black dress and red high heels. She looked like she was going to hit the Atlantic City nightclubs.

Lucy walked the rest of the way and stopped before her. Scarlet tucked an errant blond curl behind her ear, and her diamond necklace glittered beneath the overhead light. "I'm sorry if I frightened you. Can we talk?"

They hadn't spoken since the day Scarlet had arrived at the restaurant with her wedding planner, Victoria Redding, and stated that she'd wanted Kebab Kitchen to cater her wedding. All communication since then had been through Victoria.

A warning voice whispered in Lucy's head, and she tried to suppress her jangling nerves. "Is this about the latest invoice I delivered to Ms. Redding?"

"No. I understand you've been asking questions about Henry's death."

Whoa. How did she know that? "I'm not sure—"

"Victoria told me you came to see her."

"I did. Like I said, I had to deliver the final catering bill. There were some last minute adjustments because of the cost of the food."

"I don't care about the bill," Scarlet said, her voice tense.

Denial was Lucy's best option. "Then I don't know what you're talking about."

"I also happened to see you in the park the other day. Do you always make it a practice to hide in the bushes?"

Oh, no.

Denial was blown out of the water. How on earth had Scarlet seen her? She'd been careful to wait until both Scarlet and Cressida had departed before crawling from beneath the bushes. Had Scarlet turned around and spotted her with Stan Slade?

She studied the socialite as her mind whirled. What was the harm in Scarlet knowing that she'd been investigating? Maybe this was her chance to ask the woman a few questions of her own.

"You're right." Lucy folded her arms across her chest. "I have been asking questions. The police consider my head chef a murder suspect. He didn't kill Henry Simms."

"You think I did? Or Bradford?" Scarlet clenched her fists at her sides, and her face clouded with uneasiness.

"I'm not sure what to think. All I know is that Henry abused his position as bank president and stole money from accounts. Your business account with Bradford was one of them."

Scarlet touched the diamond necklace at her throat. "Henry did steal. He needed cash, and fast, but he swore that he never intended to hurt Bradford. He planned to borrow the money and then return it before we noticed it was missing. He was wrong."

"You must have been angry."

"I was. He risked the launch of Scarlet's Passion, my

new line of fragrances. But I didn't kill Henry," Scarlet insisted.

"What about Bradford? He must have been mad."

"You mean mad enough to kill?" Scarlet straightened her shoulders. "Yes, he was angry with Henry, but Bradford is not capable of murder. He's sweet and kind and doesn't have a killer bone in his body."

Bradford was a top Hollywood director and producer. Lucy doubted that a person reached that position by being sweet and kind—more likely driven and cutthroat. Was Scarlet lying? Or was she bamboozled by her new husband just as Cressida and Holly had been conned by Henry?

"What about the money stolen from your account?" Lucy asked.

"Henry eventually returned the money, and Bradford forgave him. Bradford wanted me to do the same. I admit it was a hard sell for me to forgive and forget, but I did it for him and because Scarlet's Passion is still on a timely schedule to launch. Even though picking the best man is customarily the groom's choice, we shared all the important wedding decisions. That's why I agreed with Bradford's decision and never replaced Henry as the best man."

Lucy wasn't entirely convinced. Scarlet didn't seem like the forgiving kind, even if that was what her husband truly wanted. Especially when Henry's actions had almost compromised her new business venture.

"What about the pictures that were sold to the tabloids?" Lucy asked. "You were adamant about the wedding staying out of the papers, and you went so far as to insist your guests place their cell phones and cameras in a basket before walking into the reception.

Victoria saw Henry smuggle in his cell phone. You must have been livid."

"I know where you're headed, but my anger over the tabloid pictures still didn't make me go out and murder Henry. Plus, those pictures weren't published until *after* Henry was murdered. Your theory that I saw red and turned around and stabbed Henry at my own wedding doesn't hold up."

She had a point. Still, Henry's underhanded dealings at the bank provided enough motive and Lucy wasn't convinced of Bradford's *or* Scarlet's forgiveness.

Lucy shifted her feet. "What about your maid of honor?"

"Cressida? What about her?"

"Her affair with Henry is no longer a secret."

Something flickered far back in Scarlet's eyes. "I guess you heard more of our conversation than I thought."

Lucy had learned about the affair before then, but she didn't point that out. "Cressida claims she'd convinced Henry to leave his wife, but Holly is adamant that Henry never would have left her."

"You think Cressida killed Henry?"

"Maybe Cressida figured out that Henry never intended to get a divorce. She could have killed him."

Scarlet pulled her mouth in at the corners. "No way. I can't imagine it."

At Lucy's hesitation, Scarlet's voice grew urgent. "Fine. I can't vouch for Cressida or anyone else." She pointed to her chest. "But you have to believe that I'm innocent. Bradford too."

Lucy remained skeptical, but something else was bothering her at the moment. Something bigger.

"Why do you care what I believe? Why follow me here tonight to convince me of your innocence?"

Scarlet didn't miss a beat. "You're a local. Plus, I heard you solved a murder in town a couple months ago that the police failed to figure out. You're a smart lady, Lucy. And I always place my bets on the right person."

CHAPTER 18

Pages Bookstore was located between Cutie's Cupcakes and Magic's Family Apothecary. It was a small, independently owned bookstore, and one of Lucy's favorite places—other than Ocean Crest's library—to pass extra time. She loved the cozy atmosphere of the store, which was crammed from floor to ceiling with shelves of books, magazines, and DVDs. The owner, Candace Kent, was an attractive young widow who always welcomed local authors to her store to sign their books. Her last author-signing was for local best-selling suspense author Paul Evans. Today, Candace had managed to outdo even that turnout, and the line extended out the front door.

"There he is!" Lucy's mother placed a shaky hand on her chest.

Through the throng of people, Lucy spotted a tall, handsome blond in a tight chef's coat sitting behind a table in the center of the store. A stack of glossy cookbooks rested beside him and a long line of customers were waiting to get signed copies of Cooking Kurt's latest culinary masterpiece. A young female assistant stood to his right and opened a cookbook to the title page, inserted a recipe card, and handed it to Kurt to sign as each reader approached.

"Lord, he looks even better in person," Lucy's mom said.

A middle-aged woman stepped up to the table and squealed in delight. Kurt stood to greet his fan, and his cotton coat stretched to revealed broad muscles and impressive biceps. Lucy wondered if he spent more time in the gym than in the kitchen. He smiled, revealing dazzling white teeth, and kissed the woman's cheek. She turned bright red, then looked as if she was going to hyperventilate when he put his arm around her and struck a manly pose as her friend eagerly snapped a picture with her iPhone.

Lucy's mother grabbed her arm and tugged her forward. "We better get in line before he runs out of cookbooks."

"Easy, Mom." Lucy stumbled as she was dragged to the back of the line. "Are you sure Dad wouldn't have brought you?"

"Of course he would have." Her mother stood on tiptoe to get a better look through the throng of people in line, a useless attempt with her five-foot frame.

"Then why didn't you ask him again?" Lucy asked, feeling more than a bit frustrated.

Her mom shuffled to the right, then back to the left in an attempt to find a gap in the crowd to see. "Sometimes I like to keep your father guessing."

"What's that supposed to mean?"

Her mother gave an impatient shrug. "There's nothing wrong with keeping a man a bit off kilter. That way they don't take you for granted."

Lucy wasn't sure she wanted this type of advice, especially from her mother. "That makes no sense."

"When you've been married as long as I have to your father, it makes perfect sense."

"What's wrong with telling him how you feel and—"

"Bah!" Her mother finally turned to face Lucy and waved her hand in exasperation. "When I'm dead, you'll realize just how right I am."

Lucy's response was cut off as another excited squeal sounded and the line moved up.

Candace Kent waved at them as she walked around with a wide smile greeting customers. Returning the wave, Lucy spotted a flash of red hair around one of the shelves toward the back of the store. Her heart leaped in her chest.

Only one person had that shade of hair color.

Could it be?

Lucy stepped out of line and scanned the area, but she didn't spot Cressida. "Mom, I see a book I want. I'll be right back."

Her mother let out an exasperated sigh as a group of soccer moms moved in to take numerous pictures with Kurt. She tucked a loose bobby pin that had escaped her beehive behind her ear. "Take your time. It looks like we'll be here for a while."

Lucy hurried to the back of the store, craning to look down aisles as she went. Turning a corner, she spotted her prey in the self-help aisle reading the back of a hardcover. Another book—which looked like a college textbook—was on the floor by her feet.

"Cressida Connolly?" Lucy asked.

Cressida jumped as if she'd been caught with her hand in the cookie jar. She quickly returned the book she'd been reading to the shelf. "Yes?"

"I'm Lucy Berberian. I was at Scarlet and Bradford's

wedding. I'm sorry for what happened to Henry Simms. How are you doing?"

The corners of Cressida's lips turned downward. "I'm still in shock over what happened."

"That's understandable. Henry was the best man and your escort as the maid of honor. It must have been a frightening experience."

Cressida shook her head. "Fortunately, I never saw him after he was killed. Many of us never found out about the murder until after the reception."

Any one of the bridal party could have killed Henry, including Cressida. The time of death had been determined to be near the end of the reception, when the bridal party was still present.

Lucy pointed to the textbook at Cressida's feet. "Statistics? I remember taking that class in college. Not my favorite subject."

"Mine either. I'm taking online college classes and thought this review book might help."

"Are you also here for an autographed cookbook?" Lucy asked.

Cressida chuckled. "I have no interest in cooking, even if the chef is hot. I always come here on the same day of the week. I just didn't know there was a book signing here today."

Out of the entire bridal party, Lucy knew the least about Cressida. "Are you or your family from around here?"

"Not exactly. I was born a couple towns north in Baytown, but still near the Jersey shore."

"How nice. Are your parents still there?"

"My mom died several years ago. She was a single parent."

"Sorry about losing your mom." Lucy took a step

forward. "The truth is, I've been curious about what happened at the wedding, and when I saw you in the bookstore I came searching for you. Can I ask you a few questions about that day?"

Cressida's demeanor changed, and she stiffened. "What kinds of questions?"

Cressida had a wary look now, but Lucy pressed on. "Like I said, I was at the wedding and the whole thing upsets me. I want to know more about what happened to that man."

"I've been through all this with that boorish, unattractive investigator."

"I understand, but I'm not a cop. Do you remember the last time you saw Henry that night? It would be a good help."

Cressida wrinkled her nose. "It was near the end of the reception. Maybe ten o'clock."

"Where'd you see him?"

"On the dance floor. He was shaking it up pretty good and looked like he was enjoying himself."

He'd also been very intoxicated. Lucy had been surprised he hadn't fallen flat on his face. "That was the last time you saw Henry alive?" she asked.

"That's right." Cressida's eyes narrowed. "What's it to you, anyway?"

"One more question. Do you know who would have wanted to harm Henry?"

"No."

"You sure? What about any of his acquaintances at the wedding?"

A spark of emotion crossed her face—trepidation? anger?—before it was replaced with a cool blue gaze. "That's more than one question," she snapped. "Now, if you'll excuse me, I need to go."

Lucy watched as Cressida picked up the math

textbook and walked away. She waited until Cressida was out of sight, then searched for the spine of the book Cressida had quickly shoved on the shelf. Picking up the book, Lucy read the title: *Put Yourself First and Gain the Love You Deserve.*

Whose love did Cressida seek to gain?

Henry's?

That would never happen now.

Had Cressida's self-worth plummeted when Henry refused to leave his wife? Or had Cressida's anger taken over, compelling her to stab her lover in the neck in a fit of jealousy?

That evening, Lucy showed up at Emma's house with a new box of Legos and a steaming hot pizza. Emma's ten-year-old daughter, Niari, opened the door.

"How's my favorite niece?" Lucy asked.

Niari jumped up and down in excitement. "Mokour Lucy! I'm happy you're babysitting tonight."

Niari always called her Mokour, which meant "mother's sister" in Armenian. She was Emma and Max's only child, and Lucy adored her. Niari was a mix between Emma and Max with an olive Mediterranean complexion and dark hair, but blue eyes from her father's English and Irish heritage. She wore an Ocean Crest travel soccer uniform, and Lucy knew her parents drove her all over New Jersey to play the sport.

Lucy kissed Niari's cheek. "Did you win your game?"

"You bet! Two to zip. We play at home next Saturday."

"I'll be there. Meanwhile, tonight's going to be a fun girls' night." Lucy stepped inside and shifted the hot pizza box in her hands.

Niari eyed the box. "Is that pizza from the Hot Cheese Pizzeria? They make the best pepperoni pies."

"It is. We get to eat, then play Legos." Her niece was obsessed with Legos and had an entire bookshelf of completed Lego sets that she displayed with more pride than her soccer trophies.

Niari shut the door behind her. "I have something even better to play."

"Better than Legos?"

"I got a trampoline!"

Lucy eyed her speculatively. "A trampoline?"

"Daddy assembled it in the backyard. Come see!" Stopping long enough to take the pizza from Lucy and set it on the hall table, Niari grabbed Lucy's hand and pulled her through the family room to look outside the window. Sure enough, a large, bright blue trampoline with black netting stood in the center of the backyard.

"I can show you how to do flips." Niari's face glowed with youthful excitement.

Lucy's stomach bottomed out. "I'm not so sure about that . . ."

"It's easy. I'll teach you."

Images of high school gym class came back in a rush. Lucy had attempted to tumble on one of the mats and had split her tights in front of the entire freshman class. It was the last time she'd even attempted anything close to gymnastics. "Where are your mom and dad?"

"In the kitchen."

"You go out back and warm up on the trampoline while I have a word with your mom." Lucy didn't have to say it twice. Niari was out the back door like a shot.

Lucy retrieved the pizza from the hall and found

Emma in the kitchen making a pitcher of lemonade. She placed the pizza on the counter. "Hi, Emma."

"Hey, Lucy. Thanks for watching Niari. We'll be back by midnight. Make sure she's in bed before nine. She has a soccer tournament tomorrow in Cape May."

"No worries. That gives us plenty of time to play."

Emma looked nice in a black cocktail dress. Even though Lucy's primary doctor had told her she was the perfect weight for her height, she was still envious of her sister's slender figure. Emma never worked out whereas Lucy jogged miles and miles to stay trim. Lucy glanced longingly at the pizza box. Niari's comment was right. Guido Morelli, the owner of the Hot Cheese Pizzeria, did make the best pepperoni pies.

A colorful blur outside the kitchen window caught Lucy's attention. Niari was flipping head over heels on the trampoline. Lucy's anxiety ratcheted up a notch. "Niari wants to teach me flips."

Emma's mouth drew downward as she mixed the lemonade with a large wooden spoon. "I told Max not to get it, but he wouldn't listen."

"Listen to what?"

Lucy and Emma whirled around to see Max in the doorway. He looked handsome dressed in a navy suit that brought out his sandy hair and blue eyes. "Hey, Lucy. I assume Emma is talking about the trampoline?"

"Never mind about that," Lucy said as she leaned against the counter. Emma frequently complained about Max's long work hours and Lucy didn't want to stir up trouble—especially on their date night. "How's the season going?"

"All the summer rentals were taken months ago. New sales should start picking up soon. Although news of a murder in town is going to hurt business."

"We all hope they find the killer soon." Emma put the wooden spoon in the sink and poured a glass of lemonade from the pitcher and handed it to Lucy.

"Is Calvin Clemmons even close?" Max asked.

Lucy sipped the lemonade. It was perfect—sweet with a touch of tart. "I wish I knew. One thing is for sure: he'd like to pin the murder on Azad. He still holds a grudge against our family and he knows we rely on our new head chef."

"That's my fault," Emma said as a look of discomfort crossed her face. "Why did I ever call him Clingy Calvin in high school? I never thought the name would stick."

That wasn't the only reason Clemmons was biased against their family, but Lucy dared not bring *that* up. Emma had cheated on Calvin with his best friend, Will Thomas, their senior year. Not very nice of her sister. Lucy had assumed she'd cheated on Calvin to end up with Max. Somehow, in Lucy's mind, that had seemed more forgivable since the pair had gone on to marry. It wasn't until a couple of months ago that Emma had confessed that she'd broken Calvin's heart by hooking up with Will.

"You may be right about Clemmons," Max said, interrupting Lucy's thoughts. "Members of the wedding party have contacted me about putting their houses on the market."

Lucy lowered her glass. "Who?"

"For starters, Scarlet Westwood and her new husband, Bradford Papadopoulos," Max said.

Lucy blinked in surprise. "Didn't they only recently buy a home in Ocean Crest? One of the McMansions on Oyster Street? She told me they planned to film a movie on the beach."

"They did. But it looks like their finances are not as well off as they'd hoped. Filming a movie takes a chunk of cash," Max said.

"What about her new business, Scarlet's Passion?"

"Rumor has it that the business may never launch due to lack of funding as well."

Holy cow. This was big news. Did Henry's theft cause Scarlet's Passion to go belly up before it ever launched? Scarlet had led her to believe that Henry had paid back what he'd stolen and her fragrance line would open for business as planned. But what if she'd lied? Or what if they weren't able to get an influx of cash and Scarlet's entrepreneurial dreams plummeted?

What if Bradford and Scarlet knew this *before* the wedding?

It would blow Scarlet's claims of innocence to bits.

"Detective Clemmons requested the bridal party to stay in town until the murder is resolved," Lucy said. "How can Scarlet and Bradford leave?"

Max opened the pizza box. "Just because they want to sell doesn't mean they'll leave town. They inquired about rentals. Also, the maid of honor asked to extend her own lease."

"Cressida Connolly? Do you know where she's living?"

"She's been renting a house on Oyster Street. Number Nine."

"Another McMansion?"

"Not one of the big ones, but a smaller bungalow. It's new construction, has a high-end kitchen and bathrooms with Jacuzzis and skylights. Plus, it's only a block from the beach."

Cressida had said she wasn't a cook, and a state of

the art kitchen would be a complete waste, but not the Jacuzzi or the close vicinity to the beach. "How much is the rental?"

"During the summer months, it's five thousand a week."

That was a large chunk of cash for an unemployed college student. Cressida had said she was raised by a single mother who'd passed away years ago. So where was she getting the money?

"Do you know how she's paying for the rental?" Lucy asked.

"Once rent for the first two months clears and the application is approved by the owner, I don't ask. Maybe she has a rich aunt somewhere."

Unlikely. Or maybe she'd had a rich sugar daddy. But if Henry had refused to leave Holly, had Cressida's income stream run out? And had she retaliated by killing him for it?

There was only one way to find out more. Lucy needed to pay Cressida a visit at her home.

CHAPTER 19

"Are you sure about this?" Katie asked.

Lucy looked inside the Styrofoam take-out box in her hands. "I am. According to my mother, it's neighborly to give food when someone is going through a trying time. Murder is trying." It was the following day, and Lucy had an entire lunch and dinner shift to think of an excuse to approach Cressida again.

"You think Cressida Connolly will take food from you? From what you told me, you didn't make a good impression when you questioned her at the bookstore."

"True," Lucy said. "But this is our specialty of the day, lamb and leek stew. I hope it's enticing enough to get us through the front door. I also plan to apologize and offer my sympathies with food."

Katie sniffed the stew and closed her eyes. "Umm. It smells delicious. How much garlic did Azad use?"

Lucy closed the lid. "Enough to give you bad breath for a day."

Katie rolled her eyes. "It's worth the risk."

They set off at a brisk pace. Oyster Street was ten or so blocks from Kebab Kitchen. It was a pleasant evening and they'd decided to walk after the restaurant's dinner rush. Her parents and Emma were working and they were happy to watch the restaurant so that Lucy could take a break to walk with her friend. Of course, they thought they were strolling the boardwalk, not spying on a murder suspect.

As they turned onto Oyster Street, the large mansions came into view. "Would you look at that fountain? The naked mermaids are ridiculous," Lucy said.

"The builder must have looked at dirty Internet pictures for inspiration."

Lucy grinned, her first real smile of the evening. "You have a wacky sense of humor." Katie always had the ability to make her laugh. More and more, Lucy was grateful for her friendship. How had she stayed away from Ocean Crest for so long?

Katie answered with her own smile. "I'll take that as a compliment." She halted and pointed to a modest-sized bungalow compared to the huge houses. "There's Number Nine. It's small next to the others, but still bigger than my house."

"Max said the builder put up bungalows on the remaining small lots, but they're still luxurious with new kitchens, bathrooms with Jacuzzis and skylights, and most important, they're close to the beach. Cressida's been renting this place a few months."

"I don't get it. After you learned that Cressida was raised by a working, single mom, I did some more digging into her educational background. Cressida landed a scholarship and went to the same exclusive high school as Scarlet. That's where the two girls met and became friends. Her father was never in the picture."

"She told me her mom passed away. She never mentioned her father."

"So how can an unemployed college student afford to live here?" Katie asked.

"That's what I hope to find out."

They started up the street, but before they came close to the winding driveway, the front door opened and Cressida stepped onto the porch. Locking the front door, she hurried to her car in the driveway. Seconds later, she backed out of the driveway and sped down the street.

"Shoot. We'll have to come back another time," Katie said.

Lucy placed a hand on Katie's arm to halt her when she would have turned around. "Not so fast. We can peek in her windows."

Katie looked at her in disbelief. "Peek in her windows? Are you crazy? What if the neighbors see us?"

"It's twilight and the sun's going down fast. No one will notice us."

Katie shook her head. "It's too risky."

"It's worth it," Lucy said. "We may be able to learn something. Don't they do it all the time in those TV crime shows you watch?"

"I suppose, but—"

Lucy started walking across Cressida's front lawn. "I'm going. I'll meet you back at the restaurant if you want."

That spurred Katie into action. "Don't you dare! Wait for me."

Lucy flashed a wide grin, and Katie halted. "You just played me. You knew I wouldn't let you go by yourself, didn't you?"

"I also know you need a little push sometimes," Lucy said.

Katie was initially more eager to get involved in

murder investigations whereas Lucy held back, but when it came to risky situations, Katie could get cold feet.

"All right. Let's go," Katie said. "If we get arrested, you'll have to explain it to Bill."

"I'll tell him it was all my idea."

"Like he'll believe you," Katie scoffed.

Together they walked around the side of the house. Black aluminum patio furniture with red and green striped cushions was situated around a stamped concrete patio that looked remarkably similar to stone. The dying embers of the sun reflected off two windows and a sliding glass door. Lucy peered in one of the windows while Katie glanced in the sliding glass door.

Lucy's heart pounded. Despite her bravado about sneaking a peek inside Cressida's home, she was concerned that at any minute one of the neighbors would throw open their own windows and threaten to call the police.

Thankfully the curtains were open and Lucy could see inside to a kitchen with stainless-steel appliances. Large plastic bottles of protein powder and individual protein shakes were on the granite countertop beside a fancy blender that she'd seen featured on infomercials to help lose weight and promote a healthy diet. Containers labeled "flax" and "chia seeds" and "cocoa powder" sat on a matching granite island. Cressida had claimed she wasn't a cook, but it was clear she was health conscious.

"Other than Cressida being a bit of a health nut, I don't see anything out of the ordinary," Lucy said.

"I don't see anyone inside," Katie said.

Lucy joined Katie at the sliding glass door to look inside. Reaching for the door handle, she cracked it an inch, then looked up, surprised. "It's unlocked!"

Katie's gaze flew to Lucy. "We can't go inside! What if there's an alarm? Sneaking onto the patio and peeking inside windows is one thing, but breaking and entering is another thing entirely."

"An alarm hasn't sounded. Cressida left in such a hurry, there's a good chance that if she has one she didn't put it on." Lucy opened the sliding glass door another inch. "No barking guard dog." She urged Katie forward with her hand. "Come on. This is a great chance to unearth information. We can look through her mail and personal belongings. They did it on the last episode of *Hawaii Five-O* that I watched with you."

"For God's sake. Stop talking about my favorite TV shows," Katie said. "And what are you going to do with that?" Katie lowered her gaze to the take-out box of stew in Lucy's hand.

Lucy frowned. "You're right. If I take this inside, the garlic smell will linger and be a telltale sign that someone had been inside." She scanned the patio. "What do I do with it?"

"Stuff it under a bush. We'll get it on our way out."

Crouching down, Lucy slid the Styrofoam box beneath a hedgerow.

This time, it was Katie who slid open the glass door and entered the house. Taking one last look around, Lucy followed and darted inside.

The sliding door led directly into a tastefully decorated family room with furniture that smelled new and expensive. A large flat-screen television and state-of-the-art stereo system decked out the space. Max had told her that the bungalow came fully furnished. If Katie hadn't confirmed that Cressida's mother had been a working, single parent, Lucy would have assumed she'd left Cressida with a sizable inheritance.

Picture frames were displayed on an end table by the sofa. One of the pictures caught her eye. It was a framed print of Cressida and Henry Simms at the Ocean Crest boardwalk at night. She was dressed in a low-cut sundress, and he was wearing a Hawaiian print shirt. His arm was around her and she was leaning into his chest and pressing a kiss on his cheek. The bright lights of the Ferris wheel shone behind them.

Lucy's gut tightened. Their pose reminded her of the newspaper picture the nosy reporter Stan Slade had shoved at her—only Cressida had been in Azad's arms, not Henry's.

"Check it out." Lucy showed Katie the picture.

Katie came over and took the picture frame from Lucy. "I don't get it. Even though Henry was a handsome and fit older man, what could the two of them really have had in common?"

"Maybe it was about money," Lucy said. "Henry was addicted to gambling. I'm thinking he spent a lot of his cash winnings on Cressida."

"It makes sense." Katie went to a computer sitting in a corner and pulled out an office chair. A screen saver flashed a picture of a tropical island. "I'll check her browsing history."

"Okay. I'll search here." Lucy returned the picture frame to the table and sat on the couch before the glass coffee table. Paperwork cluttered the surface along with marble paperweights and a silver letter opener. A stack of unopened mail was piled in the corner. She scanned the return labels to find mostly credit card bills. She couldn't open the personal letters but read the addresses. Pushing aside catalogs and magazine subscriptions, Lucy noticed a manila envelope. The return address read, "Staedler Insurance Company." The envelope had been sliced open and the paperwork slid out.

She quickly flipped through the stacks of papers. She came to the second-to-the-last page, and her breath caught in her throat. "My God."

Katie spun around, her eyes wide. "What?"

"It's Henry's million-dollar life insurance policy changing the beneficiary from his wife, Holly Simms, to Cressida Connolly. The change was dated a month ago."

"You're kidding."

Lucy shook her head. "It looks like a copy. Henry must have given it to Cressida."

"A million dollars is a lot of money for a college student. Maybe she decided she wanted the cash and killed her lover?"

"It's possible. Especially if Henry refused to leave Holly. Cressida could have killed him out of jealousy."

"What about Holly? Do you think she knew about the change of beneficiary?"

"Legally she'd have to sign the change of beneficiary form. But it's not uncommon for spouses to sign documents without reading them. It happens all the time with taxes." Lucy thought back to when she'd questioned Holly outside the Big Tease Salon. "But the thing is, I believed her when she told me she was the beneficiary as his wife."

"She could have lied. Or maybe she learned the

truth afterward and went ballistic? Not only had her husband cheated on her, but he betrayed her further by taking care of his mistress in case of his death. Even though Holly wouldn't get the insurance payout, she must have been furious. She claims she doesn't need the cash, but maybe she saw red and killed him."

"I don't know. But right now, it doesn't look good for either Holly *or* Cressida. One of them is most likely the killer." Lucy eyed the remaining stacks of paper on the coffee table. "You keep looking on her computer while I sift through the rest of this."

They worked in silence for fifteen minutes. Then the scrape of footsteps by the back sliding glass door made Lucy freeze. Trepidation settled low in her gut. "She's back!" she whispered.

Katie jumped out of the computer chair. "We have to get out."

Lucy sprang to her feet to grasp her arm. "There's no time! She's right outside. Find a place to hide." Panic welled in her throat, and she frantically scanned the room. A coat closet door was ajar, and she thrust Katie toward it. "In here. Quick."

They slipped in the coat closet, stepping past rain boots and shoes. Pushing their way to the back wall, they slid the coats on the rack in front of them for cover. Katie made to shut the closet door when Lucy stopped her. "Leave it ajar. She may notice if we shut it." Katie cracked the closet door a few inches just as the sliding glass door opened.

"I don't like this at all," a male voice sounded. "Do you think anyone saw us?"

"No. That's why I didn't have you come through the front door. The neighbors can be nosy in this town," Cressida said.

Through the pie wedge of light, Lucy spotted Bradford Papadopoulos and Cressida in the room. What was Bradford doing here?

Bradford started pacing the beige carpet. "How did you figure it out?"

"I saw you sneaking pictures with your cell phone at the reception. I always knew Henry didn't sell those pictures to the tabloids."

Bradford continued to burn a path in the carpet as he walked back and forth. "You have to promise not to tell Scarlet. I don't want her to know."

Cressida crossed her arms and faced him. "I don't like keeping secrets from my best friend. You're married now, and you should trust her. Why don't you tell her that it was you who sold the pictures to the tabloids?"

"I told you why. Scarlet wanted to keep the wedding private."

"Then why did you do it?"

"I didn't have much of a choice," Bradford said, a tenseness in his voice. "We needed the cash after Henry stole from our account. I lied and told Scarlet that Henry had paid it all back. I hoped the sale of the tabloid pictures would be enough to open the perfume line. And the free publicity would help, too."

"Was it worth it?"

"No. It's still not enough cash. Henry screwed me, but he couldn't help himself. He had an addiction."

"I don't understand. How can you just forgive him?"

Bradford stopped pacing. "Henry saved my butt back in college. I pulled a stupid prank with two of our fraternity brothers and stole a professor's car. We accidentally crashed into a tree. Henry came in his own car and drove me away before campus police showed up. I would have been expelled."

Cressida snorted. "That wasn't just a dumb prank, but a mean one."

"You're right. But Henry saved me, and I owed him." Bradford ran a hand down his face. "I don't want you to tell Scarlet that I sold the tabloid pictures or that Scarlet's Passion is a bust. I'm still scrambling to raise the money."

"Fine. But you're selling your house. Don't you think she'll suspect?"

"No. I told her I didn't like it and that we'd be better off renting in this market. I want you to keep it a secret."

"You're asking me to lie to my friend."

Bradford looked at her in amazement. "Oh, please. Like you don't have secrets of your own that you've been keeping from her."

"What's that supposed to mean?"

"I know about you and Henry."

Cressida's eyes narrowed to slits. "Shut your mouth. You know nothing."

Bradford took a deep breath and exhaled slowly. "Look, there's no need to get nasty. We're all under a lot of stress since Henry's death. I'm sorry about that. I know how much he meant to you."

Cressida's face crumbled. "You're right. I'm sorry. I've been uptight as well. Do you want a cup of coffee?"

"Sure. Some caffeine sounds good."

The closet was hot as Hades. A bead of sweat trickled between Lucy's breasts. She could sense Katie's nervousness. Katie shifted and bumped an umbrella from the overhead shelf. Katie reached out to catch the umbrella, but it slipped through her fingers and fell to the bottom of the closet with a loud thud.

Oh, crap.

"What was that?" Bradford asked.

"I don't know," Scarlet said. "It came from the closet. I'll go check."

Despite the heat of the small space, icy fear ran down Lucy's spine.

Lucy nudged the umbrella to the front of the closet with the toe of her shoe and then crouched behind the coats alongside Katie a split second before Cressida opened the door and light flooded the space.

"It's just an umbrella." Cressida picked it up, slid it back onto the overhead shelf, and pushed the door closed.

Darkness consumed the space as relief rushed through Lucy.

"Two cups of coffee coming right up." Footsteps sounded on the ceramic tiles in the kitchen.

Lucy cracked the closet door and pointed to the sliding glass door. "We have to get out of here," she whispered.

Katie nodded, her eyes wide disks.

"On three," Lucy whispered. "One . . . two . . . three!"

They darted out of the closet and made a beeline for the sliding glass door. Thrusting it open, they ran outside and sprinted across the patio and away from the house.

Seconds later, a shout pierced the night air.

"Stop!" Bradford's voice.

Sheer black fright ran through Lucy. They sprinted into the neighbor's backyard. "Keep away from the streetlights," Lucy called out. Katie understood. They couldn't afford to have their faces illuminated from the bright streetlights and identified.

Running from backyard to backyard, they darted past fancy fountains and immaculately trimmed hedges and freshly mulched flowerbeds. They almost made it to the end of Oyster Street, but the last house had a white picket fence. Footsteps sounded behind them. Lucy dared a quick glance behind to see Bradford in full pursuit.

He was gaining on them. They'd never be able to outrun him. Lucy made a quick decision. Home owners in Ocean Crest usually installed fences to prevent their pets from escaping and didn't always lock their gates. It was a gamble, but there was only one way to find out if her theory was true.

She headed straight for the fence and reached for the gate handle.

Unlocked.

Yes! She ran to the opposite gate and threw it open. Just as Katie would have passed her to fly by, Lucy grasped her arm.

"Over there." Lucy pointed to a beige vinyl shed that was half the size of Katie's house. Katie got the message, and they sprinted to the shed, crouching down on the grass behind it. Seconds later, Bradford burst through the gate, whirled around in the center of the backyard, and spotted the open gate on the opposite end of the yard. He ran through it and toward the street.

Thank goodness. Her ploy had worked. Lucy hoped he'd run down Oyster Street looking for them and eventually give up the search.

Lucy's heart thundered in her chest. As she inhaled to catch her breath she noticed two things: the strong smell of ocean and the distinct sound of the boardwalk's wooden roller coaster. The house was closer to the beach than she'd thought. If they could make it to the boardwalk, they could blend in with the tourists.

They waited a full five minutes, but Bradford didn't circle back, and Lucy prayed he'd think he'd lost them.

"This way." Lucy whispered for Katie to follow, and together they left the backyard and dashed for the street. They ducked behind cars, minivans, and delivery trucks until they finally made it to the boardwalk. Gasping and sweating, they ran up the boardwalk ramp. Throngs of tourists walked the boards at night and they blended in with the crowd.

Katie doubled over and panted beneath the awning of a fudge shop. "Do you think he recognized us?"

"No," Lucy said, breathing heavily. "But that was a really close call."

Katie rubbed her side. "I still can't believe it. Bradford sold those pictures to the tabloids, not Henry. He needed the cash to start Scarlet's Passion, and he hoped the publicity would work as free advertising."

"Bradford told Scarlet that Henry had returned the money he'd stolen. He'd lied to her," Lucy pointed out.

"Bradford claimed he owed Henry and forgave him," Katie said.

"He could have lied about that, too."

Katie shook her head in disbelief. "The entire wedding party is crazy."

"You need to tell Bill what we learned, but not how we learned it," Lucy said.

"I'll figure something out. Detective Clemmons

can't look the other way now. There are too many suspects with motives stronger than Azad's."

"Meanwhile, I want to have a heart-to-heart with Holly again. Find out exactly what she knew about that million-dollar life insurance policy."

"Good idea."

"I just thought of another problem," Lucy said.

A crease formed between Katie's brows. "What?"

"I forgot the stew under Cressida's bushes."

CHAPTER 20

Thank goodness no one had yet to burst into the restaurant with the Styrofoam take-out container and accuse Lucy and Katie of breaking and entering. Lucy hoped the food would stay undiscovered until neighborhood raccoons dragged it away, or until it froze solid during the winter—or better still—until she finally cracked the case.

Meanwhile, she had a "date" with Azad that night to go over what she'd learned so far and to ask him a few more questions about Cressida Connolly. A few hours later, a knock on Katie's front door filled her with a strange inner excitement.

Azad stood on the porch. "You look great, Lucy."

Her cheeks reddened under the heat of his gaze. She stepped onto the porch and closed the door. "Thanks."

She'd taken great pains with her outfit and had changed four times before Katie had helped her settle on a stylish yet casual pink sheath dress and wedge sandals. Her dark hair was loose and fell in soft curls just below her shoulders.

Azad led her to his truck. As she walked beside

him, she noted he looked good in tan slacks and an untucked, button-down, collared shirt.

He opened the door for her, then walked around to slide behind the wheel. "Our dinner reservations aren't until eight. I thought we could stop at Mac's pub for a drink and to listen to a local band, then head to dinner."

"Okay. That sounds great." She reminded herself this wasn't a romantic night out, but an opportunity to discuss the progress of the investigation.

Mac's Irish Pub was owned by Mac McCabe and was a popular Ocean Crest hangout that had a wide array of microbrews on tap and often featured local bands for happy hour. Lucy had many fond memories of the place from her twenties. But most recently, her memories were of questioning Mac about the death of the town health inspector months ago.

Azad pulled out a bar stool and joined her. Mac McCabe was tending bar. He was a tall man with brown hair tied back in a ponytail, a big smile, and a large beer gut.

"Well, if it ain't Lucy Berberian. I haven't seen you since—"

"Since I questioned you about a murder?"

"Since you found the true murderer and cracked the case, I have no hard feelings. Now, what will you be having tonight?" he asked.

They ordered beers on tap and Mac placed frosty mugs on cardboard coasters that advertised a popular domestic beer.

Azad swiveled on his bar stool and faced Lucy. "Can I be honest about something?"

"Sure."

"I was surprised, but glad, you agreed to go out with me tonight."

Lucy sipped her beer, unsure how to answer. "My mom had something to do with it."

A flicker of disappointment flashed in his eyes. "Ah, I should have known. Angela can be very persuasive."

Lucy set down her mug. "It wasn't like that. Yes, she'd be thrilled to learn that we're out together, but that's not what I meant."

"She doesn't know?"

"No. And she's not why I said yes."

"Then why?"

"My mom pointed out that the past is the past. I know I've changed since living in Philly for five years. It's only fair to believe that you've changed as well. You graduated from culinary school, worked in Atlantic City, and returned to Kebab Kitchen—just like me."

Azad's lips twitched. "There's something about the restaurant that pulls you back time and again. There's no escaping it."

"Tell me about it." She slid her fingers down the frosty mug. "It was unfair of me to judge you about Cressida. I just wish you had told me before Stan Slade showed up and thrust that newspaper picture in my face. Azad, if I'm going to help you, then I need to know *everything*."

"You're right. I'm sorry. It was so long ago, and I was worried about how you would react." He reached out to touch her hand where it rested on the bar. "I swear to you that I never started dating her until a couple months after we broke up."

Her skin tingled from his touch. "I believe you. I guess I was jealous."

"There's nothing to be jealous about. Cressida was never for me."

Lucy felt a thrill to hear it. But her curiosity was

aroused as well. Discussing the subject of Azad's past was the perfect opportunity to learn more. "Since you know her better than I do, what did you think when Stan told us that Cressida had been romantically involved with Henry?"

"The truth is I can't see it at all. Cressida was always vain."

"How so?" Lucy prodded.

"She had her hair color touched up and her nails done weekly. She liked to visit tanning salons, and she shopped a ton, but she also worked out a lot and was a bit of a health freak when it came to her diet."

Lucy recalled the tub of protein powder, health shakes, containers of flax and chia seeds, and the fancy blender that she'd seen in Cressida's kitchen.

"She always went out with a fit crowd. We used to hang out at the gym," Azad said.

Lucy could picture Azad in a weight room, muscles glistening from working out.

An image of Henry at the wedding came to mind. Handsome, but much older. He wouldn't be able to physically compete with men who were thirty years younger.

"There's only one reason I can think of why Cressida would have been with Henry Simms, and it wasn't for love or sex," Azad said.

Money.

Henry had been a bank president and lived in a pricey house with Holly. Cressida must have thought she'd hit the jackpot. It didn't matter that he'd been married.

That was until she'd learned that Henry was broke and his wife held the purse strings to her own trust fund. That must have been a huge blow to Cressida. To top it off, Henry had no intention of leaving his wife.

But Cressida hadn't given up. Somehow, she must have convinced Henry to name her as the beneficiary of his life insurance policy.

Then she'd killed him.

Clever Cressida.

Katie would tell Bill tonight, and he'd relay the information to Clemmons. Surely, the detective would have enough evidence to bring both Cressida and Holly in for further questioning.

Azad looked at his watch. "I almost forgot. I need to make a quick stop at the restaurant before we head to dinner. Do you mind?"

Lucy felt a small surge of disappointment. She'd been enjoying herself, and she didn't want to be reminded of their work. On the other hand, how could she say no? Maybe he forgot his cell phone, house keys, or some other personal item?

She slipped off her bar stool. "Sure."

The back parking lot was dark by the time they reached Kebab Kitchen and Azad parked his truck. He sat back and frowned. "The outside light is out."

"I guess I need to replace the bulb."

"No way. You need a ladder to do it. I'll do it tomorrow."

They got out of the car and walked to the back door that led to the storage room. He pulled out his cell phone and used the flashlight app to illuminate the door as he slipped his key into the lock.

So much for leaving his cell phone behind, she thought.

He opened the door, then flipped on the storage room light. "I promise this won't take long." He held the door for her.

Lucy reluctantly stepped inside.

And halted.

"Oh, my," she said.

Her eyes were drawn to the new steel shelving that lined the perimeter of the storage room. Bags of bulgur and rice, flour and salt, canned items, and jars of spices that had previously been arrayed in a disorganized jumble on wooden pallets were now neatly arranged on the shelves.

"I wanted to surprise you," Azad said.

He had.

She looked at him in amazement. "When did you do this?"

"I worked late last night and all day today when you had off. I knew how the unfinished work troubled you, and I wanted to get it all done."

Her heart took a perilous leap. "Azad, I—"

"But I can't take entire credit for it. Butch took over in the kitchen and Emma handled the dining room so that I could switch jobs from chef to handyman."

She walked the perimeter and reached out to touch the new steel shelves as she envisioned adding additional supplies. It would be much easier, now, to locate items and maintain a consistent inventory. "I don't know what to say, other than 'thank you.'"

Azad pulled a hidden bottle of champagne and two flutes from one of the shelves. "How about we just celebrate with a toast?"

She smiled. "You thought of everything."

"You bet. I want tonight to be special. A new beginning between us." He popped the cork and poured two crystal flutes of golden, bubbly champagne. He handed her a glass and raised his. "To starting over."

Thoughts of maintaining a business relationship or accompanying him tonight just to discuss the murder investigation flew out the window. She was stunned by his thoughtfulness.

She touched her glass to his. "I'll toast to that." She sipped the champagne and the bubbles tickled her nose. She felt a warm glow flow through her and gloried briefly in the shared moment.

Azad stepped close, and reaching out, plucked the flute from her hand. His gaze dropped to her mouth, and she sucked in a breath. There was only one reason a man would look at a woman that way.

His head lowered, his lips inches from hers. Her lips parted and her eyes closed in heightened anticipation.

The storage room door flew open and hit the opposite wall, rattling glass jars on the nearest shelf.

Lucy and Azad jumped apart.

"Lucy!" Michael Citteroni stood in the doorway, his tall, leather-clad frame casting a shadow on the storage room floor.

"What the hell!" Azad exclaimed.

Lucy's gaze flew to the door. "Michael? What's wrong?"

Michael's blue eyes traveled from Lucy to Azad, then back to Lucy. "Sorry for intruding. I was next door in the bike shop and saw a light."

"So you thought to barge in here without knocking," Azad ground out.

A shadow crossed Michael's face as he took in the bottle of champagne and glasses.

Uh-oh. The two men had gotten off to a rough start

months ago. From their exchanged glares, things hadn't gotten better.

Lucy stepped between them. "Michael wouldn't rush here for no reason. What is it?"

"Detective Clemmons stopped a car in front of the bike shop," Michael said. "I thought it was a routine traffic stop at first, but then Holly Simms stepped out. Clemmons read her her rights and took her away in handcuffs. Looks like Henry's murderer was finally arrested. I thought you'd want to know."

Lucy and Azad never made it to dinner. Their evening came to a screeching halt after Michael Citteroni's big news, and Azad seemed to understand. After Lucy promised him a rain date, he'd dropped her off at Katie's and said good night.

As soon as Lucy opened the front door, her cell phone rang. She dug it out of the bottom of her purse. She answered without recognizing the number. "Hello?"

"Lucy Berberian?"

It was a woman's voice, but one she didn't immediately recognize. "This is Lucy. Who is this?"

"It's Holly."

Surprise coursed through her. "Holly Simms?"

"Yes."

Lucy's purse slipped from her fingers and fell to the front hall with a thud. According to Michael, Holly had just been arrested. How could she have been released so quickly?

"How did you get this number?" Lucy asked.

"Scarlet gave it to me. After you accosted me in the

parking lot outside the Big Tease Salon, I asked her for your number."

Lucy had given both Scarlet and Victoria her cell number as a point of contact for the catering.

"First, I didn't accost you. I merely asked you a few questions after you ditched your manicure and ran out like your hair was on fire when Cressida walked into the salon. Second, I take offense at Scarlet handing out my personal information."

Holly's laugh was brittle. "It's a little too late for that."

"How are you calling me, anyway? I heard you were arrested," Lucy blurted out.

"You're my phone call from jail."

"Me? Don't you think you should call a lawyer?"

"I was told you are one."

Lucy's grip on her cell phone tightened. "I'm not a criminal defense attorney. I can't help you."

"I think you can. You know more about this case than the police. I didn't kill my husband."

Was she serious? "Tell that to Detective Clemmons."

"I only get one phone call. Will you give me the courtesy of a visit?"

This didn't make sense. Holly was a wealthy woman with a fat trust fund. Didn't she have a slew of lawyers on call?

"Please," Holly said, her tone turning surprisingly pleading.

Lucy hesitated. Part of her was wildly curious. How had Holly managed to do it? And what story would she concoct in her defense? After breaking into Cressida's home, Lucy was sure either Cressida or Holly had committed the murder.

Cressida had a strong motive after Henry had made her the beneficiary of his life insurance policy, and Holly had motive after learning she'd been duped into signing the policy over to her husband's young lover. But Scarlet and Bradford were still suspects, too.

"All right," Lucy conceded. "I'll be there."

She hung up the phone and leaned against the wall. Now what? Clemmons may be a jerk, but he wouldn't have made an arrest without sufficient evidence. Prosecutor Walsh must have given him the green light. The wily prosecutor wanted a conviction, and fast, but she was also highly intelligent and bound by certain ethical rules. If she didn't think Holly had killed her husband, then she wouldn't have condoned Holly's arrest and risked taking a losing case to court.

So, what had they learned about Holly that had resulted in her arrest over the other suspects?

"Who was that?"

Lucy turned to see Katie, dressed in fuzzy pink slippers and a robe, standing behind her. Her blond hair was in a ponytail and her face had been scrubbed clean of makeup. Clearly her friend had been on her way to bed. Lucy felt guilty for disturbing her, but she knew Katie would want to hear the news.

"You wouldn't believe it," Lucy said. "Holly's been arrested, and her first phone call was to me. She wants me to visit her in jail."

Katie sucked in a breath. "What does she want with you?"

"She thinks I know more about the case than anyone else."

"She's probably right about that."

"She thinks I can help prove her innocence."

A flash of humor crossed Katie's face. "Give me a break. Don't go. She's just going to lie through her teeth."

"I'm prepared for that, but the thing is, I almost feel sorry for her. Her husband cheated with a woman young enough to be their daughter. Then she learned he'd tricked her by having his life insurance changed to list Cressida as the beneficiary."

"Still, somehow she lured him into your catering van, stabbed him to death with your sharp stainless-steel skewers, then allowed your head chef to take the blame," Katie countered.

"But how did she lure Henry into the van in the first place?"

"He was intoxicated. Maybe she enticed him with hanky-panky."

"Seriously?"

"Who knows? But with her arrest, at least Azad is off the hook."

"True." Lucy was relieved that with Holly behind bars, Azad would no longer be a suspect. But her inquisitive mind was not something she could just turn off. Questions arose and plagued her. It was like trying to put together a thousand-piece puzzle without the picture from the box.

How exactly had Holly managed to get Henry into the van? According to Michael, Holly had been chasing him all night and had not been with her husband. Michael had said Holly had disappeared for a half hour period when she'd claimed she'd gone to the ladies' room. Had she somehow enticed Henry to join her in the van then? And how had she managed to open the van? It had been locked, and the only two people who had the key the entire evening were Azad and herself.

"I have questions for Holly. First, how did she get into the locked van?" Lucy said.

Katie twisted her ponytail. "Other than Holly sneaking into the kitchen and stealing the keys, there must have been a way. Think back to that day and retrace your steps."

Lucy's thoughts turned, and the image of the wedding day focused in her memory. "Azad had been driving and I was looking out the window taking in the sights and sounds and reminiscing about how little Ocean Crest had changed since I was a girl. Other than the mansions on Oyster Street and Castle of the Sea, I thought the town had remained the same."

"All right," Katie prodded. "You were looking out the window. You arrived at Castle of the Sea and then . . ."

"Azad hit a pole backing up the van. We jumped out to view the damage. I hoped my dad wouldn't notice, but I suspected he would. Then you arrived with Butch."

"Before you jumped out, did you close your window?"

"My God," Lucy blurted out, then looked at her friend. "That's it! I must have forgotten to roll up the window. The van doesn't have power locks or windows. Azad couldn't have shut my window, and I forgot to do it after the accident. I was concerned with the damage to the bumper, not closing my window. That's how Holly got into the van."

Katie's eyes lit with excitement. "And Holly managed to invite her cheating husband inside and stab him with a shish kebab skewer knowing it would look like someone from the restaurant was the killer."

"Not just someone. Azad. Holly must have known about her husband's troubles as bank president. What if she also knew that Azad hated Henry because of a denied bank loan?"

"Oh, that's good." Katie picked up Lucy's purse from the floor and thrust it at her. "I've changed my mind. Go talk to her."

CHAPTER 21

Officer Bill Watson was the first person Lucy saw as soon as she stepped into the police station Monday morning. Bill was standing behind the front desk sifting through a tall stack of papers and set them aside when the door opened.

"Hey, Lucy. I know why you're here, but I admit to being surprised when Holly Simms used her one phone call to reach out to you."

Lucy squirmed beneath Bill's stare. From the beginning, he'd been crystal clear that he wanted her and Katie to stay out of the investigation. But now all bets were off. He knew they hadn't listened. What she didn't know was what Katie had told Bill of their whereabouts the other evening. Lucy doubted Katie confessed that they'd broken into Cressida's home, hid in her coat closet, and fled across multiple lawns while being pursued by Bradford Papadopoulos.

Taking a deep breath, she decided to answer his question honestly. "I have no idea why Holly wants to see me."

The truth. She couldn't fathom why the woman hadn't called her lawyer.

Bill sighed and let out a puff of air. "All right. Come on. She's in the holding cell." He walked around the desk and held the door for her to enter a corridor that led to the interior of the station. Lucy's gaze immediately sought out one of the closed office doors at the end of the room, which belonged to Detective Calvin Clemmons. She prayed he wasn't inside his office.

Just as they walked by, the door opened and Clemmons stepped out of his office and glared down his long nose at her. "Ms. Berberian."

Lucy cringed. So much for hoping.

"I wish I could say I'm surprised to see you here," he drawled, "but I'm not. I just got off the phone with Prosecutor Walsh."

Lucy kept her expression bland. "Oh? Does she plan on stopping by Kebab Kitchen for lunch?"

"No," Clemmons said, his voice chilly. "She wasn't pleased to hear that you were the first one Mrs. Simms called. She told me to remind you that there could be consequences."

Lucy didn't like his threatening words or his demeanor. She straightened her spine, and her legal training kicked in. "Holly Simms is permitted to place a phone call, and she has a right to legal representation."

"Are you her counsel, then?"

"I'll let you know." She turned to Bill. "Now if you'll please escort me to Mrs. Simms's cell, I'd like to speak with her."

Clemmons's dark eyes flashed, but he didn't say a word. Lucy followed Bill down the hall and around the corner.

"Remind me not to cross you," Bill said.

Lucy's shoulders slumped. "It isn't like that. There's just something about that man that infuriates me."

Bill chuckled. "You're not the only one, but for all his brass I think Clemmons means well."

Bill stopped by a closed door, removed a key ring that was clipped to his waist, unlocked the door, and held it open for Lucy. She stepped inside. The room was a dingy white and in need of a new paint job. A fingerprinting station was in the corner. A duct tape line was glued on a cracked linoleum floor indicating where suspects were to stand to have their mug shots taken. At the end of the room were a set of sliding, outer jail doors. Lucy approached and peeked inside to see four individual cells. Three were empty.

Holly sat on a cot in the last cell.

Ocean Crest was a small town, and prisoners were booked, fingerprinted, and temporarily held here until they could be transported to the larger county jail and held until further legal proceedings. Holly would spend a day here, maybe two days at most, before she would be shipped off to the county jail.

Choosing another key from the ring, Bill slid the jail doors open. "Wait here."

Minutes later, Holly sat at a desk, her hands cuffed to a thick metal ring in the center of the desk. Lucy pulled out a chair and sat across from her.

"Just shout out when you're done," Bill said. He shut the door behind him, and seconds later, the sound of the outer bars slamming closed echoed throughout the room and made Lucy jump.

"Thank you for coming," Holly said.

Dressed in an orange jumpsuit two sizes too big for her frame, Holly looked far from her glamorous self. Her mascara was smudged beneath her eyes and her lipstick was smeared and faded. Holly had been arrested not long ago, and it was evident by her full face of makeup that she'd been headed somewhere when Clemmons had pulled her over in front of Michael's bicycle shop and arrested her.

"Hello, Holly," Lucy said. "I'm still unsure why you wasted your one phone call by reaching out to me. You need to contact a criminal defense attorney."

Holly rubbed her eyes and the handcuffs rattled on the desk. Her wedding ring was missing, and Lucy knew the police had taken and bagged all her valuables.

"My lawyer already knows. I was talking to him on my cell phone about my trust fund when that crass detective pulled me over and read me my rights. My attorney is on his way from New York City."

"Good to know. But that doesn't explain my presence here."

"Like I said over the phone, you know this case better than anyone. Don't you want to clear your boyfriend's name?"

"Azad Zakarian's not my boyfriend. He's my head chef."

"Right," Holly said in a tone that suggested she didn't believe a word Lucy said. "Anyway, you've been asking questions about Henry's death, and you are smarter than that detective."

Lucy couldn't argue with that.

"The police believe you killed your husband," Lucy said. "You knew he was having an affair with the much younger Cressida Connolly. I also suspect Henry tricked you into signing a change of beneficiary form to make Cressida the beneficiary of his life insurance, and you were shocked when you finally learned the truth. And worst of all, Cressida had convinced Henry to finally leave you. So, you see, all the evidence points to you as the killer."

"All the evidence is wrong." Holly glared at her, a fierce light glowing in her eyes.

It was Lucy's turn to arch a skeptical brow.

"I admit to being upset and humiliated when I learned about his affair with that *girl.* But I didn't learn about the change of beneficiary until *after* Henry died and I tried to collect the money. You're also right that Henry handled all our taxes and important paperwork and for years I blindly signed any documents he thrust beneath my nose. But you're wrong about one thing: Henry was not going to leave me."

Holly had been insistent about this from the beginning, but how could she be sure?

"Maybe you were clueless about the life insurance," Lucy conceded. "But as to whether or not Henry was going to leave you is your word against Cressida's. A jury may still find that you had sufficient motive and opportunity to get rid of your husband."

"What opportunity? Henry was killed outside Castle of the Sea, and I never left the building."

"I know you were with Michael Citteroni during most of the reception except—"

Holly's green gaze sharpened. "He's handsome, isn't he? Surely, you've noticed. You do have a thing for tall, dark, and handsome men."

Lucy ignored the barb. "As I was saying, Michael can vouch for your whereabouts *except* for a half hour when you supposedly went to the ladies' room near the end of the evening. A half hour in which you have no alibi during the precise time that your husband was murdered. You could have snuck outside to break into the catering van, lured your husband inside, and stabbed him."

"Impossible!" Holly's eyes flashed with outrage. "I was in the ladies' room, and I have two witnesses who will testify to that fact. I have an alibi for the *entire* evening."

"Who?"

"Edna and Edith Gray."

Lucy was taken aback. "The owners of Gray's Novelty Shop on the boardwalk?"

"Yes. Go ask them for yourself. The sisters were going at it fighting over the addition of hermit crabs to sell in their shop. Edith said the crabs stink, and Edna said that kids love them and they will attract tourists. I've known the sisters for years and mediated their argument. Talk to them and see. I never left the building that night. I couldn't have killed my husband."

Lucy had jogged the Ocean Crest boardwalk and passed Gray's Novelty Shop more times than she could count. T-shirts with various logos such as "Call Me on My Shell," "Salty Hair & Sandy Toes," and "Ocean Crest Beach Patrol" hung on racks beside shelves crammed with beach pails and sand shovels, towels, and boogie boards. The only difference was that today a large glass tank sat in the front of the shop. Lucy peered inside the tank to see a dozen hermit crabs, their shells painted different colors and designs.

Edna had clearly won the argument over the crabs.

Edna and Edith Gray were never-married sisters in
their seventies and fixtures in town. Edna was tall and
rail thin with a pointed nose, while Edith was short
and heavyset with a nose that resembled a ripe tomato.
Lucy had saved her teenage allowance and purchased
her first boogie board in their shop, and she'd spent
countless hours catching waves in the surf.

Edith's smile beamed and she stopped rearranging
bottles of sunscreen on a shelf as soon as she spotted
Lucy. "Well, if it isn't Lucy Berberian. We ate lunch at
Kebab Kitchen a couple weeks back. The tabbouleh
salad was tasty. How are your parents, dear?"

"Hello, Edith. Mom and Dad are semiretired now."

"Only partly?" Edna asked from where she was
counting change behind the register. She removed
her reading glasses and they dangled from a chain
around her neck.

Lucy shrugged, smiling. "They are having trouble
letting go completely."

"I can sympathize. When you put years into a
business, it's hard to just walk away. It's like putting
someone out to pasture," Edna said.

Lucy had never thought of it that way. It explained
why her dad kept showing up in the office and finishing payroll or meddling with inventory in the
storage room, and why her mother kept returning to
the kitchen at the crack of dawn. "I guess I see your
point."

Edith made a face at her sister. "Well, Angela and
Raffi are lucky they have you to take over the place.
Nothing like family. We weren't fortunate enough to
have children. When we retire, we will have to sell the
place." Edith placed the bottle of sunscreen she'd

been holding on the shelf and approached. "Now, what can we help you with, my dear?"

"I remember seeing you both at Scarlet and Bradford's wedding. I want to ask you a few questions about that night," Lucy said.

Edna clucked her tongue. "It was a tragedy. We were both invited because Bradford wanted to film a scene outside our shop. But we were also longtime friends of Mr. And Mrs. Simms. We took out a second loan about ten years ago to expand our store, and Henry's bank gave us the business loan. We wouldn't be as successful without his help. We were shocked to learn of his death."

Edith clucked her tongue. "Poor Holly," she said.

The sisters didn't know Holly had been recently arrested for the murder of her husband, and Lucy didn't enlighten them. "Holly said she talked to both of you in the ladies' room near the end of the reception. Something about a fight over hermit crabs?"

Edna's face grew red. Edith's lips thinned.

"It's true," Edna spoke up. "I wanted hermit crabs. She didn't."

"One or two crabs don't smell, but two dozen or so in one tank do. The smell makes me sick," Edith said. "I know it sounds ridiculous since we own a store on the boardwalk a stone's throw from the beach, but it's true."

"I couldn't help but notice the tank of hermit crabs at the front of the store as I came inside," Lucy said.

"We compromised," Edna said. "I can order them for the store, but only if I put the tank as far away from the register as possible and clean it regularly. Meanwhile"—she glared at her sister—"we've been selling them like hotcakes."

"Harumph." Edith set her chin in a stubborn line. "If you subtract the upkeep from the profit, I still think they aren't worth the hassle."

"They bring in additional business. Kids and their parents have to walk through the store to pay for the crabs and they almost always buy something else," Edna argued.

"Like I said, the smell turns my stomach," Edith said. "But they're bearable at the very front of the store, and she's willing to be the one to clean the tank and handle them in order to make a sale."

Goodness. The sisters still sounded like they needed mediation. The last thing Lucy wanted was to get involved in their bickering. "Did Holly Simms stay with both of you in the ladies' room until you sorted your problem out, then return to the party?"

"That's right. We couldn't have come to an amicable solution without her," said Edith.

"That was about a half hour?" Lucy asked.

Both sisters nodded.

"And you saw Holly walk back to the reception?"

"I remember because the band announced they would only play a few more songs and started the conga when we followed Holly out of the ladies' room," said Edna.

"We also saw her chase down Mr. Citteroni's handsome son to dance." Edith winked. "He's too young for Holly, but he would be perfect for you, Lucy."

Oh, brother. Her mother's matchmaking efforts were enough to last her lifetime. She didn't need the advice of two more old ladies.

"That's all right," Lucy said politely as her mind processed what she'd learned from the sisters.

Holly had told the truth. The Gray sisters, along

with Michael, provided a solid alibi for Holly Simms. She couldn't have killed her husband. Once Lucy conveyed what she'd learned to Clemmons, he'd have no choice but to release Holly.

"Thank you for answering my questions." Lucy wandered to the front of the shop to eye the hermit crab tank. "I'd like to buy two crabs."

"You don't have to do that," Edna said.

"Oh, but I do! My niece, Niari, would love them." If Emma didn't approve, then her sister would have to cope. As far as Lucy was concerned, Emma's past had caused more problems with Calvin Clemmons than any crime scene evidence. A pair of tiny hermit crabs was a small price to pay for all the hassle.

Lucy thought about everything she'd learned as Edna fished out two hermit crabs and placed them in a small plastic tank that would house the crabs. Holly's alibi had checked out. But the big question still remained unanswered: who had murdered Henry Simms?

Out of the remaining suspects, one had the strongest motive.

Specifically, a million bucks to kill her lover.

Cressida.

CHAPTER 22

The following day, Kebab Kitchen was opened to a crowd of hungry lunch tourists and regulars.

"Where's all the hummus?" Emma cried. "The hummus bar is nearly empty and I have customers waiting!"

Lucy rushed out of the kitchen, carrying a tray that held bins. "Here are three varieties," she said. "Lemon pucker, extra garlic, and basil pesto."

Emma made a face. "I need fire-roasted red pepper, artichoke, and two more bins of traditional hummus. It's the most popular."

"Butch is working on it as we speak. They will be right out."

Emma grabbed the tray from Lucy. "I'll refill these. You tell Butch to hurry up."

The rest of the lunch menu was traditional Mediterranean food featuring *lamajoon* or Armenian pizza—a thin, flat bread with ground meat and spices—a vegetarian bake with eggplant, onions, and mushrooms, and Greek souvlaki. For the seafood lovers, there was fresh flounder delivered by fishers who fished during the season. Flaky baklava and walnut cookies were on the dessert menu.

Lucy ran around manning the register, chatting with customers, helping Emma and Sally pack up leftovers and take-out orders, and overseeing the staff. For a few hectic hours, she'd forgotten about the murder. Then lunch had dwindled down to a dull roar just before three—the recovery period before dinner service.

She spotted Azad heading into the walk-in refrigerator and hurried to catch up with him. He was placing a tray of freshly made baklava on a wire shelf as she stepped inside. The large restaurant refrigerator might be chilly, but it was the one place they were guaranteed privacy in the busy kitchen.

As the door swung closed behind her, a memory rushed back of the two of them locked in the cold place together three months ago. For safety reasons, the walk-in refrigerator didn't have a lock on the outside, but nonetheless, they'd found themselves trapped inside. When the door had finally been opened, Lucy had learned that foul play had been involved. But for that time period, Lucy and Azad had shared body heat to stay warm and he'd almost kissed her, just like he'd come close to kissing her in the storage room the other night.

Her heart hammered foolishly in her chest. Would they ever get the chance again? And if they did kiss, would it harm their working relationship?

"You all right, Lucy?" Azad asked as he slid the tray on the shelf, then straightened to look at her quizzically.

Lucy was suddenly nervous. "I was thinking about last night," she blurted out.

His eyes darkened with emotion, and she realized

she'd made a blunder. He was clearly thinking of how they'd been interrupted by Michael. Her face heated.

"I thought about it all last night," he said.

"You did?"

Azad folded his arms across his chest. "I never much liked that bike shop guy, and I like him even less now."

"Oh." How was she supposed to respond to that? A part of her wanted to avoid talking about Michael; another part of her was flattered that Azad was jealous.

His eyes were a lighter shade of brown beneath the florescent lights. "I'd like a rain check. I'd also still like to take you to dinner."

"I'd like that."

"Great. I need to prep for tonight's service. Is there something else you needed?" he asked.

He didn't know about the latest turn of events regarding Holly. Azad thought she remained incarcerated and that he was in the clear. What was the best way to break the bad news? *Just spit it out*, she thought.

"Holly Simms didn't murder her husband."

"Pardon?"

"Her alibi checked out. Detective Clemmons had no choice but to release her. I'm sorry."

His expression clouded and she could just imagine what he was thinking. With Holly in the clear, would Detective Clemmons focus on Azad once again?

"Don't be sorry," he said. "I wouldn't want an innocent woman to take the fall. The detective has to keep investigating."

She hoped he would. "I haven't given up yet, either."

His expression was intense. "I never thought you would. If there's one thing I know about you, it's that you are determined and you never give up when you set your mind to do something."

"It's a Berberian family trait. I'm stubborn and mulish. Just like my mom and dad."

"Well, I think it's a good thing and I admire you a lot for it."

She felt a lurch of excitement. It was one of the nicest compliments he'd given her. She cleared her throat. "Azad, I need to ask you more about Cressida."

He stuffed his hands into his pockets. "She's in my past, and I thought we said all that had to be said."

"We did. But this is about the investigation."

Two deep lines of worry appeared between his eyes. "What do you want to know?"

"Has she always lived in Ocean Crest?"

"No. She lived with her mom when I knew her back then, a couple of towns over in Baytown."

"Her mom?" When Lucy had questioned Cressida at Pages Bookstore, Cressida had mentioned she'd been born in Baytown and that her mother had died several years ago.

"Yeah. Cressida was raised by her mom. Mrs. Connolly was a nice lady, but overprotective of Cressida. She used to call Cressida when we were out to be sure what time she came home. From what I can tell, she's still overprotective. I ran into her about four months ago at Holloway's. I remember because she asked me the strangest thing. She suspected her daughter was dating someone and wondered if I knew who he was."

"You saw Cressida's mother a couple of months ago? She's still alive?"

"Sure is. I bumped into her in the produce section of Holloway's. She's only in her fifties. I know because Cressida had taken me to her mother's surprise fortieth birthday party in Atlantic City back then. Her full name is Catherine Connolly."

Cressida had lied and said her mother had died. Why? Did Cressida have a falling out with her mom? Or was there another reason? Did she not want her mother to know about her affair with an older, married man? It made sense if Mrs. Connolly was asking Azad if he knew the identity of her daughter's significant other.

"Why are you asking? Is Cressida's mom important to the murder investigation?" Azad asked.

Lucy rubbed the gooseflesh rising on her arms. "I'm not sure she is. I'll let you know."

Lucy left the walk-in refrigerator and passed through the kitchen. She waved to Butch on her way. "Great lunch service, Lucy Lou!" he called out as he lifted the lid from a stockpot to add spices.

Once in the storage room, she headed for her tiny corner office, picked up the landline, and dialed.

Katie answered on the first ring. "Ocean Crest Town Hall."

"Katie, it's me. I just learned from Azad that Cressida's mother is alive. Her name is Catherine Connolly and she lives in Baytown." Lucy had already informed Katie all about Holly's alibi late last night. She'd also informed Bill, who in turn had spoken with Detective Clemmons. That was one conversation she hadn't wanted to be a part of.

"You think it's important?" Katie asked.

"It may be. Can you search her name?"

"I'm already on it."

Lucy heard the tapping of computer keys and she knew Katie was accessing the county tax records. "One-thirty-three Crestview Drive in Baytown. Catherine

Connolly is listed as the original owner and last paid her property taxes in March."

"She *is* still alive! I need to find out why Cressida lied."

"I get off at five."

Lucy knew exactly what Katie meant, and this time she was in full agreement. "I wouldn't dream of going to see Mrs. Connolly without you."

"Good. You should know Clemmons released Holly early this afternoon. I stopped by to see Bill for lunch, and I could hear her screaming for her clothes and jewelry from outside the station."

Lucy could picture an irate Holly Simms accompanied by her expensive defense attorney. "I almost feel sorry for Investigator Clemmons."

"Don't. Now that Holly has a solid alibi, Bill said that Clemmons has turned his attention back to Azad."

CHAPTER 23

Baytown was two towns north of Ocean Crest. On the bay side rather than the ocean, the town wasn't a huge draw for summer tourists and had only a few summer rentals. The houses were cookie cutter colonials built in the early sixties, with one-car garages and long front porches with rocking chairs. It was trash collection day, and garbage cans stood at every curb like shiny, aluminum sentinels. Seagulls soared above looking for food from cans that had lost their lids.

An orange and black cat darted past Lucy as she sat in Katie's jeep outside Catherine Connolly's home. "That looked like Gadoo."

"You don't think your restaurant cat travels this far, do you?" Katie asked.

"Who knows? I've often wondered if numerous families feed him."

"I doubt it. No one feeds people or animals quite like your mom," Katie said. "Bill wants to move into your parents' house."

Lucy laughed. "He can have my old bedroom. He'd gain ten pounds in a week."

"Don't encourage him," Katie chided. She leaned back in her seat. "Are you ready to do this?"

Lucy nodded. "You bet. Let's find out why Cressida lied about her mother."

Katie shut the door to the jeep and they walked up the sidewalk toward a tan house with blue shutters and an American flag flying in the breeze.

"This is it. One-thirty-three Crestview Drive." Katie pointed to a mailbox by the curb.

"It looks like a nice enough place," Lucy said.

"Have you figured out what you're going to say?"

"Yes. Just let me do the talking and you follow along."

"I'm impressed," Katie said. "You're much better at this now."

"Better at lying? I'm not sure that's a compliment," Lucy retorted.

"It is if it gets Azad off the hook."

A knot tightened in Lucy's stomach, and she struggled with an unexpected uncertainty. If she was getting better at misleading people in order to gather information, what did that say about her?

You don't have a choice, Lucy, she told herself. *Think of Azad.*

Taking a breath, Lucy reached for the brass knocker and rapped on the door twice.

Moments later, the door opened. A tall, auburn-haired woman who was an older version of Cressida stared down at them. She was attractive and dressed in a simple, floral sundress and wore light makeup. "May I help you?"

Lucy smiled. "I'm Lucy Berberian and this is Katie Watson. We went to Carlton High School with Cressida Connolly, and we are on the reunion committee.

We were wondering if Cressida still lives here. We would like her to join our committee."

"How nice," Mrs. Connolly said. "I wish I could help you girls, but Cressida doesn't live here anymore. She's been away for quite some time."

"Oh, what a shame," Katie said.

"You can still help," Lucy said. "Our homes as well as the school basement were flooded by the horrible hurricane a few years ago and our yearbooks were damaged. Do you know if Cressida left her yearbook at home or if you have any pictures at all? It would be a great help."

"Of course." Mrs. Connolly opened the door wide. "Please come inside."

"Thank you," Lucy said as they made their way inside. The home was tidy, with beige walls and country-style oak furniture. A piano was situated in the corner with framed pictures of Cressida as a baby. The decor was neat but slightly outdated, and certainly not lavish and costly compared to Cressida's current standard of living.

Mrs. Connolly motioned for them to sit on a sofa. "Would you girls like iced tea?" she asked.

"That would be lovely," Lucy said.

Mrs. Connolly left to go into the kitchen. Moments later they heard the sound of ice rattling in glasses.

"Now what?" Katie whispered.

"I don't know, but I'd like to look around."

Mrs. Connolly returned with a tray holding two glasses filled with ice and a pitcher of fresh iced tea. She poured two glasses and handed them to Lucy and Katie.

"I'm sorry I don't have any cookies. I used to bake

all the time, but now I don't bother, with Cressida not living at home."

"Does she visit?"

A wistful look crossed Mrs. Connolly's face. "Oh, not as often as I'd like. She's busy taking college courses and she runs with a different crowd now."

"Pardon our saying so, but we remember her hanging out with Scarlet Westwood in high school."

Mrs. Connolly smoothed her dress and picked at an invisible piece of lint. "Yes, they met in school. I was never thrilled with their friendship. Too much partying and not enough studying. Cressida's grades weren't good enough to get into college, and now she's trying to make up for it with online college classes."

"She was always smart in high school," Katie said.

Lucy's fingers tensed in her lap. They had no idea if Cressida had been a good student or not.

But Mrs. Connolly merely smiled. "She is a bright girl."

Lucy cleared her throat. "Can we look at the pictures?"

"Oh, yes. Of course. They are all in Cressida's old bedroom. Why don't you girls follow me and I'll let you sift through her bookshelf to see what you can find."

This suited Lucy just fine. She wasn't interested in old yearbooks, but in snooping around to learn more about Cressida. With Holly out of the picture, Lucy was convinced that Cressida was most likely the murderer.

She just needed sufficient evidence to prove it.

They followed Mrs. Connolly up the stairs to the second floor. Passing two bedrooms, she stopped at the last room and opened the door. They stepped inside. The room was decorated in shades of pink, from a pink flowered bedspread, to matching curtains, to a shaggy carpet. The walls were painted a Pepto-Bismol pink, and framed prints of flowers hung on the walls. The only pieces of furniture that stood out were two white bookshelves with children's bookends of Winnie the Pooh holding a row of photo albums in place.

"I haven't changed it much. All of Cressida's old belongings and photo albums are still on these two bookshelves," Mrs. Connolly said, motioning to the shelves. "Take your time and call out if you need anything." She turned to leave.

They spent a good half hour flipping through photo albums and Carlton High School yearbooks.

Lucy reached for an album and flipped to a page showing Holly and Scarlet with thumbs-up at a football game. Their eyes were wide and glassy.

"Looks like they smuggled beer into the high school game," Katie said, glancing at the photo.

Lucy chuckled and closed the album to return it to the shelf when a photograph slipped from the pages and fluttered to the carpet. She bent and picked it up, then took a quick breath of utter astonishment. "My God. Look at this."

"What?"

The photograph was old, taken on a Polaroid camera, and Lucy was careful to hold it at the edges. "It's Cressida around four years old with her mother and a man. A much younger Henry Simms."

"You sure?"

"There's no mistaking his face. He has a fuller head of hair and is even thinner, but it's him."

Katie looked at her in surprise. "You're right! It's Mrs. Connolly and Henry Simms, and they're hugging Cressida as a toddler. They look like . . . like a family."

"They are." The shock of discovery hit Lucy full force now.

"That means—"

"Henry was Cressida's *father*, not her lover."

A soft gasp escaped Katie. "Wow! We had it all wrong."

Lucy's brows set in a straight line. "Everyone had it all wrong."

"Do you think Cressida murdered her own father?"

"I don't know." Lucy turned the photograph over, but there was nothing written on the back. No names or dates. Making a quick decision, she unzipped her purse.

"What are you doing?"

Lucy whipped out her phone and took a picture of the Polaroid. "I'm collecting evidence. It's time I had another chat with Cressida."

CHAPTER 24

Lucy kicked up sand as she sprinted away from the boardwalk and ran onto the beach. Her nerves had been tense since leaving Catherine Connolly's house. She still found it hard to believe that Henry Simms was Cressida's father.

Why keep it secret after all these years?

Her mind turned back to when she and Katie had broken into Cressida's home. Framed pictures of Cressida and Henry had been displayed on the end table. Henry had his arm around Cressida and she'd been smiling and gazing up at him. Lucy had assumed they were lovers, but thinking back, the position wasn't a romantic one; it had been merely affectionate.

Like a father hugging his daughter.

Lucy's mind had seen what it expected to see rather than seeing the truth.

After Lucy and Katie had left Mrs. Connolly's home, they'd driven by Cressida's house but Cressida's car hadn't been in the driveway. It was Lucy's evening off and she'd decided to go for a jog. The exercise was a good way to relieve stress and to gather her thoughts.

After jogging for thirty minutes, she slowed down by her favorite lookout—the jetty overlooking the Atlantic Ocean. It was well after five o'clock, and the tourists had left to shower and change for an evening on the boards. The day visitors had long since departed for their drive home. She was alone, save for a man with a metal detector and earbuds scanning the abandoned beach for coins or jewelry lost by unfortunate tourists.

Breathing in the ocean air, she sat on the jetty and sipped from her water bottle. Seagulls circled above, and a crane searching for its next meal skimmed the water. Her body was exhausted, but her mind kept chugging away.

Had Cressida murdered her father?

Cressida didn't strike Lucy as a cold-blooded killer, but what did Lucy really know about her? Catherine Connolly had raised Cressida as a single mother. Henry had been married to Holly at the time Cressida was born, which meant Henry and Catherine must have had an affair.

Henry hadn't publicly acknowledged Cressida. If they'd reconciled, maybe Cressida was bitter that her father had abandoned her and her mother. Surely that was motive for murder.

But where did the life insurance policy come into play? Had Henry felt guilty for not being a part of Cressida's life, and decided to look after her in death?

And why did Cressida lie about her mother being dead? Was it because Mrs. Connolly wouldn't have approved of Cressida reaching out to her biological father after all these years?

Lucy still couldn't fathom killing a parent, but if Cressida wasn't the killer, then she was running out of suspects. She'd have to come up with others, but she had no idea where to start.

She left the jetty, took off her running shoes and socks, and dipped her toes in the water. The ocean water was cool and refreshing. The ocean temperature had reached seventy-two degrees, good swimming temperature for July in Lucy's opinion. Carrying her shoes and socks, she walked back on the beach, her feet splashing in the surf, her thoughts turning.

Her cell phone rang.

After her experience of jogging without her phone when Scarlet had scared her, Lucy had made it a point to carry her cell phone. She answered on the third ring. "Hello."

"This is Cressida Connolly. My mother left me an interesting message today."

Lucy's stomach tilted. "Oh?"

"Funny, I didn't know we went to Carlson High School together."

Lucy's throat closed up. This didn't bode well. Lucy had planned to visit Cressida and catch her off guard with the picture on her cell phone. Now Cressida knew Lucy had lied to her mother and visited her childhood home.

"How did you get my cell phone number?" Lucy clutched the phone tight.

"Scarlet gave it to me. You did cater her wedding, after all." Bitterness spilled over into Cressida's tone.

Good grief. First Holly, now Cressida. Had Scarlet given her private cell phone number to everyone in town?

Lucy chose her words carefully. "I think we should talk."

"I'm home," Cressida said tersely. "Don't make me wait."

The line went dead.

"You sure about this?" Katie asked.

Lucy nodded. "I am. Cressida called me. This is my chance to get to the bottom of this once and for all."

They stood outside Cressida's home on Oyster Street, but this time, they hadn't walked, and Lucy had parked her Toyota in the driveway.

"What if she's dangerous?" Katie turned to her from the passenger seat.

Lucy put the car in park. "That's why I'm not here alone."

Katie nodded, as if that made perfect sense. "Okay. Let's do this then."

Stepping out of the car, they made their way to the porch steps. The door opened before Lucy had a chance to knock. Dressed in an old Phillies T-shirt and black sweatpants, Cressida stood in the doorway. Her red hair was pulled away from her face in a simple ponytail and, for the first time since Lucy had ever seen her, she wasn't wearing any makeup.

Lucy was still in her running gear, capris and an Eagles tank top. It looked like they were both Philadelphia sports fans.

"Come in." Cressida turned and walked inside.

Lucy closed the door, and they followed Cressida into the family room. Cressida sat on one of the oversized chairs, and Lucy and Katie settled on the sofa in front of the coffee table. The family room looked the same as the last time Lucy and Katie had broken into the house. Glass paperweights held down stacks of papers on the coffee table. Lucy glanced at the paperwork, wondering if the life insurance documents were still there.

Cressida's eyes narrowed. "Why'd you show up at my mother's house?"

"Why'd you lie and tell Lucy your mother was dead?" Katie countered.

Lucy raised a hand to stop the two from arguing. "None of that matters now. We know the truth. Henry Simms was your father."

Cressida looked pained, but she didn't try to deny it. "How did you figure it out?"

"We found a picture in your mother's home." Lucy took her cell phone from her purse, pulled up the picture, and set her phone on the coffee table. "It's of you, your mom, and Henry, and you look about four years old."

"I was three and a half in that picture. Henry was my father."

"Why didn't you tell anyone? The police?" Katie asked.

"Henry didn't want anyone to know, especially Holly. I respected his wishes," Cressida said.

"Even now?" Lucy asked.

Cressida reached for a tissue from a box on the table and blew her nose. Her eyes were red, and Lucy suspected she'd recently cried.

"Holly couldn't have children," Cressida began. "Henry said that she went to a fertility doctor and had numerous miscarriages. She was heartbroken in the early years of their marriage. I was the product of a one-night stand between Henry and my mother. He knew his infidelity, combined with how easily my mother got pregnant, would devastate Holly. He wanted to protect her and keep it secret."

A partner at Lucy's former law firm had unsuccessfully gone through fertility treatments. The woman had been her friend and she'd once confessed that the hormones, combined with the desperation of wanting children, had left her devastated and feeling inadequate as a woman despite all her professional success.

"Growing up, did you know Henry was your father?" Lucy asked.

"No. My mother told me my dad had been in the service and had died overseas during a training accident. I never questioned it until years later when I was working on a family tree for a school project. My mother was very secretive and it made me curious. She finally admitted the truth and revealed my father's identity."

"You must have been shocked to learn that your father was not only alive, but that he lived only a few towns away," Katie said.

Cressida's expression hardened. "Shocked . . . angry . . . unwanted. I felt a lot of things. I finally decided to reach out to him about a year ago to see what kind of man would abandon his kid. He agreed to meet me at a coffee shop. I was bitter toward him at first, but he was genuinely happy to meet me, and he explained about the past." She blew her nose again, her eyes softening. "I realized he never wanted to abandon me, but thought he had done what was best for everyone. He *wanted* a relationship with me. We met in secret twice a week after that, and we were getting to know each other."

"Holly thought you were lovers. Don't you think the truth would have been less painful?" Lucy asked.

Cressida shook her head. "Henry didn't think so."

"What about the life insurance?" Katie prodded.

A look of tired sadness passed over Cressida's features. "He said he felt guilty for never providing for me as a kid. He continued to feel guilty that he couldn't help because Holly held the purse strings. But he was adamant that he wanted to care for me in case something happened to him. It was his idea to make me the beneficiary. I never cared about the money. I wanted more time with my father. I grew to love him."

Lucy felt a jolt of sympathy. "Do you think Holly learned the truth?"

"That I was Henry's daughter? No, I don't. We were very careful."

"But Bradford knew," Katie said.

Cressida looked at her in surprise. "How do you know that?"

Lucy wanted to elbow Katie in the ribs. She wasn't about to slip that they'd hidden in Cressida's coat closet and had overheard her speak with Bradford. He'd never come out and said he knew, but he'd mentioned a secret.

Some things are better left unsaid.

Lucy shrugged a shoulder. "It doesn't matter how we know. But are we right?"

Cressida sighed. "You are. He stopped by unannounced one night to talk about how we were going to get Scarlet to her surprise bridal shower. Henry was here, and I was telling him things about my childhood. Henry asked me lots of questions and said how he wished he hadn't missed out. Bradford overheard enough to figure out the truth. I made him swear never to tell a soul, especially Scarlet."

"Scarlet didn't know?" Lucy asked, surprised. She'd eavesdropped on the two women in the park and they'd discussed Henry. Or had they? Thinking back, Scarlet had challenged Cressida to confront Holly Simms. But maybe Scarlet had thought Cressida was sleeping with Henry, not that he was her father.

"Scarlet is your best friend. Why wouldn't you tell her?" Lucy asked.

"Oh, please. Scarlet is a gossipmonger. She may be my friend, but I know her weaknesses. She can't keep a secret to save her life."

"Do you know who was most likely to harm Henry?" Lucy asked.

Cressida's blue eyes blazed with sudden anger. "His wife. Holly is a witch, and she constantly nagged and screamed at Henry for his failures. She held her trust fund over his head. She's a bitch, and I say she stabbed him."

Lucy shook her head. "She didn't. Holly has a solid alibi. Who else would want to kill your father?"

Was it Scarlet or Bradford? Their motives were financial. Henry's unethical banking practices had put Scarlet and Bradford in a bad position for their business venture. They'd already written checks to their employees and contractors that had bounced.

"My father wasn't without his own weaknesses," Cressida admitted. "He liked to live a wealthy lifestyle and enjoyed sports betting. But the thing is, I suspected he was having an affair."

"With whom?" Lucy asked.

"I'm not sure. But one time when he picked me up I noticed flowers and perfume in the backseat of his car. They weren't for me. And I *know* they weren't for Holly."

A thought barely crossed Lucy's mind before another followed. "You said perfume. Do you recall what kind?"

"Regency Garden. I know because I worked in a department store at the perfume counter during high school. It's overwhelmingly flowery and very pricey. It's a favorite with old ladies. Scarlet's mother wears it and I smelled it on Scarlet's wedding planner, Ms. Redding. I know it wasn't one of them, but he had to be seeing someone closer to his own age."

Lucy's heart hammered in her chest. Victoria Redding was an older woman who wore strong floral perfume that made her nose twitch. Could she have possibly been romantically involved with Henry?

"What makes you think Victoria wasn't Henry's lover?" Lucy asked.

Cressida blinked. "Simple. Everyone knew they hated each other. And Henry never said a word about her to me when we met. Why?"

Lucy wasn't convinced. Henry was just getting to know his daughter. Maybe he didn't want to share that part of his life with her. Lucy's mind spun with this new information. All the pieces were there; she just needed to put them together.

She frowned as memories came back in a rush. Victoria fighting with Henry in the back of Castle of the Sea.

My God. What had they said?

Henry: *"You owe me. I got you this job, remember?"*

Victoria: *"You never let me forget it."*

Henry: *"Then we're even now."*

Victoria: *"Even? I put everything on the line for you. We're far from even."*

Lucy had thought they were fighting over his behavior at the wedding and the fact that Henry had gotten Victoria the job as the wedding planner. But it wasn't Henry's drunken antics that had set Victoria off. It was his supposed affair with Cressida.

Victoria was the scorned lover, not Cressida.

And she killed him for it.

CHAPTER 25

Lucy drove Katie back to her house and dropped her off. Bill's car wasn't in the driveway. "Where's Bill?" Lucy asked.

Katie stood outside the car and spoke to Lucy through the window. "He's at the station."

"Good. Call him and tell him everything that we learned."

Katie leaned in the window and squeezed Lucy's shoulder. "I'll give you a buzz as soon as Victoria Redding is arrested."

"Amen to that."

"Where are you going now?" Katie asked.

"Back to the restaurant. I have to finish inventory." Now that the steel shelving was installed, it would be a pleasure, rather than a chore.

Katie gave her a thumbs-up. "Good work, Lucy."

"You too. I couldn't have figured it out without you."

Katie waved as Lucy pulled out of the driveway. She thought about the day's events as she drove down Ocean Avenue. Victoria was the killer, and as soon as Clemmons learned all the facts, she'd be behind bars today. Azad would breathe a lot easier tonight.

And so would she.

Lucy parked in the back of the restaurant and stepped out of the car. "Gadoo!" She scanned the area for the orange and black cat. She'd picked up extra liver treats and had stashed them in the storage room on one of the shelves closest to the door. She called out several times, but the cat was nowhere to be found.

She was about to head inside when the sound of a car engine pulling into the lot made her turn around. A spanking new white Cadillac, parked next to her Toyota. The door opened and Victoria Redding stepped out.

Alarm bells went off inside Lucy's head. What was she doing here? Did she know that Lucy had spoken with Cressida?

Impossible.

There had to be another reason for Victoria to just show up. Lucy's best bet was to act innocent of all knowledge, get away from her as fast as possible, then call Bill or Detective Clemmons at the station.

Lucy pasted on a smile. "Hello, Ms. Redding. Can I help you with something?"

Victoria was dressed in dark slacks, a cream-colored top, and gold sandals. Without her customary high heels, she wasn't much taller than Lucy. She'd never seen the woman without fancy clothes and heavy makeup. But the scent of a flower bouquet was still present and tickled her nose. It wasn't as pungent today—but the scent was still there. Lucy wondered if it had permeated all the clothing in her drawers.

"I have the final catering payment for you." Victoria fished inside her purse and pulled out a white envelope.

Relief swept through Lucy as she reached for the

envelope. *Thank goodness.* Victoria was here to pay her, nothing more. She had no idea that Lucy knew the truth. "Thanks for delivering the check. Please excuse me, but I have a lot of work to do inside."

As Lucy turned to leave, she glanced inside the Cadillac. Two large duffel bags rested on the backseat. One of the bags wasn't zipped all the way and some clothes had spilled out. What the heck? Victoria was leaving town, and it looked like she'd packed in a hurry. A new sense of urgency fired her gut—she needed to call the police and tell them that Victoria was on the run. "Thanks again." Lucy waved the envelope and reached for the back door.

Victoria's expression hardened. "Not so fast, Ms. Berberian."

"Sorry, but I really must—"

"I have something else for you."

"Nonsense. I'm sure this payment is more than enough—" Lucy stopped short as Victoria reached inside her purse to pull out a handgun. She aimed it straight for Lucy's heart.

"You've been asking too many questions from the beginning." Victoria leveled her gaze on Lucy, her eyes taking on an ominous look.

Lucy's heart skittered at the sight of the gun—a shiny, silver revolver. "I don't know what you're talking about."

"Don't play dumb with me. You're too nosy for your own good." Victoria jerked the gun toward the Cadillac. "Get in the car."

"You can't be serious?"

Victoria's face became red and blotchy with anger. "In. Now. Or I'll shoot you."

Lucy believed her. Victoria was deranged if she

thought she could get away with this. But then she'd killed once already. She had to be mad.

Lucy scanned the parking lot, desperate to leave some kind of clue or sign. If she stepped into Victoria's car, no one would know what happened to her. She'd disappear without a trace, just like all the pictures of missing persons on milk cartons or on the walls of the post office. Her parents would be beside themselves with worry. Katie would panic. How would Azad and Michael react?

Her cell phone was in her purse. If she could just—

Victoria jabbed the gun in Lucy's side. "Hand over your cell phone."

Damn! Lucy's hopes plummeted. Now there was no way the police could trace her whereabouts using her phone's GPS. She'd have to think of another way. Lucy reached in her purse and handed over the phone.

Victoria dropped it on the blacktop and smashed it with the heel of her shoe. The cell phone case picture of Lucy holding Gadoo shattered. "Now move it."

Lucy's stomach clenched tight, and she struggled to steady her erratic pulse. She needed all her wits to figure a way out of this mess. "All right. I'm going."

Victoria followed as Lucy went to the passenger door. Her hand was so sweaty it took two attempts to open the door.

"Slide over. You're driving," Victoria said.

Lucy shimmied over the gear shift and into the driver's seat. Victoria sat in the passenger seat and closed the door. She aimed the barrel of the revolver at Lucy. "Head north out of Ocean Crest."

Heart pounding, Lucy buckled her seat belt and started the engine. She backed out of the restaurant's parking lot and onto the street.

"Obey all the speed limits. I don't want to get pulled over," Victoria said.

Lucy drove down Ocean Avenue and passed businesses and the town municipal hall and courthouse. The window was cracked, and the smell of fresh-cut grass mingled with the scent of ocean, and a pang of longing mingled with her fear. "This is ridiculous. How will kidnapping me help you?"

"Shut up and keep driving."

Lucy halted the car to let a group of surfers wearing colorful shorts and carrying surfboards cross the street. She could almost hear Victoria grinding her teeth.

They came to the third stoplight, the last one leading out of Ocean Crest, and Lucy stopped the car. Victoria's foot bounced nervously as she held the cocked revolver. Lucy feared her twitching would make the gun fire.

Out of the corner of her eye, Lucy spotted two silver-haired ladies pushing a rolling cart filled with Holloway's grocery bags. The pair began to walk across the pedestrian crossway. Lucy sat up as she recognized Edna and Edith Gray. The light turned yellow, but the elderly sisters were only halfway through the crosswalk.

"Damnit," Victoria muttered. "Can't those old hags move any faster?"

Just then, Edna looked up and spotted Lucy behind the steering wheel. She nudged her sister, and both spinsters stopped walking. "Hi, Lucy!" They called out and waved in unison.

Victoria tensed beside Lucy. "Answer them, but not a clue."

Lucy's pulse pounded. Victoria held the gun low and jabbed the barrel of the revolver into her ribs. The sisters couldn't see it. For all they knew, Lucy was driving a friend around town in a fancy Cadillac.

Lucy lowered the window. "Hi, Edna. Hi, Edith."

"We plan to visit the restaurant tomorrow to say hello to your parents," Edna called out.

"They'll like that," Lucy said, raising her voice to be heard out the window. "By the way, the crabs you sold me made delicious soup. When you stop by make sure you order a bowl."

The sisters stared at her, baffled. Then Edna frowned and turned to Edith, who merely shrugged.

"Go around them," Victoria ordered.

Lucy waved once more, then eased the Cadillac through the intersection. Would it work? Or would the Gray sisters think their hearing aids were malfunctioning and return home without a thought to Lucy's puzzling remark.

Lucy noted all the landmarks as she drove by. The lifeguard station. A bathhouse for the day tourists. The Ocean Crest Information Center. Another tenth of a mile and the sand dunes seemed to grow taller as they marked the end of the small shore town. The dunes continued into the next town, but they weren't as dense as they were at this location. The tide was highest at this point.

"Where are we going?" Lucy asked.

"Somewhere your body won't be found."

Fear knotted inside Lucy, and she swallowed the panic rising in her throat. Victoria spoke about killing without a hint of remorse. "You can't think to get away with this," Lucy said.

Victoria's lips formed a strange sneer. "Why not?"

Lucy's mind reeled, thinking of a way to delay Victoria's insane plan. She'd watched her fair share of crime shows with Katie, and the killers always liked to talk about how and why they murdered their victims. She needed to keep Victoria talking until she could figure a way out of this car. "Why did you do it?"

"I assume you mean why did I kill Henry Simms?"

"Yes."

"I don't owe you an explanation."

"No, but you were right when you said I'm too curious for my own good. It's the way I'm programmed, and law school taught me to question everything. If you plan on killing me, then what harm would it do to satisfy my curiosity?"

Victoria chuckled. Lucy's comment seemed to entertain her. "You're right. Even death row inmates get one last request before they're injected."

If Lucy had any doubts about Victoria's sanity, they now flew out the window. She eyed the gun barrel. "So why did you do it?"

"Henry was my lover. We'd been together for five years. Five! I gave up my life and my career for him. I had opportunities to date other men, but I remained faithful. I wanted to marry, not be a longtime mistress. Henry hated his wife, but his promises to leave Holly were all lies. That woman had a hold on him I could never figure out."

"Maybe he truly cared for her."

Victoria's eyes hardened. "Nonsense! He told me he loved me. I had a job offer in Paris!" she snarled. "But I turned it down because I didn't want to leave him. I was a fool! He turned around and started sleeping with that young tramp. He was a cheating jerk. I did the next woman a favor."

"How did you get him into the catering van?"

Victoria cackled, a high-pitched sound that made Lucy's hair stand on end. "You mean how did I manage to get into a locked van, then lure him inside?"

"Well, yes."

"You left the window down. All I had to do was reach inside and open the door. I approached Henry at the reception and whispered in his ear that I forgave him and that I missed and needed him, and to meet me outside. I wasn't sure if he would take the bait, not when he was sleeping with Cressida, but he did. Once I enticed him inside the van, your shish kebab skewers were the perfect weapon. I rolled the window closed and locked the door on my way out."

Lucy had been right. She'd left the window open and had given Victoria access into the catering van. The entire conversation was unnerving. Victoria spoke about killing a man—a man she claimed she loved— without an ounce of remorse. Lucy couldn't fathom the way her mind worked.

But then, she wasn't a killer.

Lucy took a deep breath. "You made a mistake."

"I don't think so."

"Cressida wasn't Henry's lover. She was his daughter."

"You're lying."

"I'm not. Think about what you thought you saw when you found Cressida in Henry's arms at the wedding rehearsal. He was holding her, not like a lover, but like a father. I went to Cressida's mother's home and found family pictures. I also spoke with Cressida, and she confirmed it. Henry was her biological father. Cressida had recently discovered the truth and had reached out to him. Over time, they'd started to have a father-daughter relationship."

Victoria's hand trembled. "Still, I—"

"Please lower that thing and we can turn the car around and tell the police it was all a misunderstanding. If you turn yourself in, you can make a deal and avoid prison."

A muscle flicked angrily at Victoria's jaw, and her grip on the gun tightened. "No! You're lying. I'm not going to jail. I'll never survive the conditions. Keep driving."

Instead of listening to reason, Victoria felt backed against a wall, and nothing Lucy could say would change her mind. Time was running out. Lucy knew, without a doubt, that she couldn't talk Victoria out of her insane plans. Victoria was going to kill her.

Lucy had to act.

Without warning, she pressed the gas pedal to the floor and simultaneously made a sharp right—straight for the sand dunes. The car tires squealed, and Victoria screamed before the car slammed into what felt like a brick wall. Everything else happened in a split second.

A shot fired, hitting the windshield, and the glass shattered. The air bags exploded as the acrid odor of gunpowder assaulted Lucy's nose.

Lucy's seat belt, combined with the air bag, held her tight. Dazed, she turned to Victoria. Blood had splattered her face where she'd collided with the air bag. The safety device had saved her from flying through the windshield, but without a seat belt, she'd flown face first into the air bag, which had knocked her unconscious.

Adrenaline coursed through Lucy's body, and deep in the recesses of her mind, she knew she wouldn't feel the pain until later. Unclasping her seat belt, she reached for the door handle and stumbled out of the car. She landed on her hands and knees and slowly rose to her feet to look at the damage. The speeding Cadillac had made it halfway through the sand dunes until it came to a halt. The dunes not only protected Ocean Crest's beaches and residences, but they had saved her life today.

A low ringing sounded in her ears, growing louder by the second, until she recognized the distant sound of a siren. She cried out, but her voice was hoarse and her mouth felt like old paper, dry and dusty.

Please, let them come here.

Her prayers were answered. A police cruiser turned down the street and came to a screeching halt by the Cadillac. Officer Bill Watson stepped out of the cruiser. The passenger door flew open and Azad emerged. He ran straight for her.

"Lucy!" Azad shouted. "Are you all right?"

Relief flooded through her, strong and steady like an ocean wave. "I am now."

Bill took one look at the crashed vehicle, reached for his walkie-talkie, and called for an ambulance.

"Thank God. What happened?" Azad asked.

Lucy took a shaky breath. "Victoria killed Henry. She was his longtime lover and she thought he was cheating on her with Cressida Connolly. She didn't know Cressida was Henry's daughter."

"That's twisted," Azad said.

"Katie filled us in on everything," Bill said. "We were on our way to arrest Victoria at the Sandpiper Bed and Breakfast when Hannah Smith told us Victoria had checked out."

"How did you know she'd look for me?" Lucy asked.

"We didn't know. We were about to put out a statewide alert, when Edna and Edith Gray called the station. They told us they saw you in a white Cadillac with a strange woman and that you said the weirdest thing. They suspected something was amiss and as good citizens they decided to notify the police."

"Thank goodness for nosy neighbors! I told them that the restaurant made delicious soup from their crabs. But the crabs they sold me were *hermit crabs*, and I hoped they would suspect something was wrong."

"It was genius and it worked." Bill squeezed her shoulder, then he hurried to check on the crashed car and left Lucy alone with Azad.

Concern was etched on Azad's face. "I'd never forgive myself if something happened to you because you were trying to save my neck. I was worried out of my mind." He pulled her into his arms and held her.

Once again, he took her by surprise. She could feel his breathing on her cheek, as he held her close. She wrapped her arms around his waist and breathed in the scent of his cologne. It was a reassuring embrace, and she needed it more than ever after her harrowing escape. Then, just as abruptly, he released her and grinned. "Thanks," he said. "I needed that."

She opened her mouth to respond, but the roar of a motorcycle engine stopped her short. Seconds later, a Harley tore down the street and stopped next to the police car. A man jumped off the motorcycle and removed his helmet.

"Lucy!" Michael shouted. "Thank God you're not hurt."

Azad shot her an incredulous look that said, *What's he doing here?*

Lucy shrugged, just as perplexed as he was.

Michael approached. "I stopped by to see you at the restaurant and found a smashed cell phone in the parking lot. I knew it was yours from the cracked cell phone case picture of you and Gadoo. Then I saw the police car race from Kebab Kitchen, and I knew something bad was up. I panicked."

"So did I," Azad said.

Azad frowned at Michael, but thankfully, neither man spoke to each other.

"It's all right," Lucy reassured them both. "I'm fine. Not a scratch, thanks to my seat belt and air bag." Her emotions were tumultuous and she felt the beginnings of a headache. She knew she'd feel every ache and pain tomorrow, but she also knew it could have been much, much worse. She could have ended up shot and dropped in the ocean. Who knows what Victoria had planned?

An ambulance arrived and paramedics began working to extract Victoria from the smashed car. Victoria awoke and began screaming for her doctor and her lawyer.

Bill returned from speaking with the paramedics, his expression firm. "They think Victoria will be okay. She's lucky, considering she was not wearing her seat belt. After she's treated at the hospital, she'll be charged with murder." Bill reached for Lucy's elbow. "You should go to the hospital and get checked out, too, Lucy."

She shook her head. "No. I'm fine." She wanted to go home, shower, and curl up on the couch with a glass of wine and watch *Murder, She Wrote* reruns with Katie.

"Lucy—"

"I promise to see a doctor if I don't feel well tomorrow."

"All right. But Katie and I will be keeping an eye on you tonight." He opened the cruiser door. "Now let's get you home."

Lucy turned back to see the paramedics load Victoria into the ambulance. Her steps faltered. "I'm glad she'll be okay. Despite everything, I didn't want to kill her, or hurt her badly, just stop her."

"Don't feel too bad. She planned to kill you and skip town," Bill said.

"If it wasn't for your fast thinking, she would have," Michael said.

"You cracked the case again, Lucy. Only this time, I'm grateful that you proved I wasn't the killer," Azad said.

"I have a feeling Katie was in on this, too, wasn't she?" Bill asked.

Lucy managed a faint smile. "I plead the fifth."

Bill sighed. "For not getting involved in solving murders, you two sure do good work."

CHAPTER 26

"I knew my girl could do it," Raffi Berberian said.

"Thanks, Dad." Lucy smiled at his bear hug and the light scrape of his whiskers as he brushed her cheek with a kiss. He released her to study her face, and he grinned.

He turned to her mother. "See? I was right. I told Lucy to solve the case."

Her mom pursed her lips. "Do not take all the credit. I gave her my consent to investigate and she listened."

"In other words, you came to your senses." Raffi gave her a smug look.

Angela faced him squarely. "No. I gave her good advice about men, and *she* came to her senses."

"Mom," Lucy whined.

"Never mind how it happened," Azad interrupted. "I want to thank Lucy. I owe her my freedom."

It was days after Lucy's scare with Victoria, and Lucy had recovered from crashing into the dunes. They'd closed the restaurant early after a busy dinner service. It was another successful day, and it was even better when all her friends and family had shown up to surprise her. Now they gathered around tables in the dining room, and Lucy's heart warmed as she gazed at everyone present. Her parents, Butch, Sally, and Azad. Emma arrived a few minutes later with Max and Niari fresh from a soccer game. Her niece was dressed in a red and black soccer uniform with cleats, shin guards, and a glitter headband printed with her team name, "Go Strikers!"

Her mother, in her usual fashion, had set out a wide array of *mezze*—hummus, pita, an assortment of raw and pickled vegetables, olives, and feta cheese. Her father had opened bottles of his favorite merlot and filled everyone's glasses. Niari's wineglass was filled with apple juice.

Bill's arm was draped around Katie's shoulders, and Lucy was grateful the couple were getting along. She'd been worried after he'd learned of the extent of their involvement in the investigation. He'd surprised them both by taking it so well.

When Bill moved away to have his wineglass refilled, Lucy motioned for Katie to help her with a pitcher of water and a tray of glasses.

"Are you sure Bill's not mad?" Lucy asked when they were out of earshot.

"Oh, he was at first, but I assured him that we never purposely put ourselves in danger looking into the case."

Not if you omitted breaking and entering, running for their lives while being pursued by a mad movie director, and in Lucy's case, being kidnapped at gunpoint by a murderer.

"He even joked that we should be consultants for the Ocean Crest Police Department," Katie said.

Lucy almost dropped the tray of glasses. "Are you serious?"

"You never know with Bill, but I think he was only half joking," Katie said as she helped Lucy place the water pitchers and glasses on the table.

The sound of laughter drew Lucy's attention to Michael Citteroni. Even he'd shown up and had struck up a conversation with her mother about his deceased grandmother's Italian recipes. Angela had immediately been interested and invited him to stop by the kitchen one morning with his grandmother's recipes so they could prepare one of her specialties together. Lucy couldn't help but notice that Azad wasn't pleased. She could just imagine the fireworks when Michael showed up in Azad's kitchen.

But that would be something to worry about another day.

"We have a surprise for you, Lucy," Emma said.

"Even more than all of you showing up together to celebrate with me?" Lucy asked.

Niari jumped up and down in excitement, then ran into the kitchen. She returned carrying a white cake box. Lucy recognized the name on the box and clasped her hands to her chest.

"Cutie's Cupcakes!" She guessed what was in the box.

"Mom helped me call in the order just for you, Mokour Lucy!" Niari lifted the lid to reveal a lemon meringue pie.

Lucy hugged her niece. "Thank you, sweetie."

"Don't forget my baklava." Her mom stepped out of the kitchen carrying a tray. "It's fresh out of the oven."

The thin pastry was cooked to a golden brown and smelled like heaven.

Lucy inhaled the delicious scent. "Hmm. Niari has to share the first piece of the pie and the baklava with me."

Niari reached for a plate and two forks. "I'm ready!"

Just then, the front door opened and Calvin Clemmons walked inside. "Hello, everyone. Sorry to intrude, but I wanted to let you know that Victoria Redding was released from the hospital and confessed to the murder of Henry Simms. She was taken to the county jail to await trial. Prosecutor Walsh will handle the case."

"Thank you for coming over to tell us," Lucy said.

Clemmons cleared his throat as he took in the group. "I'll leave you to your celebration."

Lucy's gaze went to Emma's, and her sister nodded in silent approval.

"Would you like to stay?" Lucy asked.

"Pardon?"

"It would be nice if you could stay. The baklava is fresh out of the oven and we haven't even cut the pie yet." Lucy motioned to the laden table.

His eyes roved the delectable desserts as well as the food. "Well, if you don't mind, I suppose I could sample a piece."

"We'd all like that," Angela said.

Raffi poured a glass of wine and handed it to the detective.

Lucy cut the first piece of baklava and set the plate in front of Clemmons. It was a peace offering of sorts. They may not agree on everything in the future, but today was a day of celebration.

Raffi raised his glass. "To family and friends!"

Everyone followed. Even Niari lifted her apple juice.

A warm glow flowed through Lucy. Over the past few months, she'd returned home, learned how to run a restaurant, and even how to solve a murder, but nothing was more important or valuable than the people gathered with her here today.

Lucy raised her glass. "To family and friends."

RECIPES

Lucy's Baklava

1½ cups sugar
1 cup water
1 teaspoon lemon juice
3 cups finely chopped walnuts
1 tablespoon ground cinnamon
1½ cups clarified butter
1 pound phyllo dough (9-x-14-inch sheets)

Combine walnuts, cinnamon, and ¼ cup sugar in a small bowl and set aside. This is the walnut filling.

Melt butter and coat a 14-x-10-inch baking pan. Layer 7 sheets of phyllo dough in the pan, buttering each sheet with a pastry brush. Spread half of the walnut filling evenly over top. Layer another 7 sheets of phyllo dough in the pan, buttering each sheet. Spread the remaining walnut filling evenly over top. Cover with the remaining sheets of dough, buttering each sheet. Bake in preheated 325-degree oven for 40 minutes. Cool baklava before cutting it.

Simple Sugar Syrup
Boil together 1¼ cups sugar and 1 cup water for 10 minutes. Stir often until sugar dissolves in water. Add 1 teaspoon lemon juice. Turn off flame and set syrup aside to cool. Pour cooled syrup on your baklava and enjoy.

Azad's Prized Shish Kebab

3-lb beef sirloin or leg of lamb, boned, with fat
    removed, and cut into 1-inch cubes
3 cloves of minced garlic
¼ cup minced flat leaf parsley
½ cup olive oil
¼ cup red vinegar or lemon juice
¼ teaspoon cayenne pepper or to taste
3 onions, cut in quarters
2 tomatoes, cut in quarters
1 eggplant or zucchini, cut into 1-inch cubes
red, green, and yellow peppers cut in quarters
salt and pepper to taste

Place cubed meat in a large bowl with onions, tomatoes, peppers, and eggplant. Mix the olive oil, garlic,
parsley, vinegar, cayenne, salt, and pepper in a separate bowl, then pour the mixture over the meat. Cover
and refrigerate overnight or for at least a few hours.
Thread the meat onto skewers. Because cooking times
vary, thread the tomatoes, onions, and peppers on
separate skewers. Broil the skewers over a charcoal
fire. Turn the skewers until the meat is cooked on all
sides. Serve with pilaf and enjoy.

Angela's Stuffed Grape Leaves with Meat and Rice (Derevee Dolma)

1 jar (12 oz) grape leaves

Meat and Rice Stuffing

1 lb ground beef
½ cup long grain rice
1 chopped tomato
3 tablespoons tomato paste
1 large chopped onion
1 teaspoon salt
¼ teaspoon black pepper

Combine all ingredients and mix well.

Cooking Liquids

juice of ½ lemon
2 tablespoons tomato paste
½ teaspoon salt
2 cups hot water

Rinse grape leaves. Line the bottom of a large saucepan with a few leaves, shiny side down. Then, on a cutting board, roll out each remaining grape leaf, shiny side down, and put a spoonful of the meat and rice stuffing in the center. Fold over both sides and roll from bottom up until it looks like a small sausage. Continue with each grape leaf. Place the stuffed grape leaves in rows on the bottom of the pot.

Prepare the cooking liquids by combining the lemon juice, tomato paste, salt, and water and pour over the stuffed grape leaves. Place a small inverted plate on top of the leaves to keep them in place during cooking. Cover the pot. Bring to boil, then simmer gently for an hour until rice is tender. Serve warm with cold garlic yogurt sauce (optional).

ACKNOWLEDGMENTS

I have so many people to thank. First, thank you to my family—John, Laura, and Gabrielle—for your never-ending love and support. I adore all of you!

I will always be indebted to my parents, Gabriel and Anahid, and I miss them every day. This series is truly a testament to them as hardworking owners of a restaurant for almost thirty years. Many of my scenes were inspired by my years growing up in the restaurant business. Thanks to my parents, I learned how to properly set a table at an early age and carry a loaded tray with plates and glasses without a hitch.

Thank you to my agent, Stephany Evans. Her support and professional guidance are invaluable.

Thank you also to my editor, Martin Biro, and my heartfelt thanks to the entire Kensington team for their hard work and efforts.

And of course, thank you to my readers. I'm grateful!

If you enjoyed *Stabbed in the Baklava*,
be sure not to miss the first book in
Tina Kashian's Kebab Kitchen Mystery series,

HUMMUS AND HOMICIDE

When Lucy Berberian quits her Philadelphia
law firm and heads home to Ocean Crest,
she knows what she's getting—the scent of
funnel cake, the sight of the wooden roller coaster,
and the tastes of her family's Mediterranean
restaurant. But murder wasn't on the menu . . .

Keep reading for a special look.

A Kensington mass-market paperback
and eBook on sale now!

Ocean Crest, New Jersey

"Lucy Berberian! Is that you?"

Lucy's car was stopped at a red light when the excited shout caught her attention. Her gaze turned to the crosswalk, and she lowered her sunglasses an inch to peer above the rim. A tiny old lady with an abundance of gray curls was pushing a rolling cart filled with groceries. She waved. One of the plastic bags stuck out from the cart and flapped in the breeze.

Lucy glimpsed the name *Holloway's* printed on the bag—the sole grocery store in the small New Jersey beach town. "Hello, Mrs. Kiminski," she called out her open window.

The old lady smiled, revealing pearly white dentures. "You're visiting? Your mama will be so happy."

No doubt her mother and father would be thrilled when they learned Lucy was back, not only for a visit, but longer. Lucy swallowed hard. She'd hit the first stop light out of three in town and already her nerves were getting to her. It felt like a corkscrew was slowly winding in her stomach the closer she came to her destination. And to *him*.

Don't think about it.

The light changed, and Lucy waved as she continued down Ocean Avenue. Parking spots in the town's main street were vacant in late April, and only a few people strolled about. The tourist season wouldn't begin until Memorial Day. A month later and the town would be crammed with seasonal tourists, and a parking spot would be hard to find.

Lucy drove past a ramp leading to the town's mile-long boardwalk, and she spied the Atlantic Ocean between two buildings—a blue line to the horizon. The Jersey shore was in Lucy's blood. She'd been born and raised in Ocean Crest, a tiny town located on a barrier island about six miles north of Cape May. Even off-season the scent of funnel cake drifted from one of the boardwalk shops and through her window. The bright morning sunlight warmed her cheeks, and she spotted the single pier with a Ferris wheel and an old-fashioned wooden roller coaster. Soon the Ferris wheel would light up the night sky and the piercing screams from the coaster would be heard from a block away.

The small ocean town was so different from the rapid pace of the Center-City Philadelphia law firm and apartment she had grown accustomed to over the last eight years. But now that part of her life was done, and she needed to figure out what she was going to do next. When her work had thrown her a curveball, returning home had come to mind. Other than hasty holiday visits, she hadn't stayed for longer than a weekend.

A few blocks later Lucy parked before a quaint

brick building with a flower bed bursting with yellow daffodils and red tulips. A lit sign read KEBAB KITCHEN FINE MEDITERRANEAN CUISINE.

A flash of motion by the front door caught her eye as soon as she killed the engine. Gadoo, the orange and black cat with yellow eyes her mother had adopted when he kept coming around the restaurant, cocked his head to the side as if to say, *What took you so long to come home?* and then swished his tail and sauntered down the alley.

Taking a deep breath, she got out of the car, then pushed open the door to the restaurant.

The dining room was empty and the lights were dimmed. Sunlight through the front windows shone on pristine white tablecloths covering a dozen tables and a handful of maple booths. Small vases with fresh flowers and unlit tea light candles in glass votive holders rested upon the pressed linen. Cherry wainscoting gave the place a warm, family feel. The ocean shimmered from large bay windows and seagulls soared above the water. The delicious aroma of fresh herbs, fragrant spices, and grilled lamb wafted to her. It was only ten o'clock in the morning, well before the restaurant opened for lunch, and that meant her mother was preparing her savory specials.

Lucy walked forward and stopped by the hostess stand. The place hadn't changed since she was a kid. As a young child, her mom carried her around to greet customers and kiss the staff. When she was eight, she started rolling silverware in cloth napkins and refilling salt and pepper shakers. Lucy eyed the cash register behind the counter with its laminated dollar bill showcasing the first cash the restaurant took in as well as the required health department notices that hung on the wall. A low wall separated a waitress station from the dining area, and a pair of swinging doors led to the kitchen. She recalled her days as a hostess and cashier, seating customers and handing them menus, then ringing them up to pay on their way out. A waitress pad sat on a nearby table, and she remembered how excited she'd been as a teenager the day her father promoted her from hostess to waitress. The cash tips had helped pay for her prom gown.

Footsteps sounded on the terra cotta tiles. Lucy turned to see her older sister carrying a tray of sparkling glasses.

"Lucy! What are you doing here?" Her sister set down the tray on a nearby table.

Lucy smiled and embraced her warmly. "Hi, Emma. I've come for a visit."

At thirty-seven Emma was five years older than Lucy. Lucy had always been a bit envious of her sister who was slim and attractive with long, curly brown hair. She weighed the same as she had since college, and she'd never had to worry about how many carbs or pieces of pita bread she consumed. "How's Max?" Lucy asked.

Emma wrinkled her nose. "He's the same. The king of real estate in town. He works a lot and is never around."

Emma tended to frequently complain about her husband, but they had a ten-year-old daughter they adored. "And my little niece Niari?"

"Most of the time Niari's great," Emma said. "She's good in school and likes soccer. But she's also a tween who can drive us crazy. I dread the puberty years to come."

Lucy chuckled. "I imagine we drove Mom and Dad nuts as teenagers."

Emma perched on the edge of a table and crossed her arms. "How's work? I'm surprised you could get away."

Lucy cleared her throat. "Well, that's just it. I have some time to—"

"Lucy Anahid Berberian!"

Lucy whirled to see her mother and father emerge from the swinging kitchen doors. Her Lebanese, Greek, and Armenian mother, Angela, had olive skin and dark hair that she'd styled in a beehive since the sixties. Her Armenian father, Raffi, was a portly man of average height with a balding pate of curly black hair. Both had arrived in America on their twenty-first birthdays, met months later at a church festival, and married soon after. They'd meshed cultures and languages, and Emma and Lucy were first-generation Americans with ethnic roots as strong as her parents' prized grapevine clinging to its trellis.

Lucy found herself engulfed in her mother's arms, flowery perfume tickling her nose. The large gold cross—the one piece of jewelry her mother never left the house without—was cool as it pressed against Lucy's neck. Her mother was a tiny woman, only five feet tall even with her beehive hairdo, but she was a talented chef and a smart businesswoman.

Angela passed Lucy to her father, and Lucy smiled at his bear hug and the light scrape of his whiskers as he brushed her cheek with a kiss. He released her to study her face and grinned. "My little girl, the big city lawyer."

Her mother touched Lucy's arm. "It's Tuesday. Shouldn't you be at work?"

Lucy's insides froze for a heart-stopping moment. "I'm taking a vacation," she blurted out.

Why did she have to sound so nervous? She'd rehearsed the perfect excuse over and over in her car on the way here.

"A vacation?" Angela folded her arms across her chest. Her gaze filled with suspicion as it traveled over Lucy from head to toe, taking in the worn jeans, Philadelphia Eagles T-shirt, and Nike sneakers.

Lucy's attire was far from her normal business wear, but it was surprising how quick a week of unemployment could affect one's desire to dress in anything but yoga pants or jeans.

"It's true," Lucy said. A small streak of panic ran through her at her mother's continuing inquisitive gaze.

"Well, it's about time." Her mother nodded curtly and unfolded her arms from across her chest. "That law firm works you too hard. You only visit for Thanksgiving, Christmas, and Easter. You stay two, maybe three days, and then you're off again. Plus"—she eyed Lucy with an admonishing glare—"you didn't visit last Mother's Day."

Lucy's pulse quickened. Here it was. Her family's ability to layer on guilt. She'd always made an effort to visit for the holidays, but the truth was she didn't always want to come home. The smothering could be as thick as the sugar syrup on her mother's baklava— sticky, sweet, and as effective as superglue.

"You know I had a big case and couldn't take time off. You could have visited me," Lucy said.

"Bah!" Raffi said with a disgusted wave of his hand. "What company makes its employees work so many weekends? And you know we don't like to drive into the city."

Lucy knew crossing the Delaware River via the Ben Franklin Bridge into Philadelphia was like traveling to another country for her parents.

"How long is your vacation?" Emma asked.

"A month." At their stunned looks, Lucy quickly added, "It's really what we call a sabbatical." She wasn't ready to admit she was no longer employed. Knowing her parents, they'd think she was home for good. Why give them false hope?

"You'll stay with us. I'll tidy your room," her mom said.

Heck no. Seeing her parents was good, but living with them was something else entirely. "I'm staying with Katie and Bill, Mom."

Her mom hesitated and glared at her as if she'd been denied access to Lucy's firstborn. Katie Watson was Lucy's long-time friend. When Lucy had called her to tell her that she was coming home and staying for a while, Katie had offered for Lucy to stay with her and her husband, Bill, an Ocean Crest police officer.

"Fine," Angela finally said. "I've always liked Katie, and she comes from a good family."

Raffi cracked a wide grin. "You came at a good time, Lucy. With Memorial Day in less than a month, the tourist season will begin. Millie left to have a baby. We need your help."

Lucy's smile faded. Millie had worked for her parents as a waitress for years. From what Lucy recalled, Millie had married right out of high school and started having kids. Was she on baby number four by now?

"It's her sixth boy," her dad answered as if reading

her mind. "We need a waitress. We're already short for today's lunch shift."

Lucy felt as if she were being sucked back into the fold like quicksand; no amount of professional accomplishments mattered. Family helped family, and their expectations could be stifling and overwhelming. It was partly why she'd fled years ago.

But she was older and more experienced now. "Dad, I don't think—"

"You can borrow Millie's apron and Emma's clothes," Angela said.

Good grief. Millie's apron was one thing. But how would she fit into her skinny sister's black pants and white shirt? Lucy was bigger than Emma in every way. From her breasts, to her hips, and definitely her derriere.

Angela pulled out a chair. "Sit. You're too thin." She glanced at Lucy's father behind her shoulder. "Raffi, please bring Lucy something special to eat. We can catch up while we wait."

Her dad disappeared through the swinging kitchen doors.

Lucy rolled her eyes as she sat. Their mother never seemed to notice any physical differences between her two daughters. To her, everyone appeared in need of food.

Emma smiled mischievously as she set a glass of water in front of Lucy. "Good luck," she whispered, then followed their father into the kitchen.

Lucy inwardly groaned as her mother pulled up a chair beside her. She didn't need her sister's warning. She knew what was coming as soon as she spotted the gleam in her mother's eyes. The maternal message was clear. *Let's talk about how old you are and remind you that your biological clock is ticking louder than a pounding drum and that you should be married and birthing my grandchildren by now.*

Her mother patted her hand. "You know I think you work too hard."

Once again, a nagging guilt pierced Lucy's chest for not revealing the truth. "It's okay. I'm home for a while now, remember?"

Angela's face lit up. "Good. We need to focus on finding you a husband."

"Mom," Lucy whined. "I'm not opposed to marriage, but only if the right man proposes. Meanwhile, my career is important to—"

"Posh," her mom said, waving a hand. "A career doesn't keep you warm at night when you get old. Granted, men are far from perfect. Your father is a good example," she said, motioning toward the kitchen, "but he's *there*."

Lucy wrinkled her nose. She didn't consider herself a romantic, but she'd hoped for more than just *there* when it came to a man.

"I saw Gadoo," Lucy said, hoping to change the topic.

Angela always loved to talk about the cat. "He waits for me every morning by the back door. Actually, he's waiting for his breakfast. As long as I feed him, Gadoo keeps coming."

Gadoo was Armenian for cat. Not very original, but it fit the patchy orange and black cat with yellow eyes.

Before long the kitchen doors opened again and her father emerged with a large shish kebab platter and set it before her. Two skewers of succulent lamb and a skewer of roasted peppers, tomatoes, and onions were accompanied by rice pilaf and homemade pita bread. The aroma made her stomach grumble and her mouth water.

Lucy may not have missed her mother's lectures about husband hunting, but damned if she hadn't missed the food. She picked up a warm piece of pita bread, then stopped. "Is there hummus?"

Her gaze followed Emma's pointing finger. "You have to see our newest addition."

Lucy stood and looked toward the corner of the restaurant where a long sidebar stood. She hadn't noticed it earlier. At first glance, it looked like a salad bar, but instead of lettuce, tomatoes, and salad, bins of hummus were displayed, each tray a different variety.

"Specialties of the house, and all my own flavors. Roasted red pepper, extra garlic, Mediterranean herb, lemon pucker, artichoke, black bean, sweet apricot, and of course, my own recipe of traditional hummus," Angela boasted with pride.

"Customers love it," Raffi said.

Lucy carried her plate to the bins full of the creamy dips and added a large spoonful of traditional hummus next to the pita bread, then returned to her seat. "Wow! Business must be good, Dad." She dipped a piece of pita into the hummus and shoved it into her mouth.

Heaven. The lemon blended with the garlic, chick peas and sesame seed puree perfectly, and the texture was super-creamy.

Silence greeted her. Lucy looked up from her plate to see all three members of her family staring at her. "What's wrong?" she mumbled.

Emma broke the awkward silence. "Dad wants to sell."

Lucy nearly choked on a mouthful before managing to swallow it down. "Sell?"

"Not right away, but I've been thinking about it," Raffi said.

An uncomfortable thought crossed Lucy's mind. Her gaze swept him from his balding head of curly black hair to his sizeable belly back to his face. "Are you sick?"

His brows furrowed. "No. I'm old."

The irony was not lost on her. Less than an hour ago she was hesitant to set foot in the place. But selling the restaurant? For thirty years, ever since her parents had opened it, Kebab Kitchen had been the center of their lives, socially and economically. What would they do without it?

"But I don't understand why—"

"I have no sons or sons-in-law who want it. Emma doesn't have a head for business, and Max is into real estate." Her father eyed Lucy hard, his glare cutting through her like one of his prized butcher knives. "If you'd married Azad Zakarian this wouldn't be a problem."

Lucy's stomach bottomed out at the mention of the man her parents had so desperately wanted her to marry. He was one of the main reasons she'd left to take the job in the Philadelphia law firm. It had taken months, years, to dull the heartache. Her throat seemed to close up as she felt the all-too-familiar pressure from her parents' unreasonable expectations— that the ultimate fate of the restaurant rested upon her shoulders and that *she* had to be the one to keep everything together. Lucy reached for the water glass and took a big swallow.

"Dad, stop," Emma said. "No sense nagging Lucy. Max has a buyer."

"Who?"

"Anthony Citteroni."

Lucy sat upright at the name. "The bike man next door to the restaurant?"

Every summer, Mr. Citteroni's bike shop rented a variety of bicycles to tourists. Ever since she was a kid, she'd heard stories that he had mob connections in Atlantic City, and his many businesses were how he laundered money.

"He wants the property," Raffi explained.

"Why?" Lucy couldn't fathom what Mr. Citteroni would do with it.

"He wants to open a high class Italian restaurant, but he's not the only interested buyer," Raffi said.

"A local woman wants to convert Kebab Kitchen into a diner," Emma said.

"Another Jersey diner? The state is loaded with them. And Ocean Crest already has the Pancake Palace," Lucy said.

"Don't forget that Azad's interested," Angela announced.

There it was again. *His* name.

"Why would he want it?" Lucy asked.

"Azad graduated from culinary school and is working as a sous chef for a fancy Atlantic City restaurant. He wants to buy Kebab Kitchen and keep it the way it is."

Of course, he did. He was perfect. Hand-picked by her parents. He'd started working as a dishwasher for the restaurant when he was in high school. He'd soon worked his way up to busboy, then line cook, and had earned her parents' respect. Not to mention their hopes of a union with their younger daughter. The pressure tightened in Lucy's chest.

She glared at her parents. "What will you do if you retire? Where will you go?"

Follow P.I. Savannah Reid
with
G.A. McKevett

Just Desserts	978-0-7582-0061-1	$5.99US/$7.99CAN
Bitter Sweets	978-1-5756-693-8	$5.99US/$7.99CAN
Killer Calories	978-1-5756-521-4	$5.99US/$7.99CAN
Cooked Goose	978-0-7582-0205-5	$6.50US/$8.99CAN
Sugar and Spite	978-1-5756-637-2	$5.99US/$7.99CAN
Sour Grapes	978-1-5756-726-3	$6.50US/$8.99CAN
Peaches and Screams	978-1-5756-727-0	$6.50US/$8.99CAN
Death by Chocolate	978-1-5756-728-7	$6.50US/$8.99CAN
Cereal Killer	978-0-7582-0459-2	$6.50US/$8.99CAN
Murder à la Mode	978-0-7582-0461-5	$6.99US/$9.99CAN
Corpse Suzette	978-0-7582-0463-9	$6.99US/$9.99CAN
Fat Free and Fatal	978-0-7582-1551-2	$6.99US/$8.49CAN
Poisoned Tarts	978-0-7582-1553-6	$6.99US/$8.49CAN
A Body to Die For	978-0-7582-1555-0	$6.99US/$8.99CAN
Wicked Craving	978-0-7582-3809-2	$6.99US/$8.99CAN
A Decadent Way to Die	978-0-7582-3811-5	$7.99US/$8.99CAN
Buried in Buttercream	978-0-7582-3813-9	$7.99US/$8.99CAN
Killer Honeymoon	978-0-7582-7652-0	$7.99US/$8.99CAN
Killer Physique	978-0-7582-7655-1	$7.99US/$8.99CAN

Available Wherever Books Are Sold!

Visit our website at www.kensingtonbooks.com

Catering and Capers with
Isis Crawford!

A Catered Murder	978-1-57566-725-6	$5.99US/$7.99CAN
A Catered Wedding	978-0-7582-0686-2	$6.50US/$8.99CAN
A Catered Christmas	978-0-7582-0688-6	$6.99US/$9.99CAN
A Catered Valentine's Day	978-0-7582-0690-9	$6.99US/$9.99CAN
A Catered Halloween	978-0-7582-2193-3	$6.99US/$8.49CAN
A Catered Birthday Party	978-0-7582-2195-7	$6.99US/$8.99CAN
A Catered Thanksgiving	978-0-7582-4739-1	$7.99US/$8.99CAN
A Catered St. Patrick's Day	978-0-7582-4741-4	$7.99US/$8.99CAN
A Catered Christmas Cookie Exchange	978-0-7582-7490-8	$7.99US/$8.99CAN

Available Wherever Books Are Sold!

All available as e-books, too!

Visit our website at www.kensingtonbooks.com

Connect with Us

Visit us online at
KensingtonBooks.com
to read more from your favorite authors, see books
by series, view reading group guides, and more.

Join us on social media

for sneak peeks, chances to win books and prize packs,
and to share your thoughts with other readers.

facebook.com/KensingtonPublishing
twitter.com/kensingtonbooks

Tell us what you think!

To share your thoughts, submit a review,
or sign up for our eNewsletters, please visit:
KensingtonBooks.com/Tellus.

"We'll stay in Ocean Crest. It's a peaceful place," Angela said.

Raffi waved his hand toward the window and a view of the calm ocean and blue sky. "After all, what bad things happen here?"